"You pretend

*. . . he murmured, his thumb stroking my temple.
"But you're not."*

*My heart kicked it up a notch at his touch. Was
he saying I was needy? Was he saying he liked it?
God, I needed therapy. "It's a gift."*

*His forehead came down to rest against mine.
"You drive me nuts, but I can't imagine life without you in it."*

*Now my heart was treating my rib cage like a
mosh pit—thrashing all over the place in its excitement. "That's hunger talking." I cracked wise
when faced with something I didn't know how to
respond to.*

*"You're right," he agreed and the next thing I
knew, he grabbed me by the waist, lifted me off
the floor, and plunked me down on top of the table. I'm a few inches shy of six feet, and a size
twelve on a good day, so I find it remarkably sexy
when a man can pick me up like I was some kind
of delicate flower. Noah knows this, of course.
And he does it as often as he can. I think he likes
knowing he can turn me on so easily.*

*His lips curved on one side, making his smile
mischievous and boyish. "I am hungry."*

KATHRYN SMITH

Dark Side of Dawn

THE NIGHTMARE CHRONICLES

AVON

An Imprint of HarperCollinsPublishers

AVON BOOKS
An Imprint of HarperCollins*Publishers*
10 East 53rd Street
New York, New York 10022-5299

Copyright © 2009 by Kathryn Smith
ISBN 978-0-06-163271-6
www.avonromance.com

First Avon Books paperback printing: December 2009

Avon Trademark Reg. U.S. Pat. Off. and in Other Countries, Marca Registrada, Hecho en U.S.A.
HarperCollins® is a registered trademark of HarperCollins Publishers.

Printed in the U.S.A.

10 9 8 7 6 5 4 3 2 1

This one's just for Steve.

For the flowers bought in celebration of every finished book,

For the takeout he ate without complaint,

For all the trips to the bookstore just so I could get out of the house,

For putting up with neglected housework, mood swings, and all the ups and downs of being married to a writer.

And for having the courage to sign on with me for life.

You're one brave man, babe.

Love, K

Dark Side of Dawn

Chapter One

Nothing good ever comes out of fog.

Horror movies have used it for decades to evoke fear, suspense, and mystery. And, in most cases, shroud some truly horrific beings in an atmosphere that seems to have a life of its own. I'm convinced that that imagery originally came from a dreamer who got a little too close to the border of the Dream Lands—and saw the "guard dog" that lurks there.

All this occurred to me as I narrowly escaped being disemboweled by sharp, misty fingers.

I'm Dawn Riley and the reason I'm at the mercy of this fog right now is because I'm the daughter of Morpheus, God of Dreams. I'm also human, and I'm not supposed to exist. The mist knows this. Since its job is to protect this world, it sees me as a threat—something to be destroyed.

Clawlike tendrils of fog raked at my skin, raising fat, angry welts wherever they managed to take hold. Tiny dots of crimson rose from several of the marks. First blood. Freaking mist hated me.

The feeling—"Ow! Not the face!"—was mutual, damn it.

"Are you going to let it do that to you?"

I turned toward that rumbling voice. Standing a few feet away, the mist lovingly caressing him as though he was a soft little kitten and not six-plus feet of heavily muscled, chiseled and buffed man. Verek, my trainer.

And by man, I mean his sex. He isn't a man in the human sense of the word. Simply because he isn't human. For that matter, neither am I. We're Nightmares—guardians of the Dream Realm—but Verek is a full blood while I am merely half.

The mist keeps humans from straying too far within the Dreaming, and keeps enemies from getting in. It is rare that either happens, which made it all the hungrier for me, like a pack of wolves gone too long without fresh meat. Verek says I have to learn how to make the mist see me as part of this world and not as a threat.

Basically, I have to tame it, and I have no idea how to do that.

"Easy for you to say," I snarled. "It's all over you like a horny masseuse at a rub and tug."

Obviously Verek liked the comparison, because he grinned, flashing pure white teeth in a tanned face. He really is gorgeous—and I spend my time half in awe, half wanting to break his lovely nose.

"It respects me," he replied in an arrogant tone. "It knows I'm dominant, but that I mean it no harm."

What he didn't say was that the mist should regard me in the same way. Whatever sentient creatures made their home in those creeping fingers of fog should see me as a lord and master, especially given my parentage. But instead of being treated like Queen Elizabeth—the first one—I was the butt of the joke. I was Prince Freaking Charles.

As if to prove my point, the mist wrapped around my messy ponytail and pulled—hard. Tears sprang to my eyes as my scalp silently screamed in protest.

"That is so fucking it!" I yelled. I raised my hand and suddenly a dagger appeared in it. My dagger. A Morae blade, made especially for Nightmares like me. Palming the moonstone-set handle, I felt the weapon mold itself to my hand an instant before I raised the wicked-sharp blade to defend myself.

Strong arms grabbed me before I could strike. "Don't!" Verek shouted. "That's not the way to do it!"

I froze. The incessant whispering of the mist stopped

as well. The swirling tendrils drew back, as though afraid.

"Hurting it will only make it fearsome and angry," Verek told me softly. I looked down to see one of his hands held out to the mist, like he was trying to woo a skittish puppy. His other arm was wrapped tightly around me, preventing me from drawing away when the fog moved closer. Wisps curled around his fingers and wrist, and I could hear soft inhuman whispers coming from the pale curls. "You would only prove yourself a threat by harming it."

"That's just fabulous," I muttered. I can't defend myself against it either. I pulled free of his grasp. Verek's hands felt better than I was comfortable with, and I didn't like him feeling as though he could restrain me whenever he wanted. It wasn't that long ago he'd seen me as an interloper and a foe and tried to best me in a fight. Of course, in most circumstances he could pound me silly. But not here, not if I let myself go.

It's funny—and not in a ha-ha kind of way—but thirteen years ago I turned my back on this world and swore never to be part of it again. Now I'm trying to make up for all that lost time because I have to be able to protect myself from those who would use me to get to my father. The King. And wasn't there always someone trying to get rid of the king? Get rid of him or get back at him, that was the way of all those stories. And the Dreaming was where all those stories come from.

I didn't really have a choice but to try and make this work. It was with that petulant realization that I held out my hand to the mist as Verek had done. Tentative swirls came toward me and slipped through my fingers. It felt like silk, which was odd because normally the mist was sharp and . . .

"Son of a bitch!" I cried. It's a wonder the mist wasn't blue I'd cursed so much that night. "Fucker bit me!"

Right in that fleshy bit between thumb and forefinger. It stung worse than a paper cut. Good thing I can heal myself because I knew from past experience that the mist had some nasty venom to its bite.

"Let me see." Without waiting for permission, Verek grabbed my hand and lifted it to his mouth. I barely had time to stiffen before he wrapped his lips around the wound and sucked viciously at it.

"Ew." I attempted to yank my hand away. He didn't let go. "What are you doing?"

Finally, he released me, turning his head to spit a mouthful of blood on the ground with a grimace. Swiping the back of his hand across his mouth, he faced me. "I drew out the venom." He shot me a sharp glance. "You're welcome, by the way."

I wiped my hand on the leg of my jeans and shook my head. "I could have done that myself, thanks." Then

I glared at the fog. "Poisonous bastard. Isn't that treason, trying to kill a member of the royal family?"

"Don't get angry at it," Verek advised. He treated the mist as a whole, while I had bounced back and forth between singular and plural. "It will react aggressively. You have to make yourself its superior."

"I am its superior!" I shouted at the low-lying fog. "It's just too stupid to realize it!"

He started laughing then. If my hand hadn't hurt so much, I might have punched him in the mouth. Instead, I turned my attention to healing my wounds, all the while cursing Verek and men in general, under my breath. Thankfully all I have to do to heal myself is concentrate on the area. I could do that and curse at the same time.

God, I was so angry my ears were ringing. Wait. That wasn't anger. I'm pretty sure anger didn't sound like Def Leppard.

"What is it?" Verek asked, obviously noticing my sudden alertness.

"Cell phone," I replied. I'd purposefully dreamed myself into the Dream Realm tonight rather than physically crossing over as I normally do. And Noah was supposed to call and let me know when he'd be home from LA. That's probably him calling now.

My heart did a backflip, and my entire mood shifted from storms and thunderbolts to sunshine and daisies.

"Gotta go!" I chirped, as I prepared to leave. "I'll get it right with the fog next time, promise." Right. Who was I trying to kid?

"We're not done!" Verek protested as I closed my eyes and began shifting my conscious self across the dimensions. It happened much faster than it ever had before—so fast that I bolted upright, dizzy and wide-eyed, in the mussed tangle of blankets that was my bed. My phone was on one of the pillows, serenading me with "Pour Some Sugar on Me," the ringtone I'd picked for Noah. Sappy, I know. Tacky even. But I liked it.

"Hello?" Like I didn't already know who it was.

"Doc, hey."

His voice was enough to send shivers down my spine. Low, melodic and oh-so sexy. Noah Clarke is my boyfriend. He'd been a regular at the sleep center I used to work at, but then a Night Terror had targeted the pair of us for extinction and we'd been forced to acknowledge our mutual attraction. It was a long story. "Hey yourself. How's L.A.?"

"I'm not there anymore."

When he didn't immediately offer his location—Noah was a man of sometimes infuriatingly few words—I pressed on, "Oh? Where are you?"

"St. Vincent's."

"The hospital?"

"Yeah." I barely had time to register that he was back in the city before he said, "I'm here with Amanda."

Okay, so Amanda was his ex-wife, and I admit that my first reaction wasn't concern, it was jealousy. I hid it well, though. "What happened?"

There was a pause on the other end. "She's been raped."

Oh, God. Jealousy went out the window, replaced by a feeling of deep stupidity. "Can I do anything?"

There was a hesitation on the other end of the line, as though he wasn't sure what to say. "Meet me at the hospital."

I could tell from the tone of his voice that it had taken a lot for him to say that—to request my presence. "I'll be right there."

I made it to the hospital in record time. All the while I tried to keep my thoughts focused on how awful the situation was. I tried not to indulge in my own petty feelings of jealousy, insecurity and self-doubt. Okay, and maybe a little bit of anger, but admitting to that just makes me all the worse as a person, doesn't it? I mean, I'm supposed to be non-judgmental when it comes to feelings and actions. I'm a psychologist, they teach us that in school.

And normally I can do that—in a professional capacity. I help people deal with their lives through their dreams. I can give them exercises designed to help them live their lives and be healthier emotionally and mentally. But when it comes to my own life, I'm not nearly so adept. I have to work at it.

Of course Noah would run to Amanda's side after such a tragedy. He wouldn't be the man I thought he was if he didn't. And I'm sure there was a good reason why Amanda continued to list him as her next of kin even though their divorce was long since final and her parents lived in the same city.

Long story short: Noah and Amanda divorced after she cheated on him. Apparently things had been falling apart before that. I met Noah when he joined a sleep study conducted through the MacCallum Institute where I used to work as a grunt, doing menial tasks and research while I tried to get my own practice underway.

I managed to keep my relationship with Noah professional until Karatos—the Night Terror—decided he wanted to use Noah, a strong lucid dreamer, to cross over into this realm and do some damage. Karatos was aligned with my father's political foes, who weren't above using me to get to Morpheus. Hence, Karatos decided to kill two birds with one stone—namely me and Noah. We defeated Karatos—I wouldn't be here now if we hadn't.

Noah found out the truth about me because of Karatos. An artist, Noah gets a lot of inspiration from his dreams, which is why there's a portrait of me called "The Nightmare" hanging in Noah's bedroom. He's been my rock through this craziness.

I wasn't sure where my relationship with Noah was headed, or if we had a future, but I liked him enough to not give up without a fight. I also knew him well enough to know that he wouldn't turn his back on Amanda just because they were no longer married. His knight-in-shining-armor complex wouldn't let him.

That's what made me an awful person—being jealous of a woman who had just endured the worst thing a woman physically could. After all, Noah had called me to be there with him, surely that meant something?

But for the moment, as I stepped off the elevator and hurried down a fluorescent-lit corridor that smelled of alcohol, gauze, and antiseptics, I didn't care about the whys of it all. I was scared for Amanda. Like many women I've always believed that rape was one of the worst things that could happen to my gender. You could recover, but you could never forget.

I spotted Noah waiting for me by the nurses' station. In this sterile, bland environment, he was as difficult to miss as a smear of red lipstick on a pale face.

Noah Clarke was tall enough that at five foot ten I had to look up to meet his dark gaze. His hair and eyes were almost completely black, save for a touch of brown that came out in certain lights. His skin was golden, and his jaw was covered with dark stubble. He was dressed in a brown leather jacket, T-shirt, jeans, and boots. He looked tired, but I thought he looked divine.

He also looked happy to see me, which was a plus, given the reason he was here.

I walked toward him. He walked toward me. It was almost like something out of a movie. I increased my pace, almost jogging. What was I going to say? What was the right thing to do?

Noah made that decision for me. As soon as I reached him, he took me into his arms—wonderfully strong arms—and crushed me against his chest, his face buried in my hair. It might not be the kiss I'd imagined for his homecoming, but it was just as good.

"It's good to see you, Doc," he murmured, the scent of him warming my blood with its sweet and spicy heat.

I hugged him back, savoring how solid he was beneath my hands. I might not be sure of where our relationship is going, but I know the direction I'd like to go in. I let myself indulge in these thoughts for just a second or two before shaking off the selfishness.

"How's Amanda?" I asked.

"Not great," he replied, lifting his head. "I'm waiting for her doctor."

"You haven't spoken to him yet?"

"Her, and no. I got the call this morning and I caught

the first plane I could in from L.A. on such short notice."

It was ten o'clock at night. It must have driven him crazy trying to get back here. Luckily New York had three airports including Newark eager to service the city. That would have increased his chances of finding a flight.

"Is her family here?" I asked as we walked down the corridor. Noah kept my hand tucked in his.

"Mandy didn't want them called until I got here. I think she hoped I'd handle them."

That seemed an odd choice of words. "Do they need handling?" Personally, I couldn't imagine anyone who would act like an idiot when their child needed them.

"Her mother is very . . . emotional." His brow puckered a little, as though remembering something unpleasant.

I cast a glance at him, noting the strain around his eyes and mouth. "How are you doing?"

He squeezed my hand, directing a brittle but sincere smile in my direction. "Don't worry about me, Doc."

As far as answers went, it wasn't a great one, but I knew Noah well enough to know that he was having a hard time of it. He prided himself on control, and violence against women was something that pushed his buttons, having spent his formative years watching his father beat his mother. No doubt this brought back memories of hospital visits from years ago, and his mother telling doctors she had fallen down stairs or ran into a door.

A tall woman with graying red hair smoothed into a neat twist stood beside the nurses' station as we approached. "Mr. Clarke? I'm Dr. Van Owen."

Noah held my hand with his left and accepted the doctor's with his right. "How's Amanda?"

Dr. Van Own looked at me, as though she didn't want to say anything in front of me.

Noah made the introductions, adding, "Dawn's a psychologist."

Apparently the good doctor was satisfied with that explanation and she divided her attention between the two of us as she spoke. "Your wife sustained quite a few serious injuries, Mr. Clarke. I'm going to recommend that she stay here for a couple of days."

He didn't correct her on the term wife and I told myself it didn't matter. I should be ashamed of myself for even feeling so jealous at a time like this. "How serious?"

The older woman flashed a quick look at me before continuing, as though she was glad I was the one who would have to deal with the barely restrained anger lurking under Noah's polite exterior. "Lacerations of the scalp and face. She was beaten, choked, and sexually assaulted. However, I don't believe any of her injuries will require surgery. She should be able to go home in a day or two, but I would suggest she see a specialist."

Noah frowned. "I thought you said she didn't need surgery?"

I put my hand on his arm, and kept my voice low. "I don't think that's the kind of specialist the doctor means, Noah." I was already running through my mental address book. Did I know anyone who dealt with victims of violent crime? Surely the hospital could make a referral.

Noah stiffened beside me, his cheeks flushing scarlet. For a moment I thought he might simply explode.

"The police have already spoken to her," the doctor continued, taking a wary step back. "I'm sure an officer can give you particulars. Amanda asked that you be allowed to see her as soon as you arrived. She's two doors down on the left."

Noah thanked her, and I waited until she'd left us to ask, "Do you want me to wait for you?"

"Come with me." He met my gaze with dark, worried eyes. "You know the right things to say."

I knew what he meant, and shook my head. "Noah, I don't think that's a good idea. I'm not comfortable acting in a professional capacity with your ex-wife."

He squeezed my fingers. "Okay. Come anyway."

"All right." But only because I knew deep down that he needed me in that room when he saw Amanda.

"I'm going to stay toward the back, though," I said, holding his hand as we walked down the hall. "Amanda might not appreciate my presence as much as you do." I knew that I wouldn't were the situation reversed.

Two doors down wasn't far. I walked behind Noah as he entered the room, and heard his sharply indrawn breath as he saw the occupant of the lone bed. Private room. That was good.

"Noah," a voice croaked. I recognized it as Amanda's, but it was hoarse and faint. I didn't want to see the face that went with that voice.

He released my hand to move closer to the bed. I didn't follow, but let him go. The stupid jealousy I'd felt earlier was gone, and when Noah stepped to the side, giving me a view of the woman on the bed, every emotion I was capable of fled, replaced by an overwhelming surge of pitiful sorrow.

And horror. There was a lot of that as well.

The Amanda I'd first met a few weeks ago at Noah's gallery showing had been lovely to a fault; a golden-tanned blonde with big eyes and delicate features. She was petite and I'd felt like a pale, lumbering oaf standing next to her.

This woman looked nothing like that Amanda. This woman was swollen, her skin darkened with so many bruises I couldn't begin to count. One eye was purple, shut tight. That side of her face was discolored all the way down to her throat, where a circle of purple and red formed a handprint necklace. No wonder her voice had sounded so awful—the bastard had choked her.

The bruising extended to the flesh of her shoulders. I could see the ruddy abrasions where the neck of her hospital gown had slipped down. Christ, were those teeth marks? I swallowed. Hard.

But it was her head that was the hardest for me to look at. Her golden hair was matted with blood, held back from her face by a sterile gauze head band that held a bandage to her scalp. A quarter-sized circle of blood had soaked through, terribly red against the stark white.

Years of watching *Law and Order: SVU* hadn't prepared me for that stain. TV never got the color of blood just right.

Christ. Part of me thought there were all kinds of crazy in this world. The professional part of me wondered what could happen to a person to compel them to such behavior.

I still didn't like Amanda, knowing how she had betrayed Noah, but my heart went out to her. I'd had my own control taken away from me before, when a Night Terror who tried to possess Noah forcibly "seduced" me. He'd made my body want him even though I knew it was wrong. He hadn't hurt me—not then—but the thought of what he'd done made my stomach twist like a French braid. Even using me as a punching bag hadn't left scars as thick as that violation.

But that was in the past. I had survived, and so would Amanda. Drawing another deep breath for strength, I eased myself forward, close enough to hear some of what was being said, but not enough to be an intrusion.

"Do you need anything?" Noah asked. He held one of his ex-wife's hands in his. Her knuckles were raw and swollen. She had fought back, brave thing.

"There's nothing you can do," Amanda replied in that awful voice. "Having you here is enough."

I definitely didn't want to hear this. I was an outsider. I shouldn't be here, witnessing this woman's pain, witnessing the safety she felt now that her husband—*ex*-husband—was there with her.

"Dawn is here too." Noah surprised me by glancing over his shoulder at me. Making sure I was still there, I suppose.

"Dawn?" Amanda peered past Noah, meeting my gaze with her one good eye.

No more hiding for me. I was forced to hold that battered gaze as I walked toward the two of them. She looked worse with every step. "Hi, Amanda." I should apologize for being present, for witnessing her pain, but I couldn't find the words to express it without sounding like an ass.

Her expression was a mixture of defiance and wariness that I recognized from having worked with a few victims of violent crime. Granted the last few years I'd dealt mostly with dreams, but some of those dreamers were victims of violence suffering from post-traumatic shock.

"Thank you for coming." She was all grace and elegance despite having been beaten and brutalized. This show of strength wasn't merely for my benefit, or even for Noah's. It was for herself. Amanda was determined to hold it together no matter what.

When she held out her poor little battered hand, I came forward and took it. If I had any strength in me worthy of her, she was welcome to it.

Standing there, holding her delicate fingers, feeling those birdlike bones beneath my own, filled me with a profound sense of protection. I wanted to help her, and keep her from ever being hurt again. She was so much smaller than I, in height and weight. Blond to my dark, brown to my blue, and tanned to my pale. She was like delicate gold filigree and I was sturdy brass; and yet looking at her, I thought she was the strongest woman I had ever met, simply because she held it together when I would have been a sniveling, snot-spewing mess.

A Bambi-like gaze bore into mine, but that was where the Disney comparison stopped. Bambi never looked so angry or defiant. "Have you ever been raped?"

Whoa. Hadn't seen that coming. Anyone else and I

would have told her it was none of her damn business, but this was something of a "quid pro quo, Clarisse" moment. I knew what she had been through, and in her mind that put me at some kind of advantage. And she'd had enough power taken away.

"Yes," I replied, stomping down the urge to look at Noah. As it was, I could feel the tension in his body as he stood rigid and still beside me.

Something changed in Amanda's expression—a softening for lack of better term. She looked at me like a sister of sorts, one of the other two women who helped form the "three out of four" women who were supposedly raped or victim to some kind of sexual assault in the course of their lifetime.

Three. Out of fucking four.

Noah cleared his throat. It was a ragged sound. "I thought you might want to talk to Dawn."

Amanda's gaze was blank as it turned to him. "About what?"

"About what happened."

Her features hardened, just the slightest bit as she looked at him—as someone who had just betrayed her trust. "I don't."

I respected that. Hell, I was glad for it. This was not my specialty, and even if it was, this was way too close for comfort. Part of me was annoyed with Noah for suggesting it, even though his heart was in the right place.

Thankfully, before Noah could say anything else, Amanda's parents arrived. Noah must have called them after he called me. Her father, a stocky man with thick gray hair, was white with shock. Her mother, a pretty little blonde, had obviously been crying, though she had pulled herself together before entering the room. It wouldn't be long before she lost it again—I could see it in the slight tremble of her shoulders.

Parents. Always trying to be so strong for their children. My own parents were pretty weak in the parental-support department. They were really there for each other, though.

Noah took them both aside, speaking to them quietly. Amanda's mother began to sob softly. I tried not to eavesdrop or stare, but there wasn't much else to focus on, except for Amanda.

Reluctantly, I turned to the woman on the bed, the woman who was watching me as though daring me to face her. Or maybe, like me, she couldn't bare looking at her parents.

"You can't stand the sight of me, can you?" she asked hoarsely.

I shook my head. "It's not you. It's what he did that's difficult to look at it." She deserved my honesty if nothing else.

Her mouth trembled. "Is it that bad?"

I lied. "I've seen worse."

That was when Noah finished talking and Amanda's parents came to the bed. Her father was stiff and uncertain, pain etched all over his face. Her mother was bowed, obvious in her pain, but there was no hesitation. I was removed from the situation just enough to find these subtle differences in strength interesting.

Noah and I left then. I didn't want to witness the family's interaction, and I don't think Noah was comfortable around his former in-laws. They certainly didn't try to hide the fact that they weren't impressed to see him there. Probably, they weren't impressed that he was the one Amanda wanted there first. Had I the inclination, I'd probably put my mind to all kinds of theories as to why that was.

Quite frankly, I just didn't want to go there.

Out in the corridor, Noah cupped his hand around the back of my neck as we walked, and pulled me to his side. He pressed his lips to my temple as his fingers gently squeezed.

"Thank you," he said.

I glanced up at him, my hip bumping his as we matched our stride. "For what? I didn't do anything."

"You came when I called," he replied with a soft smile. "I knew you'd know what to do if I didn't."

I was flattered that he had such a high opinion of me. "I wish there was something I could do for her," I remarked. And I meant it.

Noah stopped walking and so did I. When I turned to ask what was up, he caught me in a kiss that made my lips tingle and my heart pound. "What was that for?" I asked, slightly dazed.

His thumb brushed my cheek. "For being the best person I know."

It might not have been a declaration of love, but damn if it didn't feel like it.

We didn't immediately return to Noah's apartment as we met up with Amanda's sisters at the elevators. He had to fill them in on what had happened to Amanda and how she was doing.

All I could think about was that he had torn out a chunk of her hair. Why did I think about that? Hair would grow back. Her external injuries would heal. The injuries to her psyche should be what concerned me, but as a woman—and a rather vain, girly one at that, all I could think about was that missing chunk of hair that would take so very long to look natural again.

For a moment, I thought about what I would do in that situation. I would want revenge. I would track the S.O.B. through his dreams and give him dreams that would haunt him for the rest of his life.

But it wasn't me, and the last time I had messed with someone that way had been a girl in junior high back in Toronto. Jackey Jenkins humiliated me and I went into her dreams and hurt her way more than I ever meant to. I'd never tried to do anything like that again. I swore I never would.

We grabbed some food at an all-night diner and talked a little about his trip to L.A. He'd been there for a showing of some of his paintings. It had gone well, and he seemed genuinely pleased. I was glad for that.

Over coffee we caught up on our lives like nothing bad had happened, yet there was a dark cloud over us—that invisible film that shock and tragedy leaves behind on your skin.

It was just before dawn when we reached Noah's apartment. My aunt Eos, the goddess charged with bringing light to the earth, lightened the sky with a glimmer of golden gray that would build and intensify into a riot of pinks, oranges, reds, and yellows before the sun rose into the sky, bringing day to the world. I was named after Eos's domain—for the wonder spreading across the horizon, bathing Manhattan in a sweet, almost preternatural glow—and I was proud of that.

Sometimes it's hard even for me to wrap my head around not being totally human. Noah had taken it well when he found out what I was. He had suspicions before I told him the truth—actually it was Karatos who told him, I just filled in the blanks. He accepted what I am and asked questions when he needed to. I don't think I would have handled it so well were our roles reversed.

Noah and I climbed the stairs to his apartment in silence. He hadn't come right out and asked me to stay, but he hadn't let go of me since we left the hospital. I assumed he wasn't ready to let me go just yet.

The glossy wood, high creamy walls and huge windows of his home welcomed us with a stillness that was calming and strangely welcoming. We went upstairs to his loft bedroom, stripped and crawled between the soft, buttery sheets. Thank God I didn't have any appointments booked until eleven. I could catch a little sleep before going into work.

"Are you all right?" I asked him—finally—as he drew me close.

"No," Noah replied, rubbing his hand up and down my arm, which was draped over his chest. His fingers were warm and soothing.

"She'll be all right," I promised, though I had no right. I was sincere in my hopes that she would recover with no lasting damage done physically or emotionally.

"Can you help her?"

I stiffened. He felt it too. He had to. "Noah, Amanda said she didn't want to talk to me. I can't force her. Given my relationship with you, I think its best that I don't cross any lines. Besides, I don't have much experience with victims of rape. She deserves treatment from someone who knows what they're doing."

He looked down at me. I could feel his fathomless gaze on the top of my head. "You have experience with dreams," he said softly. "Could you help her there?"

I laughed in disbelief, lifting up on my elbow to look at him. "The man who told me to stay out of his dreams wants me to intrude upon someone else's?" So much for a pleasant reunion between the two of us.

He didn't even flinch. "If it will help her, yes." His brow puckered. "I'm not asking you to alter her thoughts or mess with her head."

"Then what are you asking?"

His frown deepened. "I don't know."

The defensiveness that had crept over me loosened its hold at the frustration in his expression. He felt helpless—a state no one liked to be in, especially a man who swore never to be helpless again. I wasn't jealous because it was for Amanda, and I wasn't angry that he asked me to use my abilities for his ex-wife. What I felt was sympathy for him—and something warm and fuzzy too. He was a good man.

"I'll check on her," I told him. "But not tonight. The pain meds will make it difficult for her to dream."

"Thank you." He yawned, his eyes closing. "I hate thinking about what Karatos did to you."

"Ssh. That doesn't matter." I wondered if he would bring that up. We hadn't really talked much about it at the time, or afterward for that matter. It was old, as far as I was concerned. I was starting to become part of the "that which does not kill us makes us stronger" club. Maybe it was because I'd watched *Steel Magnolias* one too many times, or maybe I was finally growing up, but Karatos no longer had any power over me, and I refused to give any to his memory.

Noah fell asleep before I did. I wanted to make sure he was restful before I let myself go. He didn't like me popping unexpectedly into his dreams, but I'd keep my senses open to him in case he called.

I slipped into the realm the "normal" way this time. It was just like slipping out had been earlier. At least I was getting the hang of *something*. My dream self relaxed on a nice, warm beach beneath a hot sun until a familiar shadow fell over me.

I opened my eyes. Looming over me was Verek. The last time we met on a beach he'd teased me and lost some clothes—a rather splendid sight. Right now, he looked grim.

"No more training tonight," I told him warily. "I'm not up for it."

Verek shook his head and squatted beside me. The muscles in his thighs bulged beneath the fine fabric covering them. "I'm here to serve summons on you, my lady."

My lady? Usually he called me Princess and only in the most mocking of tones. "That's a little formal isn't it?" I laughed. Verek didn't. So I sat up. "Shit, Verek. What kind of summons?"

He sighed. "Tonight you will stand before the Nightmare Council and face inquiry into your actions."

My heart gave a thud. "My actions? What have I done?"

He looked almost sympathetic. "The Warden was there when you brought Noah into our world, Dawn. You broke the rules and now you must stand before the counsel and explain yourself."

Explain myself? Part of me wanted to tell him just what he could do with his summons—what the Warden could do for that matter. I hadn't known when I brought Noah into the Dream Realm during our fight against Karatos that it was something I wasn't allowed to do, never mind that it had been something I shouldn't be *able* to do.

How could they punish me for doing something no one ever thought possible? But apparently it fell under some rule about not endangering humans. Please, I had been trying to save Noah, not hurt him.

"This is bullshit," I told him. "The Council is freaked

out by me and is looking for a way to keep me under control." I am the daughter of the lord of this realm! Just who does this Warden person think he was?

"What if I refuse?" I asked.

Verek's rugged features hardened. "Then I am to bring you back to the castle in shackles to await the proceedings."

"My father won't stand for that."

Now he looked downright pitying. "It was your father who gave the order."

Oh, damn.

Chapter Two

"You look like crap." This lovely sentiment was the first thing I heard as I stepped into the reception area of the Madison Avenue offices I shared with the Drs. Clarke.

Noah's stepfather Edward and stepbrother Warren were psychiatrists who offered me my own office within their successful practice. Edward claimed to be impressed with a paper I wrote on lucid dreaming, but I think their offer had more to do with Noah than me. Still, I hoped to prove myself worthy of their kindness and grabbed the opportunity to build my own practice.

I paused in the reception area, still a little awed by the marble floor, richly colored rugs, and elegant but comfortable furniture. Soft lighting, plush cushions, and subdued but colorful artwork kept the space from seeming stuffy, and gave it a welcoming air. I'd really lucked out when Warren and Edward offered me a spot within their practice.

Bonnie Nadalini was at her huge oak desk in the empty waiting room, smiling at me with a coy smile that seemed possible only by women of a certain age. And by that I mean women who have reached the "I am woman, hear me roar" stage of life—usually her late forties, early fifties. I'd brought her over from the sleep center—and the Clarkes gave her a position as well. I thought the world of her, and that was why I didn't take offense at her pointing out the obvious.

I shot her a patently false smile. "You always know just what to say to a girl."

She shrugged, flicking her carefully highlighted blond hair over a thin shoulder with a manicured hand. Her nails were fire engine red today. "It's only because I care, kiddo." Her tone was light, but there was real concern in her green eyes. "You okay?"

Bonnie didn't know that I wasn't all human. I mean really, how could I tell her that? However, she'd been with me through everything at the sleep institute, and she'd been there for me when Karatos killed one of my patients to get to me. She knew about my strange relationship with my family, and she knew that I was dat-

ing Noah. In fact, she was very much a mother figure to
me—especially since my own mother had been absent
for part of my life.

I nodded. "Just tired. We had to go to the hospital
last night. Noah had a family emergency." It was the
best way I could think to phrase it without violating
Amanda's privacy.

And without telling her that a Nightmare had come
to me in my sleep and told me that my father had given
him permission to forcibly bring me into the realm.

Lines etched across Bonnie's forehead. She didn't
believe in Botox and having her muscles cut and all that
cosmetic stuff. I didn't have any lines yet, so I reserved
judgment for when that time actually came.

"What kind of an emergency?" she asked. "Is Noah
all right?"

Bonnie sometimes acted like a horn-dog, especially
where Noah was concerned, but I knew she truly liked
him and wanted things to work out for us. "He's fine."
Then I added, "Everyone's fine."

The lines eased, but she still looked concerned.
"You sure, kiddo? I can rearrange your schedule for the
morning if you need to be with him."

I handed her the chai latte I'd bought for her and lifted my own huge paper cup. "What I need is appointments." I had bills to pay. "Let me down this bad boy
and I'm ready to go."

Bonnie eagerly took a drink. Pleasure softened her face. She was so easy. "I love you, doll. I really do."

I grinned. "I know it. Hey, can you pull the files for my first two appointments and bring them to my office? I want to be on the ball when they arrive."

She said that she would and I went to unlock the door to my office. At the sleep institute I'd had a little office. Here, I had a larger space—with my own bathroom! Not just larger, but nicer. No longer was I stuck in a box with white walls and nondescript furniture. Here, I had a pale carpet, a salmon-colored microfiber sofa and matching armchair. Both were overstuffed and so comfortable you could sink right into them. My coffee table was topped with light sage green satin, quilted and firm enough to hold a cup of coffee without spilling. I had curtains in the windows, softly printed, hanging from thick wooden rods. I'd handpicked the art on the wall—most of which had been painted by Noah, depicting soft, gauzy scenes in pre-Raphaelite colors that made me feel good just looking at them.

My desk—a large, heavy, very English-looking monstrosity sat in the back corner with a large bookshelf and an office chair that matched the other furniture. I set my laptop bag on the desk along with my coffee and hung my coat up in the small closet. Then I made sure there was toilet paper in my darling little loo—it even had a shower!—and that it was tidy and clean.

I was unpacking my laptop when Bonnie knocked and came in with the files. "Here you go. Your first two appointments." She paused and gazed around the room. "You know, this is nicer than most apartments."

I grinned. "We lucked out with this space, Bonnie."

She rolled her eyes. "You're not kidding. Hey, you want to do lunch today?"

I did, and I told her so. She left after we agreed on a spot. Bonnie was a welcome distraction, just as my clients would be—I didn't like calling them patients. They came to me and talked about issues they had in their lives. We talked a lot about dreams. Most of my clients were bothered by nightmares—traditional ones, not ones like mine—or disturbing dreams of one sort or another. I helped them work through the issues that caused them, and taught them to use their dreams to their own benefit. Dreams can be fantastic therapy if we as humans can make ourselves face and understand them. That's the hard part.

So I was glad that my first appointment would arrive soon. Left on its own for too long, my mind either drifted to thoughts of poor Amanda and her bloody scalp, or Verek and the announcement that the Nightmare Warden wanted to see me.

Wanted my head on a platter was more like it.

It was no secret that there were many in the Dream Realm who didn't like my father or his ways of ruling the land. They didn't like me or my mother either. We were looked upon as evidence of my father's "weakness."

Did I mention that I'm not supposed to exist? A lot of people in my father's world wish that I didn't. And I was beginning to get a little paranoid that maybe someone was trying to make that wish come true.

Before I was born my mother lost a child. She was overwhelmed by grief, and in her depression slept a lot. Morpheus was apparently struck by her sadness, and her pretty face. He began doing things to try to help her and they became lovers. My mother wasn't the first human to attract the Dream King's attention, but she was the first to give birth to a child of both realms. The only one of my kind, the Dreamkin tend to either be in awe or fear of me. And they despised my mother for making Morpheus vulnerable.

Really, shouldn't someone wonder what it was about her that made her capable of having his child? How was she capable of getting pregnant in a *dream*? No one knew the answer. Morpheus had lots of theories— the best of which was that somehow he had made my mother's dreams so real to her that she managed to make them a reality. Therefore, she wanted to have a child—his child—so badly her body made it happen.

Makes you go, hmmm, doesn't it?

While they were at it, shouldn't someone wonder why she had managed to stay asleep for more than two years, her body in stasis in Toronto, while she lived the life of a "desperate housewife" in the Dreaming? Obviously my mother wasn't a normal human anymore than I was.

Okay, maybe she was *slightly* more normal than I.

And what about me? I used to think I was immortal, but now I wasn't so sure. I can die in this world—I think. But in the Dream Realm I would have to be "unmade" to knock me out of existence. And it probably wouldn't hurt to think that someone other than my father might be able to make that happen. Keep myself on my toes, so to speak.

I didn't know for sure that someone wanted me dead, and I had some confidence in my own ability to defend myself. I also was having one of those moments when I realized that my life could be worse. I'd take my lumps from the Nightmare Warden because I had to. I would probably survive it with a lot less trauma than Amanda was suffering through right now.

I opened the first file. No way was I going to fill my head with images of Amanda before seeing a client. That just wouldn't be fair. My good intentions were thwarted, however, when the phone rang. Most of my calls go through Bonnie first, and only a handful of people had my direct number. Noah was one of them, and somehow I knew it was him calling before I even picked up the receiver and heard his low, chocolaty voice on the other end.

"Hey, Doc." My stomach fluttered like the wings of a thousand caged butterflies at his greeting. Part of it was my usual reaction to him, but the rest of it was guilt. I hadn't told him about my summons to appear before the Warden, and I had no intention of telling him anything about it unless I had to. He didn't need me adding another damsel in distress to the list.

Oh frig. As soon as the phrase filtered through my brain, I winced. Damsel in distress? That was cold of me, and uncalled for.

"Hey, Noah." Could he hear the lameness in my voice? "What's up?"

"I'm at the hospital with Amanda."

"How's she doing?"

"She's good." I could tell from the stiffness in his voice that she really wasn't—not in his opinion. "We were wondering if maybe you could stop by after work?"

We were wondering. I forced a smile onto my face, even though there was no one there to appreciate the effort. I should say no. "Sure. I should be there around four thirty. Is that okay?"

"Great." I could hear the relief and pleasure in his voice. It buoyed me a little—but only just a little. "See you then."

I hung up. We hadn't gotten to the stage where we said things like "love you" at the end of a phone conversation, and that was okay. I wasn't sure I was ready for that. But I wasn't sure how I felt about this latest development either. Referring to himself and Amanda as "we" was innocent enough, and understandable. After all, they had been married once upon a time. Those bonds, even once broken, were hard to sometimes sever completely.

Was I jealous? I could say I wasn't, but no one would believe that, would they? I was an awful person being even the slightest bit threatened by Amanda when she had been through such a terrible ordeal. Awful and petty. That didn't stop the feeling, however. I was jealous—just a little. I was jealous over the bond they had despite the breakup of their marriage. I was jealous that Noah would drop everything to help her—I wanted to be the only woman he dropped everything to be with.

But it was more than my own miserable insecurities niggling at me. I wasn't really worried that Noah would dump me and go running back to a woman who had cheated on him and brought about the end of their marriage. No, I was worried about Noah's attachment to a woman who had been horribly mistreated by a man and was vulnerable.

A woman he might see as needing protection.

I didn't know much about Noah's past. He simply didn't talk about it. I had, however, picked up enough to know that his father had been a real piece of work. And I had seen something in Noah's art, and in his dreams (that was why he didn't want me just "showing up" anymore) that gave me enough insight to guess what his mother must have gone through.

I could very easily imagine a young Noah championing his bullied mother. I'd bet that's why he learned aikido as well—so he could fight for her, be her knight in shining armor.

And that's exactly why I was a little worried about his new devotion to Amanda. Noah was a good man, but he had a thing about rescuing women, protecting them. I could see it in his work, feel it in his dreams, and hear it on occasion in his words. Maybe I was overly paranoid, but come on—I hadn't gone to school for as long as I had to appease my paranoia. I was trained to see these things. And I saw all of this in my boyfriend's actions.

I didn't want Noah to rescue me, or appoint himself my protector. But I'd be lying if I said I wasn't a little bit concerned that those feelings inside him might not overpower all else where she was concerned. If anyone needed a champion right now it was Amanda, and Noah just might indulge his need to be needed.

And I was worried about what indulging that need might do to us when we were still so new.

But enough of that. I finished skimming through the

file on my first client and glanced up at the clock. As though watching me on hidden camera, Bonnie buzzed to tell me that Teresa, my first appointment, had arrived. I'd managed to quickly skim her file and the notes her referring doctor had made. She could fill me in on the rest.

A few of those people involved in my dream studies at the old clinic had decided to visit me for dream therapy on occasion, but most of my case load came from referrals at the moment. Right now, I didn't have many cases, but that would change soon enough. I hoped. I had a really good deal with Warren and Edward, but I still had an apartment to pay for, food, and an addiction to makeup that needed to be indulged on occasion.

So I put all else from my head and applied my focus and energy on Teresa and her issues. After her forty-five minutes was up I had another client, and then lunch with Bonnie. By the time we returned to the office I was tired of having little questions pop up in my head when they weren't wanted. I couldn't shake the Warden's summons, or the fact that my father had sanctioned them. I guess I was more concerned than I thought I was. And it certainly couldn't hurt to be prepared.

I told Bonnie I had work to do and that I didn't want to be interrupted, then I locked the door to my office just in case, and went to the bathroom. I took a deep breath and gathered my energy. Then, without using my hands, I pulled open a portal between this world and the Dream Realm. I thought of it as a cosmic zipper that I could pull open between dimensions. My father would probably laugh at the comparison, but it worked for me and that was really all that mattered.

It was literally a fracture of the world, the air before me seemed solid and tangible. It separated like fabric tore down the center, revealing a world beyond this; a world shrouded in mist and darkness, where lights twinkled like stars and anything was possible.

Once the portal had "unzipped" enough, I was able to step through. It was like stepping through a hole in a wall and into another room, only this room was another world entirely. Apparently I had the power to control the Dreaming, though I had yet to really test that theory. My abilities, such as they were, were rusty at best. I had no idea what I could do—no one did. Only one of my kind, remember?

Right now that was the least of my concerns. I had to talk to my father. I'm not sure if it was proof of how much trouble I was in, but my portal hadn't taken me right into the royal palace as it normally did. It took me to the gates of horn and ivory—huge, towering gates that barred the way into the capital city. Dark and majestic, they loomed over me in the darkness as I approached. Behind me, the mist slowly crept, inching closer. Whispering.

The Dream Realm could be a dangerous place, but its first objective—in the area around my father's palace—was to protect dreamers. That was the golden rule here. There were Terrors and other entities within this world who would do harm if they could. Weren't there always? And there were those who wouldn't hesitate to use me to get to Morpheus. All the more reason not to waste time out here, despite the gorgeous view of the twinkling lights of the kingdom and the breathtaking sight of the palace lit up like something out of Disney World.

I closed the portal behind me and strode toward the gates. I held my breath as my hands reached up and grabbed the carved ivory handle. When I pushed, the air rushed from my lungs in relief. The gate swung open. At least it recognized me as a non-threat.

I walked quickly along the smooth stones that glimmered with hints of blue and gold in the moonlight. This road led straight to the palace itself and was lined with outbuildings, homes, and other places necessary to a kingdom's success. There was even a pub.

When I reached the castle, towering and winged obsidian guards watched my approach with wary gazes. Had they been expecting me? Had they been told to treat me as friend or foe? And were they afraid of me? I'd rather open hostility to this wariness, I think.

"Your highness." They each bowed to me, opening

the main door of the palace for me. "The king is in the library."

Meaning I should go directly there. Do not pass Go, do not collect $200. Look at me, witty girl.

But the guard hadn't had to tell me that. I knew that's where my parents were. I felt them there, just as they knew I had come to visit without having it announced.

I thanked the guards and entered the castle. I had but a second to appreciate the great hall and its neoclassical style before the air shimmered, blurring my surroundings until there was nothing left, and then slowly bringing them back as something new. My father had brought me to him—or rather to just inside the library door—rather than waiting for me to make the journey myself. Fabulous.

Was this just because of the Warden? Or had I done something else that was against the rules? I really had to learn more about this world, but it seemed to come hurdling at me faster than I could absorb it all.

My father stood by the hearth, like he'd stepped out of a *GQ* spread. He didn't smile, but I could see pleasure in his pale blue eyes. That made me feel at least a little better. He was rugged, built like a construction worker, with reddish brown hair and handsome features. He usually wore jeans and a sweater—the way my mother liked him. I have no doubt he changed his looks according to his audience, a fact that creeped me out a little. What did he really look like? And could I do the same thing?

"Dawn." He had a rugged voice too—deep and slightly rough. "This is a surprise."

"No it isn't," I said, slipping past him into the room. I loved the library. It had every book ever written—ever dreamed of. It had been great for school reports. "You knew telling Verek he could bring me in shackles would prompt a visit. Hi, Mom."

My mother, a petite brunette, looked as elegant as ever, though a little tired. "Hello, sweetie."

I turned on my father, who had closed the door and was watching me with that resigned expression every father seemed to know. "I had to."

"Why?" I demanded, a sudden flash of anger drowning every other emotion. "So you can hand me over to the Warden like a prisoner?"

"So I could be sure you'd understand the gravity of the situation," he fired back. Now he looked angry—and upset. "I can't show partiality, Dawn, and I can't interfere on your behalf. To do so would undermine my own position—and make things worse for you."

Well damn. All the fight went out of me, and I had to try really hard not to slouch. I hadn't slouched since I was fourteen and I'd reached my full height.

"How bad is it?" I asked.

He shrugged his broad shoulders, folding his arms

across his chest as he passed me to walk deeper into the room—toward my mother. "The Warden wants to investigate your bringing Noah into this realm."

"That's crap and you know it. How could I have known it was wrong?"

Morpheus smiled. "Yes, I know it. Your ignorance might serve as a viable excuse when coupled with your genuine concern for Noah, and the attacks launched against him by Karatos." His smile faded. "Or, the Council might see it as faulty preparation on my part. Regardless, they will judge in a manner they see fit, and I will do all in my power to help both of us weather the consequences."

I sighed. "I can't believe this is such a big deal."

"It's a big deal," he said, placing his big hands on my shoulders. "Because they're scared. You did something even I cannot do, and that kind of power terrifies the Council."

Oh yeah, I'd forgotten. Even Morpheus can't bring humans into the Dream Realm. If he could, my mother's body wouldn't be languishing in a bed in Toronto, driving my family sick with concern because she wouldn't wake up. I couldn't bring her into the Dreaming either. Well, I could, but she wouldn't be able to stay for any length of time. No human could. At least, no human that I knew of. I wasn't about to say no as an absolute.

After all, I was against all the laws of that world as well.

I managed a smile. "Think I can scare them into leaving me alone?"

"They can only affect you in this world," he reminded me. "Not in the human realm. And while I can't interfere with their process, I can make things very difficult for them if they overstep their boundaries."

That made me feel better—at least a little. Then I noticed the lines around his eyes and the circles beneath. He looked tired as well. I glanced at my mother. She was more than tired, she was scared.

"Is there something you two aren't telling me?" I asked. I admit, my fear was mostly for myself.

Mom sighed. "I went into your sister Ivy's dreams last night."

I knew she did that—in fact I had met her in one once. She did it with all my siblings. It was her way of checking in on her kids and grandchildren. No, I didn't think it was the same as actually being there for them, but I knew it wasn't an easy choice for her, and I was trying really hard not to judge her for it.

"Is something wrong with Ivy?" Screw fear for myself. My oldest sister sometimes drove me to distraction, but I loved her to death. I loved all my siblings, even though they had no idea that I was more than human.

Mom shook her head, wringing her delicate

hands in her lap. "The specialist they've called in—Dr. Ravenelli—is coming by the day after tomorrow to examine me."

Oh, shit. A while ago my family had heard of this "doctor" who claimed he could bring mom out of the coma she was in. Apparently my family believed him because they'd hired him. How this man planned to sever the hold of the God of Dreams, I have no idea, but obviously my parents were concerned that he just might do it.

Not, of course, that Ravenelli could have any idea just what he was up against, right?

Or did he? I mean, it could just be a coincidence, but given everything else Morpheus's enemies had tried, it wouldn't surprise me if they were behind this. How much effort would it take to go into a dream and convince this guy that he could wake my mother? Worse, what if they told him *how*?

I looked at my father, my heart tripping. Coming after me was one thing, but my mother . . . "He's no match for you, is he?"

Morpheus shook his head. "Not for me, no."

My attention shot back to my mother. "You?"

She was pale. "I'm scared that he will bring me back. And yet, part of me thinks I should just let him."

I raised my brows. This was new. "Really?"

She nodded. "I've missed my family, Dawn. I'm not as cold and heartless as you think."

I didn't reply. The jury was still out on that most days. I opened my mouth, but my father cut me off. "There's nothing to worry about, Maggie. I've been in his dreams. He's no threat. You're not going anywhere."

He went to her and put his hands on her shoulders, standing behind her like some great avenging angel. She couldn't see his face, but I could, and the look on it gave me a shiver. I pitied that specialist if he did manage to wake my mother. In fact, I pitied anyone who came between my parents. My father might be soft when it came to me and my mother, but he was a god, and historically speaking, gods don't like to be crossed.

Being his daughter, that technically made me a goddess—or at least half one. I didn't like being crossed either, come to think of it. And I had no idea what I was capable of—except that I could do things that even Morpheus couldn't.

No wonder the Nightmare Council was scared.

I was too.

Chapter Three

True to my word, I walked into Amanda's hospital room at four thirty-two that afternoon. She was resting—a bruised china doll against the stark sheets. Her injuries looked worse in the harsh light of day than they had the night before. There was probably some reason why swelling and bruising always got worse before it got better, but I didn't know it. It didn't seem fair.

Noah sat beside the bed, reading a dog-eared Stephen King novel. Gruesome reading made even more gruesome by the circumstances, but King was his favorite, and if the book provided a distraction from reality, I was happy for it.

He looked up as I approached, and as tired as he was, his face lit up when he saw me. I liked that. He held up his hand to stop me from coming any further, slipped quietly out of his chair and silently crossed the room to meet me. He steered me into the small bathroom and closed the door behind us.

I opened my mouth to say hello, but words failed me as he cupped my face with his hands and kissed me like his life depended on it.

My arms went around his waist, pulling him close as our lips moved together, dancing in a slow, sweet waltz that not only had me sighing, but tingling in all the right places. The sink pressed into the back of my legs, cool porcelain through my jeans, raising goose bumps on my thighs.

God he felt good. Firm and lean, strong beneath my hands. Warm. He was so warm and hard. And he tasted faintly of peppermint—hot, wet peppermint. He hadn't shaved and his jaw was rough. I was going to have a bad case of whisker burn when we finally came up for air and I didn't care. It was just so good to be in his arms—and to know that he wanted me. Sounds sappy, but it was true.

"Well, hello," I murmured when our mouths finally separated.

Noah smiled—slow and sexy. "Hey, Doc. I missed you."

Awwww. I grinned. "I missed you too." I let a few seconds pass. "How's Amanda?"

Yup, I knew how to kill a moment, but I had to ask. I

mean, we were sucking face in her bathroom—it wasn't really tactful.

"I don't know," he replied, running a hand through the thick black of his perpetually mussed hair. "She woke up screaming earlier. She won't talk to me about it. She just held my hand until she went back to sleep."

I nodded. "I doubt she'll talk to me either." Regardless of how I felt about Noah asking me to be there, I wouldn't turn Amanda away if she wanted to talk. But, she would be in charge, and I would follow whatever pace she set. Rape often left victims with a kind of post-traumatic stress, and that could manifest in many different ways. The physical ordeal might be over, but for Amanda, the mental suffering was just beginning. I didn't tell this to Noah, however.

He stroked my hair. "Thanks for coming."

"You're welcome." And then, because I couldn't help myself, "Are you going to hang around here tonight?" The minute the words left my mouth I wished I could take them back. They seemed so selfish.

He still had some of my hair between his fingers. He rubbed it, smiling vaguely. "No. Amanda's mother's going to be with her. She hates me, so if you can stand it, I'm all yours tonight."

Oh, I could stand it. "Sounds good." Especially since I was going to face the Warden tonight. A nice evening with Noah would make me all the braver.

He gave me another quick, hard kiss, tugged on my hair, and then opened the bathroom door. I followed him to the bed. Amanda stirred at our approach.

"Mandy," Noah said softly. "Dawn's here."

The Barry Manilow song started playing in my head, accessing the library of pop culture I seemed to house. Amanda's eyelashes fluttered, finally opening to reveal brown, groggy eyes—or rather one groggy eye. The other was still very swollen. They had to be giving her something to sleep. Was she able to dream? Not much, I bet. The sooner she could face the dreams, the sooner she would begin to heal.

"Dawn," she croaked. "Hi." She sounded awful, so hoarse and frail.

I forced a smile. "Hi, there. You up for a little company?"

She shrugged, then winced. I couldn't imagine the pain she was in. "Sure." Her gaze flitted to Noah and he smiled.

"I'm going to go get a coffee," he announced. "I'll be back before your mom gets here."

I tried not to show—or voice—my surprise. He was going to leave me? Here, with his traumatized ex-wife? Did he need caffeine that badly, or had I been so easily duped into playing doctor with a woman who didn't want my help?

Either way, I was a little pissed, and I shot him a look

that told him that. In return, I got a look that wasn't so much contrite as it was determined. His concern for Amanda was admirable—sorta—but his methods left something to be desired.

Noah's ex-wife fumbled for his hand with her own, and gave his fingers a squeeze before letting him go. "Thanks."

He bent and kissed her forehead. The gesture struck me as sweet, and more than a little sad.

When he was gone, and Amanda and I were alone, I eased closer to the bed. "Can I get you anything?"

She shook her head and lifted her left arm. "They've got me on tubes for everything. It hurts to eat, hurts to pee. Tubes take care of it." She laughed humorlessly and I swallowed. Hurt to pee? Christ.

Then she looked at me. "You know, you're the first person who hasn't asked me how I'm doing."

I didn't think she was offended by that either. "I guess the answer is fairly obvious."

A hint of a smile curved her swollen lips. "Noah won't let me look at myself."

I kept my expression guarded. Whether or not I agreed with Noah didn't matter. He was trying to do what he thought best, but taking more of Amanda's control away wasn't going to help her. "Do you really want to see?" I asked.

She nodded. "I do."

I rummaged through my bag and found my compact *du jour*. I opened the plastic container and offered it to Amanda. She took it with trembling fingers. "I have this kind," she remarked, with the kind of surreal observation I often experienced in my line of work.

"It's good stuff," I replied evenly, trying not to hold my breath as she angled the mirror to better see herself with her one good eye.

She was quiet as she surveyed the damage. I watched, looking for any flicker of emotion. Amanda stared at her own reflection as though looking at a stranger.

"It's not as bad as I thought," she said finally, handing the compact back to me. "Nice to know I look better than I feel."

I dropped the makeup into my bag once more, and then set the supple leather on the chair by the bed—the one Noah had been sitting in when I arrived. "Do you want to talk about it?"

She shook her head. It was a little unnerving, having that one dark eye focused so sharply on me. "Not really."

"Okay." I was relieved. I didn't want to be her doctor, and I didn't know if we could ever be friends, so her not wanting to talk took the pressure off of me to be anything to her.

I guess she figured she owed me an explanation. "I don't want your pity."

"I don't pity you."

That one-eye gaze bore sharply into mine. "After what I did to Noah, I guess you don't."

"Noah's got nothing to do with it," I told her honestly. "I feel for you, and I genuinely hope that you make a full recovery."

She was silent for a moment. Maybe she was collecting her thoughts, or maybe she was wondering if I was sincere, and how much of that sincerity came from my desire to not share Noah with her any longer than I had to. If asked, I'd say maybe fifty percent.

How was that for honesty?

"I went for a walk," Amanda rasped, her battered throat obviously kicking up a fuss at being forced to make words. She took a sip of water. "Alone, late at night. You going to tell me how stupid that was? Everyone else has."

"Like who?" I really hoped Noah hadn't said that.

Amanda shrugged. "Everyone thinks it. I can see it."

This was so not good for her. "Amanda, it's not stupid to feel safe in familiar surroundings. And even if it was, stupidity doesn't deserve what happened to you. It's not your fault. I've walked home alone at night." I'd be on my guard if I had to do it now, let me tell you.

She smiled slightly at me. "Having been raped before, don't you think you should know better?"

I wasn't sure if she was teasing or actually taking me to task. "So I should act like a frightened little girl? A victim? I should hide instead of living my life?"

She grabbed my hand and clung to it with surprising strength. I could see a little dried blood beneath her nails and wondered if it belonged to her attacker. Would that trace of DNA give police what they needed to catch this guy?

"I don't want to be afraid either," she confessed, eye wide, cheeks pale. "I'm so afraid I'll never be right again."

I gave her hand a squeeze with my much larger one. She was so delicate. "You'll be right again." And I meant it. Even if I had to go into her dreams and stitch her world back together myself.

Wait now. Where had that come from? Noah was the protector of the innocent and slayer of dragons, not me. What was it about Amanda that made me want to suddenly become her champion? I couldn't be so insecure that I'd help her just to keep her from becoming dependent on Noah.

"He held me down," she blurted. It seemed she was unable to help herself, and I knew she hadn't told this to anyone other than the police. "He came out of nowhere. I didn't even hear him until it was too late. One minute I was walking, happy and relaxed, and the next I was on my back on the ground and he was on me." Her hand went to her throat. "He choked me. Stuffed something awful in my mouth so I couldn't scream. I tried to fight. I really tried."

My heart twisted at the sight of the slow tear that ran down her face. I squeezed her hand again. "You can't blame yourself, Amanda."

She stared at me, cheeks wet. Gaze pained. "I can. I do."

Anger swept over me. I wanted the bastard that hurt her to pay. To suffer. "Did you see his face?"

She frowned. "He wore a hat pulled low. Maybe. I don't . . . I don't know." She sighed, sinking into her pillows with fatigue.

My anger fled in the face of hope. If she had seen him she could identify him. It was possible her mind simply didn't want to recall his face. "I want you to do something for me before you go to sleep tonight."

Amanda's entire expression was wary. "I don't want to think about it when I'm alone. I keep thinking he's going to find me and finish it." Her fingers went to the bandage on her scalp.

I knew what she meant. She was afraid he was going to find her and kill her. Most rapists weren't killers, but Amanda's fear didn't know that. It was only natural that she be afraid of him coming back.

"I don't want you to think of what happened," I told her. "I want you to think of me. I want you to imagine I'm there with you. Imagine I'm your personal dream guardian."

And I had every intention of being just that. Why?

Why the hell not? I could help her, so wasn't I obligated to do something? All I had to do was find her through the haze of drugs and help her through her dreams that would begin healing her emotional wounds. I wasn't just doing this so I'd have Noah back either. I was going to do this because I could, because I didn't want that bastard to hurt her anymore—and because I wanted to see his face.

Amanda began to cry in earnest, and my heart broke for her. When she leaned forward, tugging me down, I didn't stop her, but went willingly into her embrace. She needed a hug, and to be honest, so did I.

I put my arm around her shoulders and rested my cheek on top of her head, mindful of the bandage nearby. I couldn't get past that bandage—it had become the sterile representation for everything vile in the world.

My own eyes filled with tears as I held the trembling woman. Shudders wracked her slender frame and I felt her sobs dampen the shoulder of my blouse. I didn't care.

A soft sound caught my attention and I looked up. Noah stood in the doorway, a paper cup of coffee in his hand. It was for me—I just knew it. He had such a pained expression on his face—but there was more to it. And for the first time I realized that I wasn't the outsider in our little triangle. Not this time.

He was.

Chapter Four

As usual, Noah and I didn't say much on the way back to his place. Maybe it was because so much of what we talked about was personal, or just plain weird, that we didn't want to chance anyone else hearing. Or maybe all the sights passing by were too much of a distraction. Or maybe we used the time in the cab to collect our thoughts. I know that's what I did during the drive. We were still new enough in our relationship that we liked to think about what we were going to say to each other before we actually said it.

Regardless, once we were in Noah's large, open apartment with its big windows and gleaming wood floors, we began to speak. Noah first.

"Is she going to be OK?" he asked as we entered the kitchen.

No need to say who "she" was, of course. "I think so."

That seemed to give him some relief. What was it like to go through life feeling so much responsibility? I would do what I could for Amanda, but I had no emotional attachment to add weight to the burden.

How much emotional weight did Noah carry?

When he hugged me, I let him, but I was slow to put my own arms around him. I hated being jealous. I'd rather look stupid than feel this suspicion burning inside me.

"Do you still love her?" I asked, tilting my head back to see his face.

Noah stepped back, but he didn't let go of me—that was good. His expression was surprised—that was good too. "Amanda?"

I nodded. "Are you still in love with her?" That was better phrasing, because of course he loved her on some level, otherwise he wouldn't be so concerned.

He frowned. "No. Christ, why would you ask me that?"

I shrugged. "I'm jealous."

The frown disappeared, replaced by an expression of male satisfaction that made me want to give him a purple nurple just to get rid of it. "I kinda like knowing you have a possessive side, Doc."

I rolled my eyes. "I don't. And you didn't answer my question." I wasn't really all that worried about what his answer would be now that I'd seen how my jealousy affected him.

"Amanda will always matter to me," he told me with a shrug. As much as I hated hearing it, I admired him for it. "But if I loved her, I wouldn't be here with you."

Did that mean he loved me? That was one question I wasn't brave enough to ask. Besides, we'd only been together a few weeks. It was too soon for love.

God, my heart was pounding like an idiot. I wasn't going to try to analyze why. And I wasn't about to ask him why he was with me. Honestly, it just made me sound needy, and even though I was, I didn't want him to know that. I was so freaked out over facing the Warden tonight, despite my best efforts to remain calm, that I just wanted him to give me another hug and make everything all right.

The scary thing was, I knew Noah would like nothing more than to do just that—make everything all right.

His brow knitted again, pulling the black slashes of his eyebrows tight over his equally as dark eyes. "What's wrong?"

I really didn't want to bother him with my problems. Honestly. I sighed and glanced over my shoulder at him as I turned toward the cupboard where he kept the menus. "Family stuff. Nightmare stuff. Professional stuff. You name it, it's going on." When his frown deepened, I tried to smile. "I'm okay. Really."

He grabbed my arm—not hard, but just enough to stop me.

"Is it your mom?" he asked, pulling me close again.

I didn't want to be another victim he tried to save. I didn't want him to look at me that way. But, I wasn't going to lie to him either. "She's worried the specialist my family hired will wake her up."

"How do you feel about that?"

I smiled despite myself. "Why, I have conflicting emotions concerning that, Dr. Clarke."

His gaze met mine. He was smiling too, and his eyes sparkled like polished onyx. "Smart ass. What's the Nightmare stuff?"

My smile melted. I was going to have to tell him eventually—especially if I was in trouble. God, for all I knew, the Warden might question him, or worse, wipe his memory or something. Could the Council do that?

"I'm being brought before the Nightmare Council to-night," I confided.

He didn't frown again, but there was concern all over his face. "What for?"

He knew what for—or at least he had an idea. I could feel it in the sudden tension that stiffened his muscles and the thinness of his mouth. "For bringing you into the Dreaming."

"But you did that to save me."

"I freaked them out." And by them, I meant everyone who had been there with Morpheus to witness the visit. I don't know the exact head count, but some of the Council had been there.

"When did you find out about this?" Noah asked.

I didn't meet his gaze. "Last night. While we were asleep."

"When were you going to tell me?"

I tried to grin. "When I had to."

He didn't smile. "You should have told me."

Here we go. The trigger for Noah's "issues" had just been pulled. "So you could do what? Worry about me as well as Amanda?"

He stomped over to the menu cupboard and pulled a stack out. "I hate it when you try to protect me." Of course he did. His mother had no doubt tried to protect him as a child.

"Well, I hate when you get all pissy because you can't take charge!" Okay, maybe that came out a little snarkier than I intended, and maybe it wasn't totally fair, but it was true. I could have handled that better, but I wasn't Noah's doctor, I was his girlfriend. Damn it. I didn't feel like putting the effort into being totally P.C.

The cupboard door slammed shut and I winced. Noah stood at the granite counter with his back to me, shoulders stiffly bowed, pulling the worn gray of his T-shirt tight across his back. I wanted to go to him and wrap my arms around him, but I didn't.

"I'm *pissy*," he growled, not turning around, "because you shut me out of your life—like I can't handle it."

"Like you thought Amanda couldn't handle looking in the mirror?" It wasn't meant to be a low blow, it was supposed to be a reminder that we all do things that we think will protect people we care about.

He turned around, obviously surprised. "She told you that?"

I nodded, but decided not to tell him that I had given her my compact. We could argue over that another time if necessary. Instead I said, "Noah, I didn't want to tell you about it until it became an issue."

"Because you thought I'd freak out?"

"Because Amanda needs your concern more than I do." Made me sound like a martyr, but it was true. Also a hypocrite. I didn't like him spending too much time with his ex, yet here I was pretty much telling him to do just that. "I might need your support later, but right now she needs all you can give her."

He didn't look particularly happy, but he didn't look angry either. "I thought you were jealous of my concern for Amanda."

I shrugged. "I'll deal." And I would.

He came to me then, one hand coming up to cup my cheek. Anyone else and I might have recoiled, but I knew Noah would never hurt me. He would rather die than ever hurt me.

"You pretend to be so tough," he murmured, his thumb stroking my temple. "But you're not."

My heart kicked it up a notch at his touch. Was he saying I was needy? Was he saying he liked it? God, I needed therapy. "It's a gift."

His forehead came down to rest against mine. "You drive me nuts, but I can't imagine life without you in it."

Now my heart was treating my rib cage like a mosh pit—thrashing all over the place in its excitement. "That's hunger talking." I cracked wise when faced with something I didn't know how to respond to.

"You're right," he agreed and the next thing I knew, he grabbed me by the waist, lifted me off the floor, and plunked me down on top of the table. I'm a few inches shy of six feet, and a size twelve on a good day, so I find it remarkably sexy when a man can pick me up like I was some kind of delicate flower. Noah knows this, of course. And he does it as often as he can. I think he likes knowing he can turn me on so easily.

His lips curved on one side, making his smile mischievous and boyish. "I am hungry."

Was he ever! Clothes disappeared as he kissed me. He nibbled on my lips, licked the inside of my mouth where I was so very ticklish, stroked my tongue with his own until my head spun. And then his hands—those beautiful artist hands—were all over me. He could be so gentle, goose bumps raised on my skin, as though brushed by a soft breeze. And then he could inflict just the right amount of pressure to bring a gasp flying from my lips. He knew exactly how to play me. I tingled from head to foot—some places more than others.

I didn't care that we ate on that table. We were about to do a helluva lot more than that. Naked, my body tight with need, I let Noah pull my thighs apart. I watched, my mouth dry, as he stepped between in all his golden glory. Noah has quite possibly the most beautiful body I've ever seen—all lean muscle and long limbs.

He reached down between us—I could feel his knuckles brush the inside of my thigh—and guided his hard length exactly where I wanted it. The head of his erection nudged, opened me a little and I gripped the edge of the table in anticipation.

Noah lifted one hand so that it caught the back of my neck. There was just enough pressure that I raised my gaze to his, and when I did, I couldn't look away. He inched closer, slowly filling me as our gazes locked. And when he was as far as he could go, as deep as I could take him, he bent his neck and whispered in my ear, "Don't ever shut me out."

I shivered. I couldn't help it. I liked it when he got all macho on me. I wrapped my legs around him. "Does it feel like I'm shutting you out?"

He growled low in his throat and thrust deep inside me. I gasped and that was the end of the conversation, until we were both panting incoherently, grunting and groaning as orgasm rocked us both.

Afterward, we dressed, moved the table back to its original spot and decided on Indian for dinner. Both of us were starving.

We sat on the couch, entwined like a couple who'd just had the kind of sex that made everything right with the world and ate chicken tikka masala, mattar paneer, naan, and rice while watching *Say Anything* on Noah's huge flat screen TV.

"Do you think John Cusack is sexy?" he asked, dipping naan in the masala sauce.

I shoveled a forkful of chicken and rice into my mouth as I nodded. "Every woman I know thinks John Cusack is sexy—especially in *Grosse Pointe Blank*."

Noah glanced at the guy holding up a huge boom box on the screen and shrugged. "I don't get it."

I grinned. "I don't get Keira Knightley, so we're even."

After the movie, we sat together, sharing some warm gulab juman and drinking a kind of chai tea that I'd made from ingredients I'd found in the kitchen. Noah likes to cook, so he's got almost anything I could want in his cupboards.

In fact, Noah had just about anything I could want in every respect. That was as scary as it was exciting.

"When are you going to go into the Dreaming?" he asked as he offered me a spoonful of the rosewater-soaked breadlike cheese.

"Soon," I replied, and let him pop the sweet into my mouth. I chewed—bliss!—and swallowed. "I can't put it off much longer."

He gave me a concerned look. "You okay?"

"I think so." I had no idea what the Warden was going to say or do to me. Suppose he—or she?—wanted to lock me up in a cell or something? I couldn't leave this world for that long. I had responsibilities.

But, there was no point freaking out until I faced the music, so to speak. So, after dessert settled and we'd watched a couple of shows stored on the DVR (we are such TV freaks), I decided it was time. It felt like it was time.

Noah decided to paint for a while. He tried to make it sound like he'd suddenly been inspired, but I think he just wanted to wait up for me.

He went to his studio area and I stayed in the living room. Once I was alone, I took a deep breath and opened the portal I needed to cross over. I'm ashamed to think of how much courage it took for me to step through. I was so tempted to let Verek come and fetch me like a Dream Realm bounty hunter.

When I opened the portal, I wished for it to take me

where I needed to go. Sometimes this worked and other times it didn't. I'm pretty sure the problem with getting it to work consistently was with me, but at least this time it seemed to listen. I stepped out of Noah's living room, crossing the veil between the worlds. It was like stepping outside after having been cooped up in a stuffy attic. The night air was sweet—no pollution in the Dreaming. And above, a million stars twinkled in a black-as-velvet sky.

I wished to go to wherever the Council wanted me to be, and ended up standing at the base of wide shallow steps, leading up a small hill to what looked like an ancient temple complete with Corinthian columns. Torches flickered on every third step, lighting a path for me to the looming doorway where two well-muscled guards stood, looking grim and deadly. Neither of them looked at me, although I thought something changed in the female's expression.

What did they think of me? I wondered as I began ascending the steps. Did they revile me as so many others, or were they in awe of the half-breed? And what lay in wait for me beyond that door?

I struggled against the anxiety clawing at me, tightening my chest. I had never been much of one for panic attacks and I really hoped that wasn't going to change right now.

I paused for a moment at the entryway to draw a deep

breath and square my shoulders. Regardless of how I felt, I wasn't about to let it show. Like the mist surrounding this world—mist that had thankfully been elsewhere tonight—these people were not my friends, and there were no doubt some who would hurt me if they could. I had to look strong, and be ready.

The room before me was large, with a pale yellow stone floor covered with rich Persian rugs. Statues of various men and women dressed in flowing robes lined the room. More torches burned in here, snug in sconces high on the windowless walls. Flickering shadows danced along the rough walls—mine was one of them. Was it my imagination or did the shadows seem somewhat out of time with the bodies they belonged to? No, it wasn't my imagination. The shadows had a life of their own, bending and twisting to the beat of music I couldn't hear. My own dark twin moved like water toward the front of the room. I followed behind.

My heart jumped when I saw the dozen or so, very serious-looking men and women seated at the front of the room, around a large, heavy table. They barely acknowledged my presence. I didn't know if that was a good thing or not. Was one of them the Warden?

I calmed somewhat when I saw my father. He sat to the side of the Council with two other men I recognized as his brothers, Icelus and Phantasos, princes of unpleasant dreams and flights of fancy. No wonder I felt freaky. As the royal family of the kingdom, they sat apart from the proceedings, but in a spot where they could see all and be seen by all. It was a comfort having my father there, even if he wouldn't be able to intervene on my behalf.

He met my gaze and gave me a small, but bolstering smile. I tried to give him one back, but it melted when I saw Verek coming toward me, looking very fierce and official.

"Are you my guard?" I asked when he was within spitting distance.

He nodded, pale eyes serious. "I'm to escort you to the front of the room."

"Do I need an escort?"

"You don't have a choice." His hushed reply had all the sympathy his expression lacked.

Well, there you go. "When you put it like that," I remarked with forced lightness, "how can I refuse?" He'd offered his arm and I took it. This was all very civilized, and yet not. It was like they were trying to give the impression of being rational creatures, but really were just waiting until no one was looking to pounce.

Bloodthirsty bunch.

The large, rugged Nightmare escorted me to the front of the room, and left me to stand alone beside the table. For a moment I thought the Council meant to make me stand beside this empty seat for the entire proceedings, but then they stood as well. It wasn't for my benefit, that I knew. Only my father and his brothers remained seated as a robed figure came through a door in the back corner. Talk about making an entrance!

The Warden of the Nightmare Council was a woman. At first the thought gave me a rush of hope, but when I looked up into that pinched, white face I thought of my eighth-grade math teacher and I knew I was in trouble.

Her eyes weren't the typical pale blue of this realm. I'm sure eye color meant something, but I had no idea what. Mine were aqua, and I thought them my nicest feature, except when they lightened and the rims went all black and spidery. I didn't like them then.

The Warden had cold green eyes, complete with black rims, but instead of being spidery, the line was thick and bold, as though someone had drawn it there with a Magic Marker. Weird. Her hair was bright copper, and hung down the back of her violet robe like a ripple of flame.

She was scary, and she knew it. I lifted my chin as she joined us at the table and fixed me with a cold gaze. I held her attention, and though I wanted to look away, I refused to give in.

"So you are the one named after Eos," she half asked, half accused in a tone that was as scorching as her hair.

"The daughter of Morpheus and a human." She said human like it was some kind of disease.

"Yes," I answered with a slight incline of my head—all the acknowledgment she would get from me. I'd be damned if I'd be ashamed of what I was.

The Warden's peach lips thinned. She could have been a beautiful woman were it not for the bitterness etched in every feature, every aspect of her being. "You have been brought before this Council on charges of willful endangerment of the realm, wanton disrespect for our rules, and reckless disregard for the safety of our kind."

I scowled. Hell, I glared. "I haven't done any such things!" The only way I could have sounded more indignant would have been if I'd had an English accent.

Clearly the Warden didn't like being talked back to. She drew up to her full height—which was a little taller than my own—and shot daggers at me with her eyes. Thankfully, she didn't try to conjure real daggers. "You endangered this realm by bringing a human into it. A human who was fully aware of this world and totally cognizant of his time in it."

That was Noah. I had brought him through a portal into the Dreaming when we'd realized Karatos had stolen his ability to dream. "I didn't know it was wrong," I replied. "I only wanted to help him."

She was unmoved. "Your ignorance only proves your

disrespect for our customs and rules. Had you taken the time to learn these things, you would have known better, but apparently twenty-plus years of knowing what you are hasn't provided you with adequate motivation."

She was such a bitch. I managed to keep my mouth shut, even though I wanted to defend myself—and tear a strip off of her. Nothing I could say could change the fact that she was right. I should have learned more about this world. If I hadn't turned my back on what I was and what it meant, I would have known that it was wrong to bring Noah into this realm.

I would have known that I shouldn't be able to bring Noah into this realm, which was really what this was all about. I scared them. Well, bully for them. They scared me too.

"And your involvement with that same human put him directly in harm's way," the Warden continued. "Something every Nightmare has sworn not to do."

I knew that harming humans was against what the Nightmares stood for. We were protectors. "I haven't sworn anything," I retorted, ignoring my father's shaking head. "I never asked to be half of this world and half human. I never asked to be a freak. I may have broken your rules, but it wasn't my involvement with Noah that got him hurt, it was the fact that a Night Terror, working for people in this realm, decided it wanted to cross over into the human world and chose Noah to be his body. If I hadn't stopped that Terror, you'd have bigger problems right now than me."

I was mad—nostril-flaring mad—and the Warden looked at me like I was a bug on her shoe. "You claim that the Terror called Karatos acted on the orders of another?"

I took a deep breath, forcing my temper down. "I don't claim it. Karatos told me him . . . itself." I had to remind myself that the thing that had tried to kill me and Noah wasn't human.

The Warden lifted her chin defiantly. "Did the Terror reveal the name of his benefactor?"

That was an odd way to put it, since there had been nothing good about what Karatos had done. "No."

She looked far too pleased. "Then you have no proof."

I lifted my chin as well. "You don't have any proof that I acted out of disregard for this realm either."

I had her there, and from the dislike shining in her creepy eyes, she knew it.

"Indeed," she replied frostily. "And so we have this inquiry into your actions. The Council plans to watch you closely, Lady Dawn, and discuss your past behavior. If you are found to have acted out of good intent, without lasting effect on this realm, then you will be found innocent and no further action will be taken against you."

Okay, so this didn't sound so bad. I hadn't done anything wrong, so there shouldn't be any ramifications. So why did I have this sinking feeling in my gut?

"However," the redheaded witch continued, "if it is determined that you acted willfully, with the intention of harming this realm and what it stands for, then I will have no choice but to pass judgment upon you and see that punishment is carried out."

"P . . . punishment?" I sputtered like a stuttering kid on a bad sitcom. "What kind of punishment?" And why did Morpheus look so pale? He was king here, damn it, and I was his daughter! I don't care how spoiled I sounded, but I was this realm's Paris Hilton, and the worst punishment I should get was a few days without cable.

The Warden actually smiled at me, but there was no warmth in it, just the opposite. "To disregard the rules of this world is akin to treason. And the penalty for treason is unmaking."

Thank God Verek chose that moment to take my arm again, because I might have fallen flat on my ass at that moment. Oh shit. I was in such trouble.

The equivalent to unmaking in the human realm was death.

Chapter Five

I clung to Verek for maybe four or five seconds before making myself shake off his grip. Sure I was shaky, but I wasn't about to advertise the fact.

"Shame on you, Padera," came a soft, whispery voice from the side. "You'll frighten the poor girl."

Was that genuine concern or patronization I detected? Like everyone else in the chamber I turned toward that sweet voice, but not before I saw a sour expression touch the Warden's features. It disappeared as quick as it came as she too, moved to face this new speaker.

Coming toward me was the tallest woman I'd ever seen. Easily seven feet tall, she was super-model thin, with long silvery hair and skin as pale and shimmery as opals. She wore a long indigo robe that flowed languidly around her feet like moon-touched waves. At the base of her long neck was a tattoo. Small and stylized, it was a beautifully drawn spider, head pointed up, legs out to the sides, reaching for her sleek collarbones.

She stopped directly in front of me. I had to raise my chin to look at her. I'm not used to looking up at women.

"Hello, Dawn," she said, her voice a little richer than it had been.

I tilted my head. "I'm sorry, but I don't know who you are."

There were a few murmurs following this statement, as though people couldn't believe I actually said that.

The woman only smiled. "I am Hadria, priestess of Ama."

I didn't even know the Great Spider, weaver of dreams, had priestesses, although I suppose it made sense. "I'd say it was nice to meet you, but I'd hate to do that and then be proven wrong."

More murmurs, but Hadria only laughed, revealing strong teeth just as white and shimmery as the rest of her. She glanced over the top of my head. "She has your bravado, Morpheus."

I glanced over my shoulder at my father, who smiled at this giant of a woman. "Are you surprised?" He stepped forward. "Why are you here, old friend?"

Friend. Okay, so maybe she wasn't so scary after

all. Hadria's dark purple eyes—pupilless and swirled with silver—fell on me once more, and while her smile faded just a little, I wasn't anxious. "I'm here to deem what your child is capable of doing."

"Verek already does that," I spoke up. "He's my trainer." I didn't want to lose Verek. He was the one person other than my father that I knew I could trust. Don't ask me how I knew it, I just did.

Hadria angled her head—all the better to look down at me, I suppose. "I've no wish to deny you of your training, Princess. I'm here not to train you, but to gauge your power."

My spine stiffened. "Because I'm a threat?"

Her smile was patient. "Is that what you are?"

Man, I was in no mood for mind games right now, but I was still a little too intimidated to mouth off. Energy rolled off this woman, wrapping around me like a giant hand. She was strong—powerful. And I knew her bad side was not one I wanted to be on.

"The Warden seems to think so," I murmured. "A lot of people seem to think I'm out to destroy this world." Maybe that was a little melodramatic, but it was the truth, right?

The priestess bowed her shoulders, lowering her upper body until we were eye to eye. Within the indigo depths of her gaze, I could see swirls of silver and blue. She had no pupils that I could detect. Weird.

"I hope destroying our world is not your plan, Daughter of Morpheus, because there are some of us who are depending on you to save it."

"Unmade?" Noah set a bottle of beer on the table in front of me—the same table we'd had sex on earlier. It didn't seem so sexy now. And yes, it was clean. "What the hell does that mean?"

I wasn't much of a beer fan, but I took a drink of the cold, bitter liquid anyway. "It means that I will cease to exist in the Dream Realm. I'll be dead."

He paled. "I thought that was impossible." He sat down across from me with his own beer. He was in a baggy black T-shirt and the Iron Man pajama bottoms that I had found for him at Target. His hair was mussed up, but his dark eyes were alert—and worried. "You're immortal there, right?"

"Technically." I took another drink. "It's tricky. I can be unmade in that realm, which will be a death to the person I am now, but my essence lives on, and will be remade into something else."

"Like what?"

I shrugged. "Anything they want." I hoped to God they didn't decide to put me into the mist.

"You'll still be Morpheus's daughter, won't you?"

"I'll be part of him, just like any other being in the world." I met Noah's gaze. "I won't be me, Noah. I'll be whatever they want me to be." My voice rose, trembled a little. A month ago I hadn't wanted anything to do with my father's world, and now . . . Now that I was faced with the prospect of losing all that I was there, I was scared.

Never mind that my own people seemed to hate me. Never mind that I didn't fit in. I liked what I could do in the Dreaming. I liked feeling like I did there. Without that, I wouldn't be me in this world either. I had always known that I wasn't human and it shaped the person I've become.

What if I changed so much I didn't recognize myself? What if Noah didn't want me anymore? What if no one knew me anymore?

Don't lose it. Don't lose it.

I lost it. Just for a second, and just a little, but I lost it all the same. I couldn't stop it. Tears filled my eyes and fear grabbed me by the throat and shook. I sobbed once. Then twice. And then I had my head in my hands and my palms filled with tears.

Noah's chair scraped against the floor and then I felt his hands on my hand, pressing me into the firm wall of his stomach. I wrapped my arms around him, heedless of the soaking my tears gave his shirt, and let myself have a good cry out. Just long enough that I didn't feel overwhelmed by it anymore.

Noah didn't try to shush me, or stop me. I liked that. I hated it as well, a part of me seeing it as his need to be cleansed by a woman in need's tears. That wasn't it, and I should know it.

I pulled back and wiped my eyes. Sure enough, the front of shirt was soaked, but it hardly showed on the black fabric.

I sniffed. "Sorry."

He wiped at my cheeks with his thumbs—one of which had a little dried paint under the nail. Burnt umber, if I wasn't mistaken. I looked up at him, and found him watching me with such softness that my heart cracked, I swear to freaking God.

"Have you been painting me again?" I asked, taking the hand with the paint on it in mine. He'd already painted one portrait of me. "The Nightmare" hung on his bedroom wall.

He smiled. "Maybe." Then he squatted before me. "You OK?"

Another sniff. I needed a tissue. I grabbed a napkin instead and swiped at my nose. "I will be. Maybe it won't be so bad. Maybe the Council will side in my favor."

"Or you could tell your father to grow a pair and tell the Warden to leave his baby girl alone."

I chuckled. "I don't think that would go over well. Besides, he can't do anything. Even he isn't above the law."

"He's got your mother living with him. Tell me that doesn't break at least one rule."

"It doesn't. She's there as a dreamer, even if she never wakes up. It might not be ethical of him to fall in love with a human, but there's no rule against it."

Noah frowned. "There was for Antwoine and his succubus."

He was right. Antwoine was a mentor of sorts to me. The only human in New York other than Noah to know that I was a Nightmare. Years ago Antwoine had fallen in love with a succubus named Madrene. My father had forbidden them to be together because it was against the rules, he said.

Was it all right for a Nightmare and a human to be together? Then again, I didn't count. I was half human.

"Maybe he could do something," I allowed, "but lately he's had enough to worry about with my family trying to wake my mother up and his subjects conspiring against him." Some of my father's people, like Karatos, weren't happy with his rule, his human wife, or his half-breed daughter.

"You think he should let you suffer to save his own ass?"

I sighed. Every part of me that could slump did just that. "I think he needs to do what's best for his kingdom, and his position as king."

Long, warm fingers touched my face—so softly tears burned the back of my eyes again. "You've said a lot lately about people doing what's best for them or other people. What about you?"

"He's the only one with the power to unmake me." I swallowed hard over the word. "If he can find a way to stop it, he will."

Noah leaned forward and kissed my forehead. "I hate that I can't do anything to help you when I'm the one who got you into this."

I looked up. "I got me into this, not you. All I need is to know you're there for me, that's all."

A bitter smile curved his lips. "Once again you have to do it on your own."

Color me defeated. "Trust me, I wouldn't if I didn't have to. I really hate being put through a court marshal by myself."

"You have whatsherface on your side—the one with the freaky eyes."

So he hadn't forgotten Hadria or her prediction. "Yeah. I sensed a shitload of power from her. Maybe she has some pull. The Warden would be really sorry that she had me unmade before I could save the world."

That got the grin I wanted from him. He stood and offered me his hand. "Let's go to bed."

Yawning, I stood as well, taking his hand. "That sounds good. I want to go into Amanda's dreams."

"Yeah?" He sounded surprised. "Haven't you been through enough tonight?"

I leaned against him as we walked through the living room, toward the stairs that led up to the loft. "I made a promise to her. I have to keep it."

Noah was silent for a moment, but he squeezed my hand. "You think helping her might help your case with the Council?"

I hadn't thought of that. Why hadn't I thought of that? Probably because my brain had a tendency to turn to mush when it was overloaded. "Maybe. I guess it can't hurt."

Then again, with my luck, it just might.

I didn't plan on spending a lot of time in Amanda's dreams. Not only because I had other things on my mind—I wasn't *that* selfish—but because I wanted her to be able to heal herself, to regain her strength and confidence on her own and take back as much as she could of what the rapist had taken from her. She wouldn't thank me if I just handed it back—not in the long run.

Noah insisted on staying up while I went in. I wasn't sure whose benefit his attention was for, and I told myself that it was for both Amanda and myself. Maybe even a little bit more for me, because I knew he was worried I was going to get in more trouble for this.

I didn't open a portal. I was too tired, and that would

be noticed by my father and possibly others. I wanted to keep this as far under the radar as I could, so I was going to enter the Dreaming like any other human—in my sleep.

I stretched out in bed, with the blankets tucked up around me and Noah reading beside me. And then I willed myself into sleep by humming a "dee-dee-dee" song in my head that my mother used to sing as a lullaby when I was a child. It was a great focus for me and pulled me into the world with relative ease—so long as I managed to keep my mind clear of other thoughts, which wasn't as easy as it should have been.

As darkness reached for me, the trappings of this world slowly dropped away, pulling me through the mist. This time neither tooth nor claw came at me. As the mist cleared I found myself standing on the street. I was uptown—a street where most of the buildings were walk-ups. It was late, I could tell, because it was relatively quiet and many of the buildings were in darkness except for the outside lights.

Raising my face to the glow of the streetlight above, I took a moment to savor being so isolated and alone in this city. I could see why Amanda thought she would be safe. And I understood why her attacker chose this neighborhood. It was hard to imagine anything bad ever happening here.

The soft scuff of heel on pavement got my attention

and I lowered my chin before opening my eyes. I didn't
have to adjust to the darkness—I could see perfectly. I
was practically omnipotent in the realm of the human
subconscious while in the dreaming state. It was that
whole "goddess" thing at work. And for now, I kept myself shielded from Amanda as she came down the steps
of her building in a pink tracksuit and ponytail.

She looked so young and cute and fragile. And whole.
She didn't look anything like the battered woman I'd
seen in the hospital and I suddenly didn't want to be
there.

But I couldn't leave her. So, I moved from my spot
beneath the light and fell into step beside her, slowly revealing myself and allowing her to notice me. I clothed
myself in jeans, sneakers, and a sweatshirt so I wouldn't
look out of place.

"Dawn?" Her steps faltered. "What are you doing
here?"

"Walking," I replied. "Can I join you?"

Amanda hesitated as memory and dreaming col-
lided. I felt her confusion and indecision. Part of her
knew this was not how it happened, and yet another
part wanted to rewrite events.

"Um, okay."

I fell in step beside her, and accompanied her down
the street, where it suddenly seemed much darker and
much less inviting. That's where it had happened. I was

seeing the surroundings the way Amanda's mind now interpreted them.

It was obvious Amanda didn't want to go there, but she began to slowly walk toward it, pulled by her memory. She might not want to go, but her mind knew she had to.

I didn't talk. Really, I wanted to ramble like an idiot, but I was scared that I would say or do something that would do her more harm than good. I hadn't gone into someone's dreams for the purpose of guiding them in a long freaking time, and I didn't want to mess up.

The night grew darker, the lights more dim. Suddenly the night didn't seem so inviting as it had. Then Amanda grabbed my hand. Before I could clutch her fingers with my own, she was pulled from me. I saw a flash of an arm in a black jacket, and then she was pulled between two buildings. I could hear her cries, but they were muffled by a thickly gloved hand. There was no way anyone in these buildings could have heard her. I wouldn't have heard her in the middle of nowhere, let alone in a neighborhood of a city that "never sleeps."

Instinct took over and I ran into the alley after them. I ran up behind the man who now had Amanda on the ground. He knelt between her legs and all I had to do was kick him hard in the back of the head to stop him.

But this wasn't real-time and me hurting him wouldn't change anything in Amanda's world.

Instead I moved around behind Amanda and knelt at the top of her head. The alley was rough and pebbles dug into my knees through my jeans. I willed them away and reached out for Amanda.

He had shoved a gag into her mouth and held her arms above her head with one hand as he pulled at her track pants. She struggled and he hit her—hard. I could hear her sobs mixed with his harsh breathing. I felt sick.

I placed my hands on her head and stroked her temples and hair. "Look at his face," I said. "Look at his face and see him."

Amanda whimpered and shook her head. Her attacker hit her again. He had her pants off now. I couldn't do this. I couldn't just sit here and watch . . .

I took her fear, bit by bit. I took her pain. I gently rubbed her forehead with my thumbs and held her still so she had to look at him. "See him," I told her. "It's all right." And then I drew that fear and pain out of her and into myself. It rolled over me like oil, thick with grit, coating me. I'd never felt anything like it before in my life.

I cried out. I couldn't help it. But I kept my hands on Amanda. I was slowly peeling back the darkness Amanda's mind had placed over his features to reveal his face, not just to her, but to me as well.

She struggled, gasping for air. He drew back his arm once more, lifting his head, and as his fist came down,

I saw his face. Amanda saw his face. It was so normal, so unremarkable except for the hate twisting it.

Fear raced through my veins—Amanda's fear. This prick couldn't hurt me. I pushed her emotions aside and concentrated on why I was there. It wasn't to play voyeur, or analyze this bastard's sociopathy, it was to help Amanda.

"Remember his face," I told her. "You want to tell the police what he looks like. And when the police catch him, you'll put him behind bars. You're stronger than him." Yes, I had rehearsed this bit. I wanted to make sure I planted the right suggestions in her head. It was important that she identify the rapist, but more important that she know that she would go on.

And now it was time to end this horror. I wasn't going to witness anymore of this—and I wasn't going to let Amanda suffer anymore than she had to. I could give her a partial reprieve, just this once.

I drew a deep breath, summoning whatever power I had in this world. It came over me like warm water, washing away the greasy dirt of the rape. Inside I felt as though I had grown to an enormous size, ripe with strength and knowledge.

"You're at City Bakery," I said, capturing a memory of Amanda's that rose to greet me. "You're having hot chocolate with Noah." Normally I would shy away from witnessing a happier moment between my boyfriend and his ex-wife, but given what I had just watched, my wants didn't amount to crap. I could deal.

"Remember how nice that day was." I "pushed" the thought into her subconscious, replacing this dark alley with the well-lit, chocolate-scented interior of the shop. "It was cold, and the hot chocolate was so good."

Suddenly Amanda was whole and unhurt, and sitting on a chair in a pair of jeans and a blue sweater. Her blond hair was loose and she held a huge cup of chocolate.

And she was smiling at Noah like he'd hung the moon and stars. And he was looking at her like he would do anything she asked.

I had no business being there. I had no business feeling guilty for seeing, or jealous over what I had seen.

"For the rest of the night, you'll dream only of happy things," I told her, touching her shoulder gently as I turned away from the obviously in love couple. "Sleep well, Amanda."

And then I left. I actually walked out of the shop out onto the sidewalk and took a few steps before I remembered that this was a dream. Amanda's dream. And I needed to get the hell out of it.

God, I was such a mess.

I panicked. Amanda's fear and pain—her rage— was too much for me. I was like a rabbit running from a wild cat. In fact, I actually began to run. I had to escape the unknown hunter tight on my heels. As I ran down the street, past the nameless people and endless stream of cars in Amanda's subconscious, I prayed for an out.

"Open," I begged, breathless and sweating. *"Open."*

Ahead of me the sidewalk cracked, splintering like the shell of a hard-boiled egg. Yes! I focused all of my will on that crack as I picked up pace. My lungs were going to freaking burst soon.

One good push and that fracture turned into a rupture, and then a crevice, ripping the concrete apart like it was nothing—and while the Dreaming might be ever changeable, that pavement was as real as the actual streets of Manhattan. It was me tearing the sidewalk apart like paper. My power.

Whatever pride I might have felt disappeared as the ground beneath me opened and swallowed me whole. I fell—and like an idiot, I fell screaming.

Just like in the movies, I bolted upright on the bed with a large, harsh gasp.

Noah was there beside me in a second, taking my shoulders in his strong, warm hands. "Dawn, you OK?"

I was breathing like I'd just run a marathon, but I nodded. I was OK. Now that I was awake and out of Amanda's head I was more than OK. I was fan-freaking-tastic.

Noah hovered over me, frowning, his dark brows

pulled tight over his fathomless eyes. "Jesus, Doc. You look awful."

. I chuckled—more from relief than humor. "I feel it." I slumped against him, relishing the heat of his body as I closed my eyes in total mental exhaustion. "It was one of the worst things I've ever experienced."

I felt his body shift and knew he was looking down at the top of my head. "You saw it?"

There was an edge to his voice that warmed me despite its brusqueness. He wasn't angry at me. He was angry at what I had witnessed.

"I felt it," I explained, glancing up into the pitch black light of his eyes. "I took her emotions into myself."

He hugged me then—fiercely, and so tight I could barely breathe. "You scare the shit out of me."

I hugged him back, fighting the rush of tears that flooded and burned the back of my eyes. I scared myself sometimes, but I knew Noah meant it as a backhanded compliment. "I hope the police find him soon," I heard myself say, even though I didn't want to talk. I was pretty much myself again, but that fear clung, like a bad taste in the back of my mouth— a nightmare not quite remembered, but you know it was bad.

"Five minutes alone with the bastard," Noah muttered. The muscle in his jaw ticked. "That's all I want."

Noah was trained in aikido, and despite the defensive nature of the martial art, there was no doubt in my mind as to what he would do in the span of those five minutes.

"Would you kill him?" I asked, not sure if I wanted to know or not.

He shrugged. "I'd like to."

This would have been a great time to keep my mouth shut, but I couldn't help myself. "Because of what he did to Amanda, or out of general principle?"

Confusion deepened his frown. "Is this about you being jealous again?"

Was I angry at myself for wanting to say yes, or angry at him for not seeing the big picture? I wasn't quite sure. "A little, but more about you saying you could kill someone."

He chuckled humorlessly. "I should have known better than to say something like that in front of you. Now you're going to pick it apart."

"Yeah," I replied honestly. "I am. You'd save yourself a huge pain in the ass if you just told me yourself."

Noah sighed, and flashed me what I interpreted as a begrudging grin. "You're impossible."

"Don't forget scary," I reminded him glibly.

His laughter was more genuine this time. "Yeah, I'd like to kill the guy for what he did to Amanda, for hurting people who are smaller than him, weaker than him. Could I actually kill him, yeah. I think I could."

I appreciated his honesty. "And that's why I hope you never get your five minutes alone."

"Okay, miss morally superior, what would you do to him if you got the chance?"

I didn't miss a beat. "Make him dream about being raped every night for the rest of his life until he repented and begged for mercy."

He wore a smug expression that made me want to flick him in the eye—and jump his bones. "I just want to kill him. You want to make him suffer. Maybe you should analyze your own feelings, Doc."

I poked him in the ribs. "Maybe I should make you dream about the perils of arguing with me." I was only half joking. I hadn't messed with anyone's dreams since Jackey Jenkins bullied me into torturing her thirteen years ago. Hell hath no fury like a picked-on fifteen-year-old.

He pulled me closer. "You going to punish me, Dr. Riley?" A sexy glint lit his eyes. A teasing glint.

I pushed him away, but the effect was ruined by my laughter. "You'd deserve it."

Noah looked down at the bedsheets before raising his gaze to mine once more. "You shouldn't be jealous of Amanda. Really. I'm where I want to be."

I swallowed against the lump in my throat. I gave a jerky nod. "It's hard not to envy that history—what the two of you once had."

He raked a hand through his thick, inky hair, his expression almost incredulous. "I think I should tell you why Amanda and I divorced."

"I thought it was because she had an affair."

"It was, but there's more."

I looked at him, seeing the uncertainty—and was that guilt?—in his gaze. "How much more?"

Noah looked down at his hands. "Amanda and I divorced because when I found out about the affair I reacted badly. I hurt her."

"Did you hit her?" I asked, even though I wasn't sure I wanted to know the answer.

He shook his head. "No. I wanted to." His laughter was harsh. "I wanted to. I even raised my hand . . . but I didn't. I tried to walk away and then she got in my face and was crying. She begged me to forgive her."

I was so relieved he hadn't actually struck her that it took me a few seconds to find my voice. "Then how did you hurt her?"

He was silent for a moment as well, as though pondering whether or not to tell me. "She tried to keep me from leaving. I pushed her away, and she bruised her legs on the coffee table. I told her I wanted a divorce and then I left." When his gaze met mine, the dark depths of his eyes were bright with guilt. "I didn't leave her because she fucked someone else. I left because at that moment, I wanted to hit her."

I frowned, then forced my expression to soften as I took his hand. "Noah, I don't think there are too many people out there who wouldn't have felt the same kind of anger faced with the same situation." Last time a guy screwed around on me I wanted to kick him in the balls so hard he'd have to call a search party to find them again. What made me a reasonably sane person is that I didn't kick him. And Noah, despite growing up as he had, proved that he wasn't like his father by forcing Amanda away from him rather than hitting her.

Noah pulled his hand from mine. "Don't try to make it okay, Doc. It's not."

"No, it's not," I agreed. "You both hurt each other, but you've gotten past it enough to be friends. You've been there for her when she needs you most, if that doesn't alleviate your guilt, I have to think there's more to it than what you're telling me."

He glared at me, but oddly enough, I didn't take it personally. "I hate it when you're so fucking calm and professional."

A little spark of anger kindled inside me, but I pushed it down. He wanted me angry. Anger he could deal with. Patience was what needled him. I smiled instead. "It won't happen again."

He was still chuckling when I drew him down onto the bed beside me, and we fell asleep wrapped around each other, smiling.

Chapter Six

Over the next few days my life was fairly quiet. The Warden didn't bother me, although I heard from Verek when we met for a shape-shifting session—something I'd seen Karatos do but hadn't tried yet myself—that she was asking a lot of questions about what had happened with Karatos.

That made me so angry I turned into the Warden—which kinda freaked Verek out. It seems that taking on the forms of humans is normal, but not so much taking on the visage of other Dreamkin. One more item in the "freak" side of my tally sheet. I had been trying to concentrate on someone to "become" and my rage had filled in the rest.

On the other hand, this shape-changing thing could come in handy if I wanted to assume the form of someone a dreamer knew while I was in their dreams. Imagine how I could help heal old wounds if I could give my clients someone to actually confront? Anyway, it was still a new thing to me.

He said the Warden was also asking about Noah, which bugged me despite my expecting it. She could ask all she wanted. I hadn't done anything that I wouldn't do again.

Well, maybe I wouldn't bring Noah into the Dreaming again, but I had done it out of fear for him, and I wasn't going to apologize for wanting to save his life— even though he spent most of his free time lately glued to Amanda's side.

(I will not be bitter. I will not be petty.)

So it wasn't really a surprise when I felt the familiar buzzing in my brain—my father was calling me to him. Good thing it was Friday afternoon and I had no other appointments scheduled for the day.

I stuck my head out into the waiting area. "Hey, Bonnie, if I get any calls just take a message, please."

The older woman saluted me as she reached to pick up the ringing phone. "Aye, Captain Kiddo."

I shut the door with a snort of laughter. What would I do without her?

I grabbed my purse and went into the bathroom—

my usual spot for complete privacy. I made sure the lid
was down on the toilet before I sat—best way to avoid
all kinds of embarrassment—and tried something
new. Instead of opening a portal big enough for me to
walk through, I took today's compact from my bag and
opened it. Benefit Some Kind-a Gorgeous foundation
has a *huge* mirror. That mirror was what I planned to
use as my own personal comm link to the Dreaming.

A silver bowl full of water probably would have
worked better, but I was low on scrying supplies.
Snort.

Anyway, I concentrated on the smooth surface that
reflected my face, looked beyond myself to what lurked
beyond. Think about it—the realm of the Dreaming is
a world behind ours, a world that lives in shadows and
reflections. What I saw in that mirror wasn't really me,
it was a me made of light and shadow—my interpreta-
tion of myself.

Basically, it's all about illusion, and that's what my
father is king of. It made sense, and I remembered my
mother using a similar trick before pulling her Sleeping
Beauty routine.

The surface seemed to ripple, waving like the molten
stuff the evil Terminator was made of in the second
movie. Pretty. Colors flashed along the surface, bending and swirling until they took a clear shape. It was
my father.

"Look who's remembered how to call home!" He grinned, obviously proud.

I grinned back. "Like riding a bike," I quipped. I wasn't very good at the bike thing. Really, it was just dangerous to trust two skinny little wheels and spindly brakes with the considerably uncoordinated woman that is me. "What's up?"

"I've come to issue an invitation."

My eyebrows rose. "How very Jane Austen of you."

He chuckled. "Ah, Jane. Interesting dreams, that one."

I'd rather keep my opinion of Jane as high as it was, so I didn't ask. "An invite to what?"

"Hadria's home. At your earliest convenience."

Polite euphemism for "get your ass there pronto." How was I supposed to feel about this? Her power was scary and her eyes were freaky, but I didn't sense any danger from the priestess. "Does she report to the Council?"

Morpheus nodded, but he obviously sensed my indecision. "Hadria is highly respected, Dawn. The Council will take her opinion very seriously."

I stared at him for a moment. "You asked her to meet with me, didn't you?"

"I did."

I scowled. "Is it so bad that you need to call in your old girlfriends?"

He laughed—not that I took much solace in his humor. "Hadria is an old and dear friend. I think very highly of her, but she won't lie for me, if that's what you're thinking. Her recommendation to the Council will be unbiased and based solely on her opinion of you."

Though his tone was easy, my father's words chilled me. "So if she doesn't like me I'm toast."

"If she truly thinks you're a threat she will say so, but I don't think that's what she'll find."

I thought of the Warden and the vitriol in her tone as she accused me of basically being the Dreaming's equivalent to the Anti-Christ. "Do people really think I'm out to destroy your world?"

"It's your world too," came the soft reply. I didn't argue, even though I wanted to. I was only half of that world. Half of this. Whole of neither. "See Hadria as soon as you can. I think you'll find her extremely helpful."

"I will." If for no other reason than to get some straight answers. Hadria would have no reason to want to protect me from the truth, unlike my father.

"Good girl." He gave me a quick grin. "I have to get back. Your mother doesn't know I snuck out."

"Trying to keep her in the dark are you?"

He gave me a droll look. "I'm trying to worry her as little as possible."

"She's not some delicate flower, you know." I thought

of Amanda and all she had suffered. "It won't hurt her to face reality."

The God of Dreams tilted his head and gave me a strange look. I recognized the expression as one of my own. In fact, his entire posture was like looking in a mirror. Which, of course, I was doing. Weird. "You don't know how she's suffered since leaving her family."

I sighed and rubbed my forehead. "I'm not having this argument again."

He nodded, surprising me by backing down. Normally he'd launch a hot defense in Mom's honor. Maybe he was as tired of the argument as I was. "Take care of yourself, my sweet dream."

He hadn't called me that in years. Damn him for choking me up and then disappearing, because that's exactly what he did. One second he was there and the next he was gone.

Leaving me staring at nothing but my own watery-eyed reflection.

Why did everyone in the Dreaming seem to hate me? What had I done to deserve this?

Feeling sorry for myself was not an attractive trait, but I seemed to indulge way more than was healthy. As a fat kid I was picked on a lot—and disliked for no reason. I don't think I was a brat, but other kids never seemed to like me. All I ever wanted was to be liked.

I had that feeling now. I just wanted the people of my

father's world to like me and accept me. I wanted to be one of them. I wanted to belong.

My eyes stung as a tear trickled down my cheek. Great. Now I was bawling. Sniffing, I grabbed a tissue from the box on the bathroom vanity and dabbed at my eyes, careful not to smudge my mascara. Vain even in the face of self-realization.

I left work shortly after that. Bonnie didn't ask, but I could tell from her expression that she knew something was up. I wonder if she knew what it was. God knew I didn't.

I went to Noah's rather than my own apartment. I didn't want to be alone. I needed . . . something. Something good. Something I could hold on to. It didn't make sense, but I was going to run with it.

He answered the door a couple of seconds after I pressed the buzzer. Thank God he was there. I don't know what I would have done if he hadn't been home.

"What took you so long?" Noah demanded lightly, rumpled and barefoot in the entranceway.

I went to him and put my arms around him. The door closed behind me, sealing me into the tiny vestibule where there was nothing but Noah. I was surrounded by warm, firm flesh that smelled of warmly spiced vanilla and felt like heaven.

I don't know what came over me, but I began to shake. I needed him so badly at that moment—needed him inside me. Needed to feel his skin against mine. Needed to feel something. I fumbled with the button fly on his jeans.

He stared at me a second. I held his gaze as my fingers tore at his clothes. He must have seen the desperation in my eyes because he didn't say a word, but his mouth came down on mine—hot and hard. There was no gentleness in the kiss, and I returned it with equal fervor. His lips were insistent, fierce even, and a thick rush of emotion pushed through my veins.

"You kill me," he growled against my lips as he held my face in his hands. Then he kissed me again—softer this time, but no less intense. I kissed back, meeting his tongue with mine, letting him taste how much I needed him—wanted him.

"I want you," I whispered. "Here. Now."

There were probably some men who would have suggested going upstairs, to where a comfortable sofa, and an even more comfortable bed waited, but I wasn't interested in comfort and Noah seemed to sense that. Luckily for me, he was adventurous.

Noah backed me against the wall, squeezing my ass with both hands before sliding them up to my chest. He pinched my nipples through my sweater and bra and I was so turned on I gasped. It felt so good, even through all the layers.

Only the clothes that needed to be gotten rid of

were removed—and quickly. My jeans and panties were tossed aside, but my socks stayed on. I could have laughed were I not so desperate to have Noah inside me.

He turned me so that my back was to the stairs. Then, he wrapped his arms around me and lowered me so that I sat on one of the steps, my legs instinctively coming up around his hips, urging him closer. God, between my legs practically *ached* for him.

So when he slid into me, I almost exploded right then and there. I wrapped my legs around him, and leaned back against the hard edge of the stairs behind me. I braced my elbows beside me, lifting my hips to better accommodate him.

"Noah," I rasped, feeling the ache swirling and tightening inside me. "Oh, *God*. Noah!"

He claimed my mouth with his own, swallowing my moans and adding his own. The stairs creaked beneath us. I was going to have bruises along my back from the steps and I didn't care.

I pulled my mouth away. "Please," I pleaded. I never used to talk during sex. Never used to make demands or take initiative. Noah changed all that.

He shuddered, and I felt the humid skin of his forehead press against mine. "Christ, you're tight." He thrust again. "I've never felt anything like this."

Moaning, I arched as much as I could against him. I

just wanted him to keep talking. And he did. We came together so swiftly and powerfully I didn't even notice that I'd actually slid up a couple of steps. When we did notice, we both laughed so hard tears sprang to our eyes.

Our laughter eased the tension of the moment, but there was no hiding from the smell of sex that surrounded us or the memory of how I'd talked, or the realization that it had been some of the best sex we'd ever had—and we had amazing sex. I'd never been like that before. Only with Noah.

And now, I felt a peace that I hadn't felt for a very long time, if ever.

We half sat, half lay on the stairs as he ran his fingers through my hair, combing it. He kissed me again, so sweetly I could have cried. Then we gathered up our clothes and headed upstairs. We shared a bath and he rubbed my shoulders until I felt as limp as a noodle. Then he dried me off and carried me to the bed, where he proceeded to do all kinds of naughty things to me, until I couldn't even think of stress, let alone experience it.

And then we ate! There's nothing quite like Chinese food after sex. We sat on the couch in sweats with containers on the coffee table and loaded plates in our hands as we watched *Shrek II* on TV. We had a couple of beers, stayed up late, and fell into bed sometime around three. Cuddling led to more sex and by the time sleep claimed me I was too tired and too damned relaxed to do anything but fall into the abyss. For the first time in a while I actually liked my life. In fact, I loved it. I felt like everything just might be okay.

And then we woke up late Saturday morning and learned that there had been another rape.

Chapter Seven

Noah and I decided to get out of the city.

There was a craft show going on in White Plains, so after checking in on Amanda (her mother was with her), we jumped in Noah's car and headed for the I–87. Traffic was heavy, but moving steadily.

"Did Amanda seem upset?" I asked, watching the large white van ahead of us.

"Angry," Noah replied. His voice was tight. Amanda wasn't the only one reacting to the news of another attack.

I only nodded. I didn't have to say that I hoped the police caught the guy soon. And I knew that both of us were wishing there was something we could do—Noah for personal reasons and me because, as someone who was half immortal, I was feeling pretty damn useless.

The black cloud that the morning's news account of the attack had brought couldn't last forever, and by the time we reached White Plains, our collective mood had lightened considerably, although neither of us could entirely shake the gloom.

If I had to put it to words I'd say that it was a feeling of defeat—that this guy would get away with what he did, and that Amanda would never have her justice. That she would go through life knowing "he" was still out there.

Did I mention feeling useless? Sigh.

It only took a few steps inside the door to start the distraction. Tables and booths went on as far as the eye could see, each displaying more food, art, clothing, and jewelry than a girl with my weak willpower should have to be tempted by.

Noah and I bought butterscotch scones and ate them as we walked around. I couldn't help but buy a turquoise and silver jewelry set. The large stones were polished to a rich shine and set in handcrafted bezels of bright silver. It was definitely worth the money. Besides, I put in on my Visa. I'd worry about paying for it later.

I bought a bright orange silk wrap-skirt as well. It would be perfect for wearing around the apartment or next summer. Noah pointed out a dress that he thought would look good on me, but it was too rich for my wallet, even with my good friend Visa. What did the foolish man do? Bought it himself, of course.

"That's a lot of money to spend on someone you've been dating for, like, a month," I told him, and I meant it.

His lips curved at one corner as we left the booth, dress bagged and in his hand. "Guess you'll just have to stick around for a while."

I grinned like an idiot—not hard to imagine, is it? "Okay."

He took my hand and we walked some more. We should have brought a shopping cart. Noah bought homemade jams and sauces, loose tea, and a Danish pastry ring that I knew wouldn't survive the drive home. He also bought a metal wall sculpture, a shirt, and a glass spider that he caught me admiring.

"The weaver of dreams, right?" He made the comment with a smile as he slipped the wrapped and boxed palm-sized arachnid into one of my bags.

"I'm impressed." And I was. "The mother of all, Ama, wove the universe and created the Dreaming."

We walked around for a few more minutes before Noah spotted a booth of swords that he wanted to look at. My attention was grabbed by a display of porcelain dolls, so I told him I'd meet him in a bit.

The dolls were amazing. All shapes, sizes, and colors. There were Nubian princesses and geishas, Native beauties with shining braids, and fairylike delicate creatures with gossamer wings. The attention to detail was exquisite. Each face was different, with a distinct personality. And the hair was soft, silky, and obviously real. The doll maker had styled each head with loving obsession, making each doll look as though she might come to life at any moment.

One doll in particular caught my attention. Clad in a pale pink gown encrusted with Swarovski crystals, she looked like a giant Barbie—only more perfect. She was slender, but curvy with a golden complexion and large eyes with thick lashes. Her hair was long and blond, shimmering under the lights.

Huh. She looked familiar . . . Amanda. She looked like Amanda. Maybe it was because I had been thinking of her, but the resemblance was uncanny. Even the hair was the right shade.

"She's lovely, isn't she?"

I looked up at the man who had spoken. The smile I'd been prepared to give him froze to my lips as the world seemed to tilt and distort beneath me.

Oh. Fuck.

It was him. I'd know his face anywhere. He looked so calm and serene. So fucking friendly—as though he wasn't a monster underneath that perfectly ordinary veneer.

Were all of these dolls facsimiles of his victims?

"Yes," I croaked hoarsely. "She's beautiful. Did you make all of these?" God, I couldn't believe my voice actually sounded relatively normal when inside I was shaking. I was scared and mad and so very tempted to whisper a waking nightmare for him alone. I had done it before—to a poor girl in a coffee shop. I'd made her think there were spiders on her.

Spiders were too good for this guy.

He smiled at me. "Yes. Every one by hand."

I shuddered, but kept the smile on my face. "How much for this one?" I pointed at the doll of Amanda.

His face changed when he looked at the doll. His expression became almost loving. I'd never been so disturbed by another human in my entire life as I was at that moment. "I'm sorry, but she's for display only."

"Oh," I tried to sound disappointed rather than disgusted. "Is she part of your private collection?"

He nodded, light brown hair catching a slight green tint under the fluorescent lights. "She's one of my special girls, yes."

My stomach rolled. "That's too bad." What would I have done with it if he had sold it to me? It wasn't like I could give it to Amanda.

My gaze jumped to Noah just a few booths away. He was busy talking to the guy there as he held a samurai sword in his hands. Here I was, with Amanda's rapist in front of me. I should tell Noah. We could call the police.

And then what? Tell them that I had saw the guy in

Amanda's dream? We had no proof. Nothing except that I knew without a doubt that this was him.

For that reason, I couldn't tell Noah. I wanted to kill this guy, what would Noah want to do to him? That sword would get tested real quick. Noah would be up on assault charges at best, and we'd still have no proof that this guy was the rapist.

No, I couldn't tell Noah. Not yet. I'd rather risk his being angry at me than risk him doing something he'd regret.

"You know," he was saying, eyeing me like Noah did sometimes when he was in artist mode. Except, this made me feel uneasy rather than desirable. "You have gorgeous hair. If you ever decide to cut it, I'd be interested in buying the ends."

He wanted to buy my hair? Gross.

And then, it was like a puzzle piece literally snapping into place. *Hair.* I looked at the Amanda doll again. The hair wasn't just the same shade as Amanda's, it was Amanda's!

I could just puke I felt so sick. No wonder he wouldn't sell it. This doll was one of his trophies. He not only made dolls of his victims, but he used their hair as well.

I really hoped there was a hell.

My gaze went to a little plastic card holder on the table. "Mind if I take a card? In case I do get a haircut."

"Of course not," the son of a bitch said with an easy, aw-shucks grin. "I do custom work as well."

So I noticed.

Mother, a voice whispered in my head. It was that same voice I'd used to bring about the spiders at Starbucks. I wondered why his mother would be the stuff of nightmares? Or more to the point, the kind of stuff a Nightmare could use against him. Exploiting fear was more of a Night Terror thing, but it was yet another talent I seemed to have that no one could explain.

"Thanks." I forced another smile and took one his cards. Then I took two more just in case I lost that one. Phillip Durdan. He had a shop in Brooklyn. Now the police would know where to find him.

And now *I* knew how to find him too. I might not be able to turn his sorry ass over to the cops, but I could do something almost as good. Now that I had met him I could go into his dreams.

Do no harm, I reminded myself as I walked away, his card tucked in a zippered compartment in my purse. I was still shaky, but that gave way to sheer determination as I approached Noah.

I wasn't going to harm Phillip Durdan.

But that didn't mean I couldn't make him pay.

Noah dropped me off at my place. He was going to visit with Amanda and make sure she had dinner before his younger sister Mia arrived to stay the night. He asked me if I wanted to come with him. I didn't.

I couldn't face Amanda after meeting her rapist. Couldn't sit there and resent the fact that she had my boyfriend wrapped around her finger when I could see what she had suffered—when I knew what she had suffered.

I didn't want to be jealous of her, but I was. And I'd rather saw off my own eyelids than watch Noah fuss over her when his reaction to my possible unmaking had seemed so . . . less knightly. Not that I wanted him to fuss over me.

Yes, I'm an idiot. Despite Noah telling me I shouldn't be jealous. Despite him saying that I was who he wanted to be with. See, the thing was that even though I knew he believed these things, I also knew that he felt guilty for wanting to hit Amanda for her affair. Guilt, coupled with his need to protect, was a powerful motivator.

And I'll admit that there was a part of me who figured he'd only be with a freak like me for so long before he wanted a "normal" girl again.

Yep, just one towering pile of pathetic insecurity—that's me.

Normally in this situation I'd put on some sweats, get a huge bowl of cereal—I'm talking a Jethro bowl—and watch *Sense and Sensibility*, reciting all the best lines at the right moments while Fudge snored on my lap.

Instead, I decided to do my waistline and Jane Austen a favor and accept that invitation my father had "issued" the other day in my office bathroom.

I was going to visit Hadria. I had to anyway, so now was as good a time as any, and maybe visiting with her would give me a better idea of the trouble I was in—and what I could do to set things right. Plus, she was old, and she could no doubt teach me a lot.

I needed to learn about the Dreaming if I was ever going to be considered part of it—a good part. Imagine people actually thinking I was a villain! I'm nowhere near sophisticated enough to play the villain. Now, the Warden on the other hand . . .

Nope, wasn't going to think of her. Not now when I was already feeling so down on myself. If my lower lip dropped anymore I'd be able to wear it as a balaclava, and while I might often indulge in self-pity, I wasn't about to let it rule my life. I had choices to make and a fight to win.

I went into my bedroom, so inviting with its Mid-eastern orange walls and purple bedding. I flopped on top of the bedspread and cradled a pillow beneath my cheek. I felt so tired inside I knew it wouldn't be hard to fall asleep. While my body recharged in this world, I'd recharge my mind and spirit in the Dreaming.

Normally when I slipped into the Dreaming, I could "put" myself where I wanted to go—or within a reasonable distance. I had yet to really play with this ability, but if memory served, I could teleport within the Dreaming, just like Morpheus. It made for easy transportation, but I wasn't sure just how to do it. I still felt more comfortable making the motions of travel, or bending the world to my needs—which was way more work. All I could think of was the scene in *Galaxy Quest* when the creature came through the transporter inside out.

Anyway, it seemed that the Temple of Ama was not a place I could just let myself into, for whatever reasons. I ended up entering the Dreaming just outside the gates to the palace. The ivory and horn gates gleamed in the moonlight. Myth said that true dreams passed through the gate of horn and false dreams through the gate of ivory. I don't know if that's true, but both gates opened for me whenever I approached.

Tonight, however, there was a carriage waiting outside those gates.

Or at least, I thought it was a carriage. It was a large spherical vehicle covered in what looked like smooth purple, silver, and green scales, pulled by two massive pewter-colored griffins with ebony-tipped wings. They were harnessed to the carriage by delicate silver chains that didn't look hardy enough for the job.

The door to the carriage, as circular as the vehicle itself, opened and two steps lowered to the ground. The interior glowed with soft light from opalescent sconces, revealing pale gray walls and lush violet padded seats. If I hadn't suspected before this, I'd know that Hadria had sent this for me because of its sheer awesomeness.

Damn, she was good if she sensed my presence and sent a ride for me this fast.

I only hesitated a moment—a little part of me wasn't too keen on trusting Hadria totally. Who could blame me? The people in this world hadn't exactly done anything to inspire or claim my trust. But I didn't really see that I had a choice. Hadria's opinion of me would influence the Council, and I could use the help.

I climbed into the shiny scaled orb and settled on the padded seat. It was just as comfortable as it looked. The griffins waited until the door clicked shut and the interior lights dimmed before setting off.

I leaned back against the cushions, looking out the porthole windows at the distant lights of the palace. The griffins began to pick up speed, and soon they raced along the smooth rock road. Then, there was a jolt, and I was pinned to the back wall as the carriage lifted off the ground. The griffins were taking flight.

Oh. My. *God*.

I was in the air, in a big shiny ball with nothing keeping it attached to the mounts but little tiny chains. I should have been terrified, and for a minute I was—until I caught a glimpse of the view out the window to my right.

Below me, the palace and its surroundings looked like something from Disney World—so pretty and twinkling in a sea of dark. And then, fanning out from that central area, was the rest of the kingdom. I could see the lights of distant duchies—such as those belonging to my uncles—and little hamlets and towns. I had never seen it like this, and I was struck by how gorgeous it was. I was in awe—and I have to admit, my heart swelled a little at the sight.

Home.

The griffins turned, swinging the carriage to the right, giving me another postcard-perfect view. Too soon the lights grew closer, the darkness less dim, as my flying vehicle drew closer and closer to the ground.

A slight bump—touchdown—and the carriage was still. I climbed out as soon as the door opened.

I was standing on the side of a mountain; a wide ledge that jutted out over the almost sheer cliff face. There was no road that I could see, nor any kind of path that could lead to this spot. There was enough room for the griffins and the carriage—perhaps another as well—and me. Obviously the temple didn't get a lot of visitors.

As for the temple itself, I could only assume it was in the cave behind me. The wide mouth yawned invitingly, dark rock smooth and worn. Iron sconces were driven deep into the walls, lighting the sloping path inside.

I went in. Not like I could go anywhere else.

The ground beneath my feet was scuffed from thousands of years of shuffling feet, and buffed to a soft finish. It gradually eased deeper into the cave, taking me into the mountain. I could hear music coming from the depths below.

The walls sparkled with little grains of crystal, flashing dots of blue, white, and pink when the flickering torchlight hit them. I kept walking, one hand tracing this shimmery wall for balance.

Finally, after what felt like forever, I reached the bottom, entering a large open hall. The floor was set with different color tiles—all purples and grays as I had come to expect from Hadria. The walls were glossy and dark—like onyx. Stalactite-like cones of light dripped from the ceiling, bathing the room in a rich, golden glow.

And alone, in the center of this room, sitting at a rough table peeling fruit that looked like a cross between a pomegranate and an apple, was Hadria.

"A pleasant evening to you, Princess," she spoke, her rich voice filling the room. "You honor me with your company."

"Call me Dawn," I said. Only Verek could call me Princess without me squirming. And if she was so damned "honored," how come she never looked at me?

She stilled in her peeling and then turned her freaky

gaze in my direction. "All right. Won't you sit, *Dawn*?"

I took the chair to the left of hers—back to the wall, watching the entrance. Of course, there were probably other doors to other chambers leading from here, but I'd take what security I could.

There was an extra knife on the table in front of me. "May I help?" I asked.

"Thank you."

I picked one of the ruby-red fruit from the large silver bowl and began peeling, separating the discarded flesh into a wooden container. "I've never seen fruit like this before."

"No? It began to bloom here around the same time your human stories of the fall of the Garden of Paradise began. We call it Eve."

I stared at the fruit in my hand. Huh. The fruit of the Tree of Knowledge? What would happen if I took a bite . . . ?

"It is very good, but potent. We use it in our truth-seeking ceremonies."

"Truth seeking in a world built on illusion." I couldn't help but chuckle at my own wit as I slid the blade of my knife through the thick rind. "That must be an interesting bag of tricks."

I looked up and found Hadria watching me, a smile on her iridescent face. "You are welcome to join us some time. If you wish."

Oddly enough, I would like to do just that. "Thank you. There's still so much I don't know about this world."

Her smile grew. "You'll learn."

I dropped my gaze and kept peeling. Tart smelling red juice ran down my hand. "Not if the Warden succeeds in having me unmade."

"I don't believe that will come to pass. The Warden leads the Council, but Padera does not speak for it."

Oddly enough, her words gave me some comfort. I finished peeling the Eve fruit in silence, placed it in the bowl, and reached for another. I was almost finished with it, my hands sticky and delicious smelling, when something caught my attention from the corner of my eye.

I raised my head, and sitting on the table beside me was a huge train case filled to overflowing with cosmetics—the good stuff too. Every brand and pretty color I could ever drool over sat there in brand-new bottles and tubs and containers—like treasure—in a MAC professional case.

"Um, what's that?" It hadn't been there before, so it seemed a pretty safe assumption that Hadria had brought it there.

Hadria barely acknowledged the case. "See something you want?"

I laughed. "All of it."

She stilled, watching me with those swirling purple

and silver eyes. "You could just take what you want. Take it all."

Frowning, I glanced from her to the case. Shit, had it gotten bigger? Was that Prada perfume I saw on the top tier? Ohhh, and Lancôme lip gloss. I love Juicy Tubes.

And suddenly, like a great revelation, I knew that it was very, very important that I did not take a single thing from that glorious case—no matter how much I wanted to.

"No, thanks." I turned away before I could change my mind. "I don't need anything."

"You are quite a remarkable young woman, Dawn."

"I'm almost thirty."

Hadria smiled sweetly. "Infant." She held up the bottle of wine. "Drink?"

"Please." I probably shouldn't, but was it even possible to get drunk in this world? Besides, it was good. "What do you think makes me so remarkable?" Pardon my ego, but I wanted to know.

Hadria handed me a towel for my hands. "The flesh of Eve fruit has great powers of temptation."

Something in her tone made me glance at the case again, but it was gone. I was surprised, but not much as I directed my gaze back to the priestess.

"Eve brings out your every desire, no matter how small or how vile and offers them to you. But every time you give in, you lose a little bit of yourself, until there's nothing left but a shade."

"A shade."

She nodded to the darkest corner of the cavern. "A ghost."

Following her gaze I thought I saw something moving in the darkness. I looked away, my heart pounding in my throat. "So this was a test?"

She nodded. "And you passed."

I stared at her. I was hurt. I had thought . . . well, I had thought that she liked me. "You bitch."

She set a glass of rosy wine in front of me, not reacting at all to my proclamation. "Do you know how many people succumb to Eve's temptation? Almost everyone who comes in contact with the fruit. You've had its juices on your skin, handled its flesh, and yet you were able to resist. Only your father and myself have that ability, and I have had to work hard to acquire it over the years."

Another trait only me and Morpheus had. Swell. It didn't take the sting out of being duped. "What if I hadn't resisted?"

Hadria shrugged. "Then I would know how easily you could be corrupted."

Understanding began to edge through my thick skull. "But now you can tell the Council that I can resist?"

"Yes. That your soul is untainted will make it difficult for them to think ill of you."

I wiped my hands and took a sip of wine, not really pissed off anymore. "What's the damage with people thinking I'm some kind of destroyer?"

Her gaze met mine. "Because long before you were born, back in the days when humans first developed the ability to dream, a priestess of Ama received a vision. She saw Morpheus give his heart to a mortal, and she knew a child would be born from that union—a child that could walk between both worlds. This child was to be born and grow in a time of change, and soon after reaching maturity, she would become involved in great strife and either bring upon the destruction of our world, or be the savior of it."

She had mentioned before that she thought that I was going to save the Dreaming. Personally, the obliteration or salvation of this world wasn't a responsibility I wanted to shoulder.

"So all this crap is because of a vision some old woman had, like twenty-seven centuries ago?" I shook my head. "I mean, *come on*. Doesn't that strike you as stupid?"

Hadria reached across the table and refilled my glass of wine. Her expression was sympathetic. "It might, if I hadn't been the 'old woman' who had the vision."

Chapter Eight

You'd think that given my true nature—and the total fantasticness of it—that I would be really good at keeping secrets. Not to mention that my job requires a degree of discretion. But no, I'm awful at sitting on something that I know I shouldn't share, especially with people I care about.

I wanted so badly to tell Noah about Hadria's prediction, but I didn't know how. Hell, I couldn't quite explain it to myself when I thought about it later.

I mean, really. Imagine me destroying a world. Now imagine me saving it. Hard, isn't it? Still, I couldn't stop thinking about it. That prophecy took almost as much of my brain as Phil the doll maker did.

I still hadn't told Noah about him either. It had only been a day, though, so it's not like I'd had long to feel guilty about it. Not only did I want to avoid a fight, but I didn't know what he would do with the information. I thought he would be able to control himself. I *hoped* that he would do just that, but I also knew that it was a lot to ask. It would be very tempting for him to take the law into his own hands.

I'm not trying to make excuses for myself, or for Noah. It was human nature to want revenge—an eye for an eye. If someone I cared about had suffered what Amanda had, I don't want to tell you the things I'd be tempted to do. Even the memory of Jackey Jenkins wouldn't be able to stop me.

So, I was going to do it my way. That made me something of a hypocrite, I know, but I was more willing to risk myself than him. My way was outside of police jurisdiction, and if I was careful, which I planned to be, not even the Warden would be able to find fault.

Or rather, I didn't think she'd be able to find fault.

So, here I was, sitting on Amanda's couch, having accompanied Noah on his daily visit. She'd been home a few days now. As my attention refused to leave that bandage on her scalp, I knew I was right to keep my silence. My way was better for all involved. And it was certainly safer.

Noah was going to stay with Amanda for the eve-

ning since I was having a girl's night at my place. She
didn't like to be alone, he'd said, and he didn't mind
keeping her company. I tried very hard not to be resentful. After all, it wasn't like he was standing me up
to be with her. Still, it wasn't easy to sit there while
he looked so totally comfortable in her home—like he
belonged there.

So, after half an hour I decided it was time to leave.
I had to go home and shower, and get ready for the arrival of my BFFs.

I said my good-byes to Amanda, and then Noah
walked me to the door. He braced a hand against the
frame, preventing me from leaving right away. His
back was to his ex-wife, preventing her from witnessing our exchange.

The black T-shirt he wore pulled tight against his upper body. The arm beside my head was strong and taut,
despite a lack of tension in his posture. He wasn't big by
any stretch, but he was all muscle. Compared to him I'm
helplessly out of shape, but he seems to like my curves,
so I'm not going to complain or go all insecure.

He smelled good, and he looked even better. He had
the shadow of a beard on his jaw, giving him a rough
look. His wide mouth was set in a soft curve as his dark
eyes sparkled. Sometimes I got the feeling like he was
constantly amused by me—or maybe it was the way I
drooled whenever he was close.

"Will you be in my dreams tonight?" he asked, voice low and gravelly.

Goose bumps. *Everywhere.* So long resentment and jealousy. "Do you want me to be?"

"I want you, Doc." He leaned closer, so that I could feel the heat of his breath on my cheek. "Very much."

I was mush—literally. I was also curious. "What is it with you and dream sex?"

He arched a brow, and the onyx of his eyes glinted even brighter. "I can do everything I want to you in a dream. I can stay inside you forever in a dream."

Oh God. When he put it that way . . . I swallowed, my throat suddenly dry, damn him.

"You kill me," I muttered. My voice was so hoarse I sounded like Joan Rivers.

Noah smiled, his gaze flitting over my face in the sweetest way. "Funny. I think you save me."

Yup, I was going to fall so hard for this guy. Who was I trying to kid? I had already fallen hard for him. I'm surprised I didn't have bruises.

"What?" he taunted sweetly. "No comeback?"

I shook my head, grinning. "Nope."

He came in even closer, brushing his lips against mine with the softness of a butterfly's wing. It was enough to make me shiver, but not enough to satisfy the craving for him.

"Mandy, I'm going to walk out with Dawn." He said

this over his shoulder as he straightened. I was able to open the door then. Good thing because I needed the air.

I called another farewell to Amanda and left the apartment. Noah walked me downstairs and out into the street.

"You don't have to do this," I told him, even though I thought it was sweet.

He frowned, shoving his hands in his jeans pockets. It was a chilly night and he hadn't put on a coat. "Are you kidding? I'm not letting you out of my sight at all if I can help it. Not while that bastard's still free. Not ever."

I arched a brow, fighting a little spurt of guilt. "Now, if you could just thump your chest I'd be really turned on."

He shot me a glare—not much of one, but it was there all the same. "Don't be glib."

With a sigh, I lifted up on my toes and kissed his cheek. "I appreciate the concern, really."

"Do me a favor."

"Anything." And I meant it. Oh, I knew the protective thing was all part of his own issues, but I was only human and the guy I thought the bestest of the best wanted to be all alpha for my benefit.

The look he gave me was coy. "Don't do anything that could get you in deeper shit with the Warden."

I blinked—and it wasn't a fake one either. Why would he assume I was going to do something that could get me in "deeper shit"? And how in the hell did he know me so well? "Like what?"

He smiled again. "You know what. Anything that requires you going into the Dreaming. You're already doing enough for Mandy, you don't need to risk yourself."

Now, I knew all of this was said because he wanted me to be safe. However, there was a part of me that thought he was suggesting that maybe I didn't have enough sense to be careful. That maybe I was stupid.

Like he knew that I would do something—which of course I was going to.

"Because Amanda already has one protector, right?" Oh, I sounded snarky. "She doesn't need another one?" Wasn't he the one who had wanted me to help her in the first place?

His hand whipped out of his pocket and wrapped around my back, pulling me tight against him in a cobra-fast motion that stole my breath. "Because I don't want you to get hurt," he informed me hotly. "Because I'd go fucking nuts if anything happened to you."

Well. Those were certainly better reasons than mine. And really, I was just as bad. I hadn't told him about Durdan to protect him—keep him from doing something stupid. "Okay," I squeaked.

He kissed me then—long and hard. And when he lifted his head, mine was still spinning. He hailed a cab—that seemingly magically appeared at exactly the right time. He even closed the door for me as I slid into the backseat—after checking out the driver, of course. Paranoia, thy name is Noah. And I loved him for it.

I arrived home safe and sound, of course. I even called Noah's cell phone to let him know the good news. When we were about to hang up, he wished me "sweet dreams" for later that night. I actually blushed at the blatant innuendo in his tone.

My roommate Lola—mixed race and curvy (she calls herself a bucket of chicken—all breast and thigh)—laughed as she walked by me into the kitchen. She was wearing low-riding lounge pants and a tank top. Her dark hair was in pigtails. She was so cute I could have backhanded her.

"Talking to Noah?" She grinned.

I smirked. "My dentist."

Her expression was appreciative. "I gotta change dentists."

I grinned because I couldn't help it and practically skipped off to my bedroom to change into my own comfy clothes.

Julie—another petite brunette—arrived a few minutes later. I felt like a giant next to the two of them, but I've become fond of my height so I didn't mind. In fact, I was becoming fond of a lot of things that used to bother me. I hardly thought about my size anymore, and had settled into a solid size 12. I could be skinnier, sure, but Noah liked me the way I was and I had to admit I kinda did too.

Weird, huh? I wasn't sure if Noah was to blame for this sudden confidence, or if facing my dual nature was the culprit.

I hugged Julie and then the three of us sat down with various menus, searching for the right food for the evening. We decided on Chinese—yay!—and I placed the mountainous order while the other two picked through DVDs to watch. No worrying about Wardens or being the destroyer of worlds tonight.

I wanted to watch *Devour* but was vetoed by my friends. "It's awful!" Julie wailed.

"But it has Jensen Ackles." I pointed to the too-pretty-to-be-legal face on the cover. "We love Jensen!"

Julie rolled her eyes and I sighed, putting the movie aside. I'd have to watch it—again—on my own.

Lola suggested *French Kiss* with Meg Ryan and Kevin Kline, and Julie and I gave it a big thumbs-up. I knew what would happen. We'd watch, recite dialog in all the right places, and be in love with Kline by the end. Then we'd spend the rest of the evening talking to each other with very bad French accents.

Are we wild or what?

Julie grabbed *The Replacements* as the second on our double bill. A good choice. Not only did it have Keanu at the pinnacle of his hotness, but it had Rhys Ifans, who I think is totally adorable despite his obvious attempts to be anything but.

The food arrived within the first half hour of *French Kiss* before KK's charm reached full throttle. We glutted ourselves on fried wontons, General Tao's chicken, pork lo mein and garlic vegetables. And for dessert— Lindt chocolate. As if that wasn't bad enough, cocktails followed.

By the end of the night, I was still full and half tanked. I felt lovely. Lola and I sent Julie home in a cab—watching from the window as she pulled away. I guess we were almost as bad with her as Noah was with me—but I hadn't been drunk. Julie was trashed.

I went to bed after washing my face and brushing my teeth—habits that I never broke no matter how bad the state I was in. Once my head hit the pillow I had another dilemma. Did I go after Noah first or did I try hunting down Amanda's attacker?

It didn't matter that I was tipsy. I probably wouldn't be in the Dreaming. Booze didn't seem to matter there, as I'd learned when having wine with Hadria. I didn't want to give up this lovely feeling, but I had to at least try to find the rapist—if for no other reason than because I could.

Okay, and I was just looped enough to admit that the sooner that S.O.B. was behind bars, the sooner Amanda could find closure, and Noah and I could go back to trying to build a relationship that only included the two of us, and didn't include either one of us trying to save the world or a small portion of it.

It was decided. I'd go check in on Noah and then I'd go after Durdan.

I settled in, letting my foggy brain drift further and further away from this world. I was going in the old-fashioned way—less risk of doing something that would get me into "deeper shit" as Noah so eloquently put it.

Sleep came with ease. I was getting better and better at putting myself to sleep when I wanted, although I had my sleepless nights just like anyone else. Fortunately, I could whip open a portal to the Dreaming and rejuvenate my mind and body that way.

Since Noah was expecting me, I reached out to him with my mind. We'd done this a few times now, so he easily opened his dream to me. He had already set the stage, and was in a dream version of his bed—bigger, with sheets that felt like butter—waiting for me.

Clad in a little tank top and boy-cut panties, I climbed in beside him, slipping eagerly into his warm arms. God, he felt good. Because of his amazing ability as a lucid dreamer, this was as real to him as it was to me. Almost.

He gave me a squeeze. "How was your night with the girls? Did you get loaded and have pillow fights in your underwear?"

I laughed at the thought. "No. But we did make out."

Now he was the one chuckling. "Did you take pictures?"

I shook my head. "Video. It's on YouTube."

He was silent as we both enjoyed the light moment. Then of course, I had to ask, "How's Amanda?" So much for levity.

"Better." A man of many words, my Noah.

I patted the hand that rested on my stomach. "She's going to be all right." It wasn't a promise or a platitude, it was something I knew in my gut. She had to be all right or he and I were in trouble. I felt that in my gut too.

"You can't fix everything," he said quietly, with just a touch of bitterness that I had to tell myself wasn't directed at me.

"Sure I can." Look at me, trying to force lightness into our conversation again. I didn't want to spend this time with him letting the real world intrude. I should have known better than to open my mouth in the first place.

"You can't make sure that bastard pays for what he did."

I wasn't thinking clearly, otherwise I never would

have said what I did. "Sure I could. I could make him think he was a sewer rat if I wanted. I could make him spend the rest of his days in the grip of nonstop nightmares."

Noah went still against me. His gaze locked with mine. "Isn't that against the rules?"

I shrugged. "Without a doubt, but they never said anything before." I should have said yes, it was definitely out of the question. Shouldn't let him entertain the idea—or myself for that matter. But it was out there, hovering between us now.

"Jackey Jenkins." I was surprised he remembered her name. "What exactly did you do to her?"

I kept my eyes closed. Tried to remain calm and not let my mind go there. "I don't remember."

God love him, he left it at that. We both had our secrets and for now we both respected that. Some day he'd want to know more. And someday I'd want to know about his father, but not today.

"Promise me you won't do anything," he said softly, a gentler tone than he'd used outside of Amanda's earlier, when he asked basically the same thing of me. "He's not worth the trouble you'd get into."

I couldn't promise to not do anything. And part of me was perturbed that he asked. He would do something if he could. There'd be no stopping him. "I promise I won't do anything to get into trouble." I hoped.

He pulled me tight against him. "I mean it, Dawn. I don't want to find out that you made him jump off the Brooklyn Bridge or in front of the six train."

"I wouldn't do that!" Death was too good and too quick for the sonuvabitch. And someone would have to clean the track up afterward.

I felt the tension ease from his body. "Good."

"You don't think much of my common sense do you?" I cast a wry glance at him.

He nuzzled his face against my hair. "Of course I do. It's your sense of justice that worries me."

I laughed—I had to. "*My* sense of justice? You'd beat the snot out of the guy if you had half a chance."

"That's different."

"Give it up." I scowled, but I was glad I hadn't told him about meeting Durdan. "It is not."

"Is too." I could hear the grin in his voice and I could have smacked him for it. "Beating a guy up might land me in jail, but if you do something you could end up having your life altered forever. No one's worth that."

He was. That thought hit me crisp and clear. It was because of him that I did much of what I was doing. Sure, I did what I could for Amanda, but a lot of my motivation lay in trying to keep Noah from feeling responsible. Forgive me if I sound like a broken record, but I was really afraid that he was getting something he needed from Amanda that he couldn't get from me. It had nothing to do with sex or love. He could be all protective of her. She needed someone to look after her. I didn't. Part of me couldn't understand how Noah could just let that go, given how much he needed to be a hero of sorts.

I looked at him—really looked at him—and saw nothing in his earnest face that gave me any cause to doubt his feelings for me. He was mine and I had no reason to question that. So why did I feel I had to do so much for Amanda? Why did I personally take it upon myself to bring her attacker to whatever justice I could bring him to?

I guess Noah wasn't the only one with a hero complex.

"I think I just fell a little more," I whispered.

His eyebrows came together for a second, before smoothing out in understanding. He smiled that crooked smile that made my stomach do flip-flops. "I'll catch you," he promised, raising his hand to cup my cheek.

Then his lips were on mine and my last thought before I shut off my mind completely was that I hoped Noah would forgive me when he found out I lied. I really would try to stay out of trouble. But I had to do *something*.

And now I knew what.

* * *

Because of my unique abilities, I could consciously control my dreams right down to the last detail. Usually I didn't do this because it really sucked all the fun out of dreaming—and really, I had issues to work out just like everyone else. Tonight, however, after leaving Noah, I put myself into darkness. It wasn't a room or a box, or even a cave. It was just darkness—like standing in the sky on a night with no moon and no stars.

Then, with nothing to distract me, I focused on the information I'd taken from Amanda's memory, and my own recollection of having seen Durdan in person. I concentrated on how he "felt" and followed that vague sense. Once I've met a person it's relatively easy for me to latch on to their dream self. It's hard to describe—it's not exactly a feeling, or a taste, or a smell, yet it's like all three. Let's just say that every human has a signature within the Dreaming that makes someone like me able to track them down. So, once I got a whiff of Durdan, I picked up the trail and followed it with my senses until I located the point of origin. Then, I followed, until I let the darkness drift away and found myself standing inside a shop. His shop.

Polished, dark planks gleamed beneath my shoes. It was clean, not a dust bunny or speck of dirt to be found. A large counter in the same wood appeared before me, complete with antique cash register. The debit/credit machine was new, however, as was the computer off to the side.

The rest of the interior filled in, and I stopped to take a look at my surroundings. And what I was surrounded by was dolls. A hundred faces ranging from stark white to chocolate brown stared at me from beneath glossy, fully styled hair.

When I turned the corner of one showcase, I noticed a young dark-haired boy sitting in a large leather armchair—one of two—not far from the large front window.

He had a doll in his hands. She was dressed like a flapper, complete with sequined headband around her shiny black bob. Her fringed dress had no doubt been beaded by hand. The boy peered underneath the skirt—and looked disappointed at what he found there. I almost smiled.

Footsteps from the back of the shop grew louder—*clomp, clomp, clomp.* They were heavy shoes—the kind with a thick heel, but I could tell from the brusqueness of the stride that it was a woman coming toward us.

"What are you doing?" she demanded in a harsh voice as she stomped over to the boy. "Sitting here, playing with dolls when there's work to be done?" She snatched the doll from the boy's hands.

The boy was silent. He didn't even look at her. But it was obvious that they were mother and son—the resemblance was uncanny.

"I swear, you're going to end up like your father." She shook the doll in the boy's face. "Did you look up her skirt?"

Her son still didn't look at her, but he took the doll from her once again. He didn't really have a choice, she was practically forcing it on him.

"Yeah, just like your father." She sneered. "You'll probably run off too some day and leave me to take care of this shit hole by myself. Don't know what we'll do when we run out of dolls."

She glanced around the shop and her pinched expression gave way to one of calculated relief. "You know how to make dolls, don't you?" She gazed down at the boy with a mixture of greed and contempt.

The boy nodded and she laughed bitterly. "Looks like you'll prove more useful than he ever was."

So this was where it started. She overpowered him, bullied him. That kind of experience—an overbearing, abusive female figure—was bound to have an adverse affect on a young man.

As if following my thoughts—which was impossible, wasn't it?—the dream changed. When I turned my head to look at the boy again, the child had been replaced by a teenager—lanky and sullen. He still had the doll in his hand, and the shop was much the same as it had been, though there were some different dolls on the shelves. These dolls were even more amazing than the others.

The woman was beside him now, touching him. She was older too, but still thin and attractive in a bitter kind of way. She stroked the young man's hair and face in a way that made me feel like an eel was slithering down my spine.

"Come out back, little man," she purred. "There's something I need you to do for me."

Shit. Not only a bully, but she molested him as well. He tried to shrug off her hands. "I'm busy."

She made a sound like a sob. "Don't you love your mama?"

Oh, this was so very twisted—like something off a soap opera. You know it can't possibly be right, but you can't change the channel.

The young man looked up, and suddenly he didn't look so sullen anymore. He looked guilty and strangely eager. "Sure I do, mom."

And she smiled prettily—her tears all gone—and offered him her hand, he took it, letting her lead him into the back of the store.

I didn't want to stick around for what came next, but something compelled me to pick up the doll he'd left discarded on the chair. Her little beaded dress wasn't as pretty as it had been before, and it looked as though some of her hair had come out.

I froze. Some of her hair had come out. There was a small bald patch on her white skull.

Suddenly I knew I had to look under the dress. I didn't want to—no way did I want to. Swallowing, I pinched the delicate silk beneath the beads and lifted. The side of my thumb brushed a powdery-soft thigh and I shuddered. This was seriously creeping me out.

Holding my breath I looked under the sparkling beads. Heat rushed to my head.

Someone had painted a realistic vagina between her legs. I didn't need to guess who that someone was. He'd even attached pubic hair. From the appearance and the slight odor coming from it, I'd guess it was real pubic hair. Gross.

But that wasn't the worst part. The worst part was that her thighs were streaked with something the color of rust. I wanted to think it was paint, but I knew it wasn't. Just like the pubic hair, I knew the stuff painted on this doll's delicate thighs was real as well.

It was blood, and I was willing to bet it had come from his first victim.

Chapter Nine

If I were the heroine in a movie or TV show, I would have a friend at the police department to whom I could give the information I'd uncovered so far in Durdan's dream. As it was, I didn't know anyone in the department, except for Bonnie's boyfriend, and I don't really think I wanted to go down that road—even if there was a snowball's chance he'd believe me.

I suppose I could pretend to be psychic, but I had my doubts that they'd believe that any more than they'd believe I actually went into the asshole's dream.

Or maybe I could call in an anonymous tip, give them Phil's name and the address of his shop. Tell them I had seen something weird, but that wasn't a sure thing either.

What was a sure thing, was me.

So maybe I was acting in a "too stupid to live" manner by taking such a risk, but I couldn't let this go. I wasn't trying to be stupid. I just wanted to do the right thing.

And as long as I didn't hurt him, everything would be okay.

I followed down the hall where Phillip Durdan and his mother had disappeared. I really hoped they were done with whatever it was they were going to do. But just in case, I sent a little nudge out into the Dreaming. When I opened the last door at the end of the hall, I crossed my fingers and hoped that time had moved on.

Phil was alone in what appeared to be a workshop. Doll parts were all over the place—it looked like an Alice Cooper stage show. He was washing something at a sink. I looked over his shoulder to see a length of red hair in his hand. The water running down the drain was brown. Blood.

He hummed as he worked, and I could feel the serenity of his mood. Whatever demons drove him were calm right now as he gently shampooed and conditioned his trophy.

I looked around—it was either that or try to take his eyes out with my fingers. On the table, a doll body was laid out, a selection of clothing beside it. Its head was bald, waiting for the hair he cleaned, and would eventually style.

I glanced over my shoulder at Phil. He still hadn't noticed me. I needed a moment. Needed to figure out how to do this. I already knew the best way to solve this was to convince him to confess. But how? My brain was whirling now, adrenaline started whishing through my veins. Verek and I had played around with shape-shifting—something most Dreamkin could do, but I'd never done it under this kind of pressure or circumstances. To be convincing I would literally have to become another person, not just a reasonable facsimile.

I could make myself look like one of his dolls, but he might like that. He wasn't afraid of his dolls—they had no power. Ditto for his victims. If I turned into Amanda, he would probably look at her fondly. He certainly wouldn't be afraid of a woman whose power he had already taken.

But what about the woman who had taken *his* power away?

Yeah, that would do it. But could I?

Time to find out if, like Morpheus, I could change my appearance so completely I became another person. Closing my eyes to better focus, I drew her out of his subconscious, her every expression, word and touch. I let that essence flow over me, cover me, seep into me. I became her with surprising ease. I felt her venom. I felt every twisted little emotion.

Somewhere Jackey Jenkins twitched in her sleep as this aspect of myself leapt to life once more, gleeful at being released from its cage. I knew because I felt that little bit of her that still had my hooks inside it.

If every human had a Shadow archetype, this was mine. This was the part of me at home in the dark corners of the Dreaming. The part of me that knew what it could do and liked it.

I tried to push aside the pleasure I felt and concentrate on what I needed to do. I couldn't harm him—I *wouldn't* harm him.

God, I wanted to. I wanted to tear at him with razor teeth, remind him of the damage this woman had done. I wanted to fuck him up so badly he'd spend the rest of his life drooling and whimpering—trapped inside a never-ending nightmare. I could do it. I could make sure he was never the same again.

But I knew the better course would be to make him aware of the terribleness of what he'd done.

"You've been a very naughty little boy, Phillip," I said in that smoke and glass voice I'd heard her use.

Phil stiffened, his shoulders snapping back. He didn't turn and I tasted the tang of fear on my tongue. It tickled me like downy feathers in the sweetest spots.

I approached him, feeling my hips move in a haughty sway, my hands clenching into fists at my sides. She hated him. Hated him and depended on him. He represented everything she despised about her missing husband. And yet, Phillip looked so much like the man she had fallen in love with. Having him sexually was like having his father again. And it made sure he would never leave her—yet it made her despise him even more.

Shit, I couldn't stay this woman for long. I shouldn't have taken so much of her into myself.

My hands uncurled to come down on his shoulders. He was so warm and muscular beneath my palms. So deliciously young and strong. I was shorter than him in this form, but I felt as though I was ten feet tall. "Look at me, Phillip."

He didn't move.

"Phillip."

Slowly he turned. I lifted my hands from him, running them down his arm as he came to face me. His face, which had looked average to me before, now looked so handsome and vital as his mother.

His *mother*. God.

"What have you been doing?" I asked.

"N . . . nothing." But I saw the lie in his eyes.

I smiled at him. "Don't lie to mama. I know about those girls." It was the right thing to say, because Phillip's face lost all color and his eyes grew very large.

They had fought about girls before. His mother didn't like it when he looked at other girls. Didn't want him dating other girls.

"No one wants you but me, Phillip darling." I heard her voice in my head as clearly as Phillip heard them in his own. She had told him that time and time again. *"I'm the only woman who loves you."*

Now I knew where Phillip got his particular brand of crazy. Not very professional of me, I know, but I wasn't myself at that moment.

"I didn't mean to . . ."

"Shhh." I put my finger to his lips as he tried to explain, pushing so that I could feel the hard wall of his teeth behind the soft flesh. He trembled. "Don't lie to me."

He nodded—like his neck was stiff—and I took my finger away. Part of me wanted to wipe the moisture that clung there on my clothes, but I fought the urge. "Mama" wouldn't do that.

"I couldn't help it," he said.

I smiled and patted his shoulder. "I know. You've never learned how to control yourself. I thought I taught you better."

And the things this woman had taught him about "control" made my spine slither. Ugh.

"I'm very disappointed in you, Phillip." As I spoke I combed my fingers through his hair. It would have been a very maternal gesture from anyone else, but I felt menacing as I did it. "You've been a rotten little man, and now someone has to clean up after you—again."

That slipped out of its own accord as I followed the dream as Phillip dictated. What had he done that she had to clean up after him in the past? How much did his mother know about his crimes? And why the hell didn't she stop him?

Maybe because knowing gave her more power over him.

He hung his head. "I'm sorry."

"Sorry doesn't cut it this time, Phillip." I kept saying his name, knowing how he hated it. "This time you have to be a man and take responsibility."

Faded eyes lifted and met mine. He looked like a scared little boy. "What do you want me to do?"

"You have to go to the police and tell them what you've done."

He shook his head, jaw set mulishly. "No. I won't. You can't make me."

"Phillip."

He kept shaking his head as he pulled away from me. "No!" His face contorted into a mask of frustration and rage. "I won't! I won't!"

I slapped him—hard. My palm stung and his cheek blossomed with crimson. He was calm.

"You have to," I told him. "I'm not cleaning up after

you this time. They know it was you. They'll be easier on you if you confess."

"They don't know it was me." He was shaking his head again. "No one knows."

For a second, staring into those eyes, I knew true emptiness, and it terrified me. "The police know, Phillip." I sought to take control again. "They found evidence. They know what you are." It was a lie, but he didn't know that. "They know what you did. You have to confess."

If he shook his head again I was going to back hand him. He did. I did. It felt good—too good. I had to end this soon. "You will confess," I said.

"No."

I grabbed his jaw in my hand, forcing him to look at me as I snarled in his face. "You will, or I'll tell them all about you. I'll tell them what you did to me, you rotten little bastard." And I knew as soon as the words left my lips that "Mama" was dead. I was very much afraid that Phil had killed her.

I bet somewhere in this workshop there was a doll wearing her face and hair too.

He was shaking now. Tears welled in his eyes. "I didn't mean to hurt you, you know that."

That's when I knew I had won. I let go of his jaw and wrapped my arms around him. "I know, baby. I know. Shhh. That's a good boy." I held him against me as he sobbed into my shoulder, feeling far more self-satisfied than I should have. "You know how you can make it up to me, pretty boy. Don't you? You know what will make me happy."

He nodded, and when he lifted his head, his tears had stopped. He looked dejected, like a kicked puppy—or a sorry little boy.

"What are you going to do?" I asked softly, stroking his hair again. "What are you going to do for Mama?"

"Go to the police," he replied hoarsely. "I'm going to tell them everything."

And he would too. I smiled in pleasure and hugged him again. "That's a good boy." And then my lips were searching for his and I knew I had to get the hell out of Mama before this dream finished playing out.

I shucked her off as quickly as I could and left the dream. Phillip was too busy screwing his mother to notice my departure.

I woke up, my eyes snapping open in the darkness. I eased out of bed and headed for the bathroom. I needed a shower.

Problem was, I wasn't sure if I would ever feel clean again.

Just before sunrise I heard Phil Durdan in my head. Whispering to his mother, he told her he would confess just as she wanted. Wasn't he a good boy?

Before I could stop myself, I answered that yes he was—or rather his mother answered. It was me, but it wasn't. I had been so convincing that when Phil sent out his little "prayer" to Mommy Dearest, I was the receiver. That creeped me out.

But, I wasn't going to let weirding myself out ruin this good news! I jumped out of bed, cleaned up, put on a spectacular face, if I do say so myself, and hightailed it over to Noah's.

He had sleep in his eyes when he answered the door, and his hair stood straight up on end. He never looked better to me. He left me in the kitchen and went off to shower with little more communication than a grunt. That was okay. I had woken him up after all, and it wasn't even seven thirty yet.

I was pouring myself a cup of coffee when Noah sauntered back into the kitchen a little while later. He took one look at me and stopped in his tracks.

"What did you do?" he demanded.

I looked up from pouring him a cup from the carafe. "What do you mean?" My expression was all innocence, I was certain.

That I was guilty of something, however, seemed obvious to Noah. "You're up before me and ready for work. And you made coffee. Either you've done something, or you're not really Dawn."

Since he'd already tussled with one faux me in the course of our relationship, it wasn't really an odd thing for him to say. And having seen the pounding he gave that fake me, it wasn't a big surprise when I caved.

"I talked Phil into confessing," I blurted.

That explanation only made him look more bewildered—and annoyed. "Who the hell is Phil?"

I stirred cream into my coffee, unable to meet his dark gaze. "Amanda's rapist." I held my breath.

Silence echoed in the kitchen. Then, "You're on a first name basis?"

I braved a quick glance at him. He was still as a statue, in nothing but Batman pajama bottoms and a frown. "Sort of."

Suddenly, he was beside me, his hand on mine, stilling my stirring. "You'd better tell me all of it. *Now*."

A deep breath later, I turned to him. "I didn't hurt him. I didn't do anything the Council could take me to task for."

Noah closed his eyes and took a breath. When his eyes opened, he looked calm and serene. "What did you do, Doc?" He couldn't be that mad at me if he was using his nickname for me.

"I went into his dream and sort of talked him into confessing."

Noah's jaw tightened. "Go on."

"I pretended to be his mother and I convinced him that he had to confess."

He stared at me. "You convinced him to confess by pretending to be his mother?"

I admit it sounded pretty farfetched. "Well, I sort of became her—as he saw her."

His brow furrowed again. "Became her?"

I sighed. I needed a drink of coffee. I lifted my cup and took a sip. I could see his impatience, so I didn't keep him waiting any longer. "I used residual dream matter from his subconscious and made myself into the perfect image of her. I even thought like her." I winced at the memory.

Noah saw my reaction and reached for me. "You can do that?" And then, "Are you okay?"

I leaned into him and wrapped my arms around his waist. "Yeah. She was one sick woman. Her son's worse."

Warm hands rubbed my back. "And you're certain he's going to confess?"

I lifted my head to smile weakly at him. "As certain as a mother can be of her son."

He didn't share my humor, however dark it was. "You took a big chance."

"It's worth it if it works."

When he didn't immediately agree with me, I felt foolish, as though I was missing something.

"How did you know how to find him?" There was

a stillness to his tone, a hesitancy that told me he was bracing himself for the answer.

This was what I had been dreading. There was no getting out of it, however. I might be a coward when it came to discussing this with Noah, but I wasn't going to become a liar.

"I tracked him through the Dreaming," I replied, working up the courage to tell the whole story.

Noah released me, stepping back to look at me with an expression I didn't like. He looked surprised, hurt, and wary. "I thought you could only do that to people you've met."

He really paid attention when I told him these things. He was right. Unless the person was a Dreamkin, I had to physically come face-to-face with them in order to pick up on their dream selves.

"He was at the craft show," I whispered, unable to bring my voice up to its normal volume. "He's a doll maker."

If Noah had flown off the handle I think I could have handled it. Instead, he looked at me with disappointment, and maybe just a little disgust. I really hoped the latter was a figment of my guilty conscience.

"How did you know it was him?" No recriminations, just a simple question.

"I recognized him from her dream. I saw his face. He had a doll that looked just like Amanda. I think he used her hair on it."

"I see." He turned away from me then, taking a couple of steps away to brace a hand against the wall. He kept his back to me, rigid and still. Was he angry at the rapist, or at me? Or both?

I opened my mouth to say something—anything that might make him understand why I did what I did.

Noah spoke first, "He told Amanda she'd make a beautiful doll."

"What?" Now it was my turn to feel broadsided. It wasn't a good feeling. "When?"

He turned, face so blank it scared me a little. "When he raped her. Didn't you hear him say it in her dream?"

I shook my head. "Dreams aren't always exact replays . . ."

He didn't let me continue, cutting me off with sharp precision, "And if you had told me he was there, I could have seen the doll for myself and called the police."

That was true. So was this: "If you had told me he'd said that to her, I would have told you I saw him."

Muscular arms folded across his chest. Classic defensive posture. "You should have told me regardless."

"Probably." I folded my arms across my chest as well. This was headed in a great direction, wasn't it?

"But you didn't."

"No, because at the time I was freaked out and you were holding a huge sword that you might have been tempted to use."

He looked like he didn't know whether to laugh or scowl. He did a little of both. "You think I'm some kind of idiot?"

I frowned too. "Of course not, but I would have loved to kill the bastard and I don't have the connection to Amanda that you do."

His eyes widened. "Kill him? Sweet Jesus, Doc. Am I that much of a monster?"

For a second, the therapist in me raised its head and started to analyze his choice of words. I batted her aside and concentrated on the argument. How like me to try and distance myself emotionally by becoming Dr. Dawn. "You're not a monster. Trust me. I've been in his head. I know who the monster is."

"Once again, you risk your own safety because of me." His arms uncrossed and he raked a hand through his thick hair, mussing the inky strands.

I guess he was referring to all that Karatos crap. "I did it because I thought it was the best way to handle it."

Dark eyes locked with mine. It was difficult to hold that gaze, mostly because I didn't really like the reflection I saw there. "The best way being not to tell me."

"The best way being taking care of it myself." I sighed. "That didn't come out right."

He shook his head, a bitter smile twisting his lips. "Don't bother. I get it."

I moved toward him, putting my hand on his arm. He didn't shrug it off, so I took that as a good sign. "Noah, I didn't take any risks. No one got hurt, and we didn't have to deal with police questions. It seemed like a good idea at the time."

He watched me for a second, and this time it was easier holding his gaze. I let him see the sincerity in my own. I hoped how much I thought of him—how much I never meant to upset him—was obvious.

He sighed. "Look, I think I've been pretty fucking understanding and patient given the extraordinary circumstances surrounding our relationship, but if you can't be straight with me, what's the point?"

My heart flipped. That sounded like break-up talk to me. "I am straight with you."

He snorted. "When you think I won't go psycho."

"I didn't think you'd go psycho."

Pinned again by a gaze that held me tighter than two-sizes-too-small Spanx. "But you were afraid."

Boy, he just wouldn't let go. I guess I deserved it. I hadn't thought that he'd see it this way. All I'd thought was of him losing it. Of course he'd take that as an insult, when he liked to think of himself of controlled. "I was. Yeah." How could he be surprised? He was the one who said he'd like to have five minutes alone with Durdan.

I saw some of that control now, in the stiffness of his

posture, the careful movements as he stepped back, away from me. "I don't want a girlfriend who's afraid of me."

"I'm not afraid of you. I just didn't want you to do something stupid."

"Because doing stupid stuff is your job." There wasn't any heat in his voice, no anger, but I felt as though there was. His eyes were bright—glittering even—and I knew we were headed for a fight of epic proportions. He was hurt and I wasn't handling this well at all.

"I'm going to go to work," I said softly, "Before this turns ugly. Will ten hours be enough for you to figure out whether or not you can forgive me?"

"It's not about forgiving you," he replied likewise. "It's about whether or not you want to be with me. Do you think you can figure that out in ten hours?"

Before I could say anything, Noah took his coffee cup, turned on his heel, and walked away, toward his bedroom. "Have a good day at work."

Right, I thought, gathering up my things and stomping toward the door like a chastised school kid. Like *that* was going to happen.

Chapter Ten

I went to work feeling a little bit like a kicked dog. I totally deserved the feeling, I know. But that didn't stop me from resenting Noah for it. Had I expected him to fall to his knees and thank me for taking matters into my own hands? Maybe praise my abilities and the ease with which I manipulated a sociopath? Sure. I'd be lying if I said there wasn't a part of me that had wanted him to do just that. I felt bad, but there was a part of me that wasn't the least bit sorry for what I'd done. He hadn't been totally honest with me either. Right?

Ahhh, relationships. This was why I'd never had many. I really wasn't good at them.

Okay, enough whining. Noah and I would fix this if

we wanted to be together, and if we didn't . . . well that was that. But sitting around here worrying about it wasn't an option. I wasn't going to let a fight wreck my day.

When the phone rang a few minutes later, I put aside my latte (full of fatty-feel-goodness, no skinny today) and the file I was reading, and answered with a peppy, "Dawn Riley speaking."

"Good morning, Dawn Riley," came a familiar low and slightly gravelly voice.

I smiled, feeling better already. "Antwoine!"

Antwoine Jones and I had met right before Karatos began screwing with my life. He was the only human, besides Noah and my mother, who knew what I was. Antwoine had been in a long-term relationship with a succubus before my father put an end to it years ago. Antwoine knew a lot about the Dreaming—way more than I did. I don't know what I would have done without him when I faced Karatos.

"Girl, what kind of trouble have you gotten into this time?" I don't know how he knew these things but, God love him, he seemed to know me better than I knew myself at times.

"I don't know what you're talking about."

"Word has it that the Warden had you brought before the Council."

See? He's human, banned from the Dreaming and he

still knows stuff no human should. He refused to tell me how he knew these things either.

"She did, but I'm good." I hesitated. "I think."

His low chuckle made me smile again, despite how foolish I felt. "You know, I know someone who might be able to give you some information about Miz Padera."

He knew the Warden's name. Huh. "Who might be able to give me information?"

"Madrene," came the soft reply.

Madrene was the succubus Antwoine loved. He hadn't seen her for years since my father banned him from the Dreaming. Of course, Antwoine had his own little "cell" within the Dream Realm—humans can't survive without dreams. I had promised Antwoine I'd try to track down his former lover in return for all he'd done for me. So far, I hadn't kept my word.

Now would be a good time, I think. I risked pissing Morpheus off by doing so, but even he couldn't deny the debt owed to Antwoine, so I didn't think he'd give me too much grief. Besides, I'd rather have my father be angry at me than renege on a promise. And if Madrene could help with the Warden, it was so worth the risk.

"I'm sorry," I said. "I've been preoccupied lately. I'll look for her, okay?" I wasn't sure exactly when, but soon. Tonight was going to be dedicated to getting things right between me and Noah. "Tomorrow."

"You're a good girl, Dawn."

I didn't feel it. "Hold the praise till I deserve it."

He chuckled. "Meanwhile, you wanna have lunch tomorrow? You can fill me in on what you've gotten yourself into while I've been gone."

"That could take a while," I replied with a grin. "You buyin'?"

"Maybe."

I knew he was teasing. He would rather bite off his own arm than let me pay for his meal. Antwoine was fairly well off, and he had some old-fashioned notions about things. It would be a fight just to get him to go Dutch.

"Then I will clear my social calendar."

"Great. I'll meet you at that Thai place we went to last time. One o'clock."

When I hung up I had a more positive feeling about the day than I had ten minutes ago. It would be good to see Antwoine again—he made everything seem right with the world.

My last appointment of the day was at four o'clock. Deandra, a sophomore at a city high school, had been sent to see me by her mother who was an old friend of Bonnie's. Deandra's father died seven months ago and the girl had been experiencing reoccurring dreams of her father ever since. Most would probably assume that this was Deandra's mind's way of letting go of her father, but since in all the dreams her father continuously stated how he wished they could be together again, I looked at it from a different perspective.

The Dreaming existed between the human realm and that of Death. After all, if you know your mythology, you know that my father is the nephew of Death. I'm not sure if that's the actual relationship or not, but regardless, I had a very strong suspicion that Deandra's father was caught in the Dreaming, unable to move on. Like one of those shades in Hadria's cave.

I also suspected that he was going to unintentionally talk his daughter into killing herself, because that was what she thought he wanted her to do. I urged her to realize that her father would not want her to hurt herself, no matter how much he wanted to see her.

Deandra left after promising me she wouldn't try to kill herself, and with several possibilities of other things her father might be telling her firmly (I hoped) rooted in her mind. Hopefully I had done my job, because if that little girl hurt herself, I was going to need a very long leave of absence.

I leaned back in my chair and took a deep breath. Any minute, Bonnie would come in to let me know any changes in my schedule for tomorrow, and ask how my day was. But for now, I was alone, and my thoughts closed in on me like hungry wolves.

Thinking of Deandra's father and what I would say

to him made me think of what I had done to Durdan and that, of course, led to the inevitable thoughts of Jackey Jenkins. All she had done was embarrass me by pointing out that my period had spotted through my jeans. What I had done in retaliation was way worse.

I should never have been able to do what I did. A fifteen-year-old kid should never have that kind of power. What had felt so satisfying at the time, now left a sour taste in my mouth and a horrible sense of shame and regret in my soul.

I could probably try to go into Jackey's dreams again and attempt to make it right, but I hated to think what dreaming of me might do to her. And I had no idea how to fix something that had happened thirteen years ago. I didn't think I could. Some scars went too deep.

And frankly, I was too chicken-shit to face the damage I'd done.

At exactly 5:15 I was saved anymore self-introspection by Bonnie's light tapping on the door. She didn't wait for me to tell her to come in, but rather swooped in immediately after lowering her fist. This was why I opened portals in the bathroom—with the door locked.

"You must be beat," she remarked, as she set a small stack of folders on my desk. "You've been here since before me."

I smiled wearily as she scooped up the folders for today's appointments out of the basket. She kept me organized to a fault, God love her. "I am beat."

"That's too bad." She flashed me a coy grin. "Noah's here."

Oh crap. I wasn't thinking I'd have to face him quite so soon. "I guess I'd better perk up then, eh?"

She didn't respond in the salacious manner I'd come to expect from her. Instead, she gave me a close, and scrutinizing look. "You okay, kiddo?"

I nodded, like I was fifteen and trying to convince my mother that I hadn't been smoking. "Fine. Just a little tired."

Bonnie had kids—though you'd never know it from her figure—and it was obvious I wasn't fooling her. She let it go, though, with a, "Hmm."

"Give me a minute," I told her as she reached the door.

Again with the close look. She saw way more than I was comfortable with. "Do I need to tear a strip off that boy?"

I couldn't help the smile I gave her. "No. I just need to take care of some stuff first." "Stuff" being my face, my nerves, my courage.

"Just buzz when you're ready." I knew at that moment that Bonnie would keep Noah on ice for days if I needed her to. "Do you need anything else?"

"Thanks, but I'm good."

The second she shut the door, I stood up and headed for the bathroom. I just needed a moment to pull myself together, and nothing gave me more courage than an impeccable face. A touch up of perfume, and antiperspirant helped too.

I barely reached the bathroom door when I felt the world give out beneath me. No, the world was *ripped* out from around me. I was yanked into the Dreaming without finesse, without care, and without my permission.

"What the hell?" I whirled around, still dizzy, to face my host.

The Warden smiled at me with bitter satisfaction, her crimson lips thin and wide. "Hello, Dawn. You just can't stay out of trouble can you?"

I was too pissed to be as scared as I probably should have been. Not even Morpheus had pulled me in without my permission. I didn't know that anyone could. If the Warden had that kind of power, she was not someone to screw with. "What do you want?" I demanded.

The Warden's smile widened. She looked like a cross between Nicole Kidman and the Joker in my mind. "I want to talk to you about what you did last night."

My spine stiffened and I rose to my full height. I didn't actually think I'd intimidate her, but it didn't hurt to make myself as big as possible—mostly for my own benefit. "I appreciate the interest, but I'm a little busy right now." I turned to leave. Could I leave? What if she was strong enough to hold me there?

I didn't get a chance to find out, because she spoke again, "Did you really think you could get away with going into Phillip's dream and manipulating him like that?"

Something in her tone grabbed my attention with an oily fist. Slowly, I faced her, all thoughts of leaving on hold for the moment. "I didn't hurt him."

"You could have."

"But I *didn't*." I met her gaze with an unflinching one of my own.

Apparently she was in the mood to toy with me. "I cannot imagine how you even came to exist let alone how you managed to survive all these years. One more example of the ruination you'll bring down upon our world. And your father allows it."

Ruination? Nice. "Is that discontent I hear?" I kept my voice neutral. "Sounds like you're one of the assholes trying to make my father's life difficult." Karatos had told me that there were people in the Dreaming who were unhappy with my father and how he ran things—mostly that he had my mother living with him, and let me run around loose. Morpheus had no idea how deep it went—or obviously how seriously he should take their little revolution.

The Warden shrugged. "I never meant to give any such impression."

I smiled grimly. "That's it, cover your ass."

Bright eyes narrowed. "It's not my ass you should be concerned with."

"Don't threaten me unless you can back it up." Where was all this bravado coming from? "And don't give me any of this 'rules' crap. The reason you're so scared of me is because there aren't any rules for what I can do." And that was true. I hadn't broken any rules by bringing Noah into the Dreaming because no other Dreamkin could do that—not even my father. And my kind influenced dreams all the time. So maybe I had bent the rules a bit, but I hadn't broken any.

"Scared of you?" The Warden—Padera—sneered. "I don't fear you. I despise *you*."

"Why is that anyway?" I truly wanted to know. "Because I'm half human? Or because you believe some prophecy that I'm going to destroy the world?"

Her features hardened. "Before Morpheus brought your mother into our world, there was order and balance. That all changed once you were born. More and more humans have been able to interact with the Dreaming. The veil between the worlds is thinning, bringing destruction ever closer to our realm."

Great. She considered that proof that I was a destroyer of worlds. What bullshit. "None of that has been my intention."

"But it's your fault."

Could she prove that? "The Council doesn't seem to think so."

"What do you suppose their reaction will be when they learn of this latest stunt? It's the second time you've done this kind of thing, isn't it? Of course, this time to a lesser degree. Do you know that poor girl still dreams about what you did to her. Her mind has never fully healed."

I so did not want to hear this. "I was a kid. I didn't know what I was doing."

"But you do now, don't you?"

She had me there. "So, what are you going to do about it?" Was there anything she could do? If there was, wouldn't she have the Council with her? Instead, she'd come to me alone.

Again with the creepy smile. "I've already done it. I took away what you did to Phillip. He doesn't remember any of it."

My hands curled into fists. "You stupid cow! You let a rapist go on his merry way because you had a score to settle with me?"

That erased some of her glee. "I released a dreamer from the manipulations with which you bound him."

"Bullshit. If you were that magnanimous you would have done the same to Jackey years ago. You did it out of spite. You bitch."

She went dark—almost like a negative image—for a split second before whipping herself toward me. "You pathetic half-breed! You have no right to wield any power in this world! You never should have been allowed to live!"

Half-breed? Shouldn't have been allowed to live? I leaned close, putting my face in hers. And I smiled as coldly as I could. "But I do have power. Lots of it. You might be the head of the Nightmares, but I am still the daughter of Morpheus, and you will treat me accordingly or I will fuck you up." Obviously I was still carrying some of that darkness with me, because normally I'd be at least a little scared right now.

"How dare you," she whispered.

I was all shock and amazement—in a mocking kind of way. "You've got some nerve, lady. I convinced a serial rapist to turn himself into the police and now you've let him run free. The blood of his next victim is all over your hands."

The Warden sneered at me. "Knowing that causes you the least bit of distress gives me the greatest satisfaction."

I could have killed her. Honest to God. If I thought I

had the power to unmake one of my kind I would do it right on the spot. But my father was the only one who had that power, lucky for the Warden.

"And don't even think of going after him again," she warned me. "If I catch even the faintest whiff of you in that man's dreams, I'll report you to the Council— and I'll tell them about Miss Jenkins. They won't be so quick to think you an innocent then."

It was almost worth the risk until she said, "And once you're unmade, who will look after your mother when your father is busy trying to keep his kingdom?"

My eyes burned. Any minute I was going to lose control and rip this bitch apart just for the sheer pleasure of it.

And then she was gone. All of it was gone. It was like some giant hand gave me a huge shove and knocked me out of the Dreaming back into the mortal world. I even stumbled as I hit the ground.

I was in my office. Alone. The Warden had tossed me out like a bag of dirty laundry.

I could tell Morpheus what she'd said, but then I'd have to tell him what I had done. He had to be told that the Warden was part of the group who had set themselves against him. Somehow, I'd find a way to tell him that. And if I had to, I'd tell him everything.

God, what was it with me? Why was I so afraid of

the men in my life that I wasn't completely honest with them until I had to be?

As my anger dissolved, I slumped into the chair I used during sessions and buried my face in my hands. She'd let Phillip go free. He wouldn't confess, not now. And there was nothing I could do about it.

How was I going to tell Noah that I'd failed? How could I face Amanda knowing that I had fucked up so very royally?

I'd let Phillip's vileness—his mother's evil—coat me like a film. I'd let my own dark nature seep through and take over. I'd been a proper bitch to Noah, and all of it was for nothing.

And I wish I could say it was residual darkness that made me want some kind of revenge on the Warden, but it wasn't. It was one hundred percent all me. She and I had a score to settle, and some day, I was going to settle it.

Time passed differently in the Dreaming, so only a few moments had gone by when I finally buzzed Bonnie and told her to send Noah in.

I'd touched up my makeup—enough to hide most of the flush my confrontation with the Warden had brought to my cheeks—and my knees had stopped trembling by the time Noah walked in.

He must have had a meeting or something because he was wearing a crisp white shirt and black jacket with his jeans. His boots had been polished as well, and his hair, while spiky, was artfully so. He looked nice. Good enough to eat.

I forced a smile and stood as he shut the door behind him. "You're all dressed up." What a conversationalist I am!

"Meeting with a gallery owner," he said. "Are you busy?"

"No. I'm done for the day." We just stood there, looking at each other. "Are you still mad at me?"

"A little," he replied with a slight smile. He ran his hand through his hair. "I thought you might want to go out. It's been a while since we've done anything like that."

Okay, so I guess he wasn't going to dump me. That was good. "I'd like that," I replied. "But first I have to tell you something."

A frown pulled his brow. "Okay. What?" A man of many words was Noah.

I went to him. I only meant to close the distance between us, but somehow I ended up in his arms. I don't know which one of us embraced the other first. "I'm sorry I didn't tell you about seeing Durdan. You were right. I fucked up, Noah."

He went very still, but his arms were strong and

warm around me. "Yeah, you did. But it wouldn't have happened if I'd told you what Amanda said."

I looked up, forcing myself to meet his gaze. That fear nudged me again, but I fought it. I would be honest this time. "No, I mean I really fucked up. The Warden found out what I did to Durdan and she reversed it. He's not going to confess now." I was on the verge of tears. I felt like crap and I didn't want him mad at me and I was tired, damn it! "I'm so sorry."

"You're sorry?" He caught my face in his hand, and lifted my chin with surprisingly gentle but firm fingers. "Dawn, you don't have to apologize."

I can only imagine how awful I looked with my face as squished up as it was. "But I wanted to help Amanda, and now he's going to get away with it unless the cops get a clue." And I meant that literally as well as figuratively.

Was he laughing at me? "Doc, no one has done more for Mandy than you."

My face smoothed out. "You're not mad?"

He tilted his head. "That you tried to help Amanda? No. That you seem bound and determined to get yourself in shit? A little. You don't have to take these risks."

I really couldn't believe my ears. "If I don't, who will?"

"Doc, it's over. I found one of Durdan's business

cards and called the police. I told them about the doll you saw. I told them everything."

My eyebrows rose. "Everything?"

He chuckled. "Maybe not everything, but enough that he's a person of interest."

Giddiness washed over me. The Warden's interference didn't matter. My own actions hadn't really mattered. Score one for the humans.

"Thank God," I murmured. Once the police searched Durdan's workshop they would find all the evidence they needed. They had to.

"So," Noah said, giving me another squeeze before letting me go. "Let's go grab some dinner and go back to my place so we can make up the right way."

That sounded so unbelievably good to me. I grabbed my coat and purse and turned off the lights before locking my office. There was no one else around so I set the alarm—the night cleaning crew knew the code—and we left.

It was a cool evening, but pleasant enough. I hated that it was starting to get dark so early. I missed the long, bright days of summer. Soon it would be dark at four o'clock. Ugh. I'd get more clients in the winter, though. It never failed. All that darkness, cold, and holiday cheer drove most people into depression. I guess that was something to look forward to.

My office was on Madison between Forty-second and Forty-third, all of which were heavy with pedestrian traffic at this time of day. Lots of people heading toward Grand Central Station for their train, or various streets for a bus. I was glad that I lived a few blocks south and east, in Murray Hill. I didn't have to train to work anymore unless the weather was crap.

We walked along Forty-third toward Fifth, holding hands, talking about our day. It was like nothing bad had ever happened between us, although I knew we'd talk about it later when we were at his place. There were still some things we needed to discuss—and apologize for.

I was happy that Noah had another gallery interested in obtaining some of his work. Even though we hadn't been together long, I was very proud of his work and how successful he had become.

And of course, I was very honored to have been one of his subjects. I looked almost angelic in "The Nightmare" as I held a sleeping man in my arms. The man was Noah. Showing me the painting was how he broached the subject of finding out exactly what I am.

Funny, but if it weren't for Karatos, the whole of which had been one of the worst experiences of my life, I probably wouldn't have gotten together with Noah. See what I mean about positive things coming out of the negative? I should write a book on it. Maybe it would hit the *NYT* list and make me a superstar. I could go on *Oprah* and never have to worry about having a full case load again.

Hey, a girl could dream. Couldn't she?

We were on our way out of a Starbucks, each nursing a piping hot latte when Noah's cell phone rang. He checked the number before flipping it open. I don't think he would have picked up if he hadn't thought it important. "Hey, Mandy."

Amanda. Yeah, she was definitely important. I sipped my latte and watched him out of the corner of my eye as he talked.

"What . . . ? Yeah, she's with me. Hold on." He turned his face toward me. "Amanda wants to know if we have time to meet her for a drink?"

"Of course." She either wanted to celebrate or commiserate. "What happened?"

He held up his cup, gesturing for me to hold on, and went back to his phone. "Did you hear that? Yeah, we'll meet you there. Bye." Then he snapped the phone shut and tucked it in his pocket.

"What's happened? Is she all right?"

Noah's normally smooth, golden brow wrinkled. "I'm not sure. She sounded weird."

"I hope the police didn't let Durdan go." I knew without him saying a word that Noah hoped the same. We walked the rest of the way in tense silence. When we reached the hotel where Amanda wanted to meet, she was already in the bar waiting.

She looked up when we entered, her gaze going from me to Noah. And then she burst into tears.

She was also laughing.

"They got him," she said as she rose from her seat. Tears ran down her cheeks as she laughed with unbridled relief. "I picked him out of the lineup and he's been charged."

She held her arms out to me first and I hugged her so hard I thought I might snap her spine. I think we might have jumped up and down too. I'm not sure.

"Let's celebrate," I said when we broke apart and Noah took his turn with the hugging. I glanced at him to see if it was OK, and he nodded. "Amanda, come have dinner with us."

As she withdrew from Noah's arms I thought her expression looked strangely sheepish. "I'd love to, but I can't. I already have plans for dinner." She cast a quick peek at Noah. "Warren is taking me out for Italian."

Now, this was a surprise! Noah and I exchanged surprised glances. "Great," I enthused. "Say hi to him for us."

She said she would, and after our good-byes, Noah

and I walked her to the street, where she caught a cab, and we decided to head over to K town to a little Vietnamese place I'd found there that served great pho.

"You must feel pretty good about yourself," I remarked as we walked inside. "Your call to the police paid off."

He gave me an assessing look. "You waiting for me to say I told you so?"

I looked sheepish and I knew it. "You could."

He shrugged. "Hearing you say it works for me." Then he grinned. "Let's eat. Celebrate. Talk later."

Sounded good to me. A few minutes later we were seated. I waited until the appetizers arrived before I brought up another potentially tricky subject. "Warren, huh?"

Noah chuckled and snatched up a chunk of spring roll with his chopsticks. "I wondered how long you could last before you brought that up." He popped the crispy morsel in his mouth, chewed and swallowed. "My brother's always had a thing for Mandy."

"You don't mind?" I dipped my own chunk of spring roll in a small puddle of hot sauce and hoisin. "I suppose it's not really a date. I mean, she's still recovering . . ."

He cut me off. "I don't care." He said it like a man who really didn't, not in a jealous way at any rate.

"They're much better suited than she and I ever were. Warren will take good care of her, and right now he's being a friend, which is exactly what she needs."

I couldn't argue with that. I raised my chopsticks and their sauce-covered prize. "To breakthroughs and budding romances."

Noah clicked his spring roll against mine. Our gazes locked, and I knew he was about to make his point. "And to staying out of the Warden's way."

I stuffed my food into my mouth before I could say anything—such as make a promise I might not be able to keep.

Chapter Eleven

Antwoine Jones was a little shorter than me with a lean and wiry build that could be mistaken for frail, but was just the opposite. His dark hair was graying, but his eyes were keen. He had a kind of Morgan Freeman vibe about him—like I thought Will Smith would be in another twenty years or so.

He was one of the few humans who had ever tangled with my father. I was pretty sure Antwoine was one of these anomalies that seemed to start popping up before my birth, but had become more and more common. They were people who had some power within the Dreaming—like Noah.

Anyway, Antwoine had fallen in love with a succubus, apparently tried to kill Morpheus, and got himself banished to his own private corner of the Dreaming for the trouble.

His face lit up when he saw me, and I knew mine did the same. It had been too long since I'd seen him, even though we hadn't known each other very long. Antwoine had realized what I was the first time we met—seeing what even my siblings didn't know.

"Child, you are a sight for these sore eyes." He laughed as he hugged me.

I laughed too. "You talk like you're ancient."

He released me. "Some days I feel it."

We took our seats and the waiter came by with water and menus. We didn't need them. I wanted shrimp pad thai, and Antwoine ordered the same with chicken. We made small talk until the food came and we were relatively certain we wouldn't be interrupted.

"Much as I've missed you, I have a feeling there's something you're not telling me." Antwoine twined noodles around his fork—like he was eating spaghetti. "What's the deal, little Dawn?"

I brought him up to speed on what had been going on since we last spoke—my meeting with Hadria, how I convinced Durdan to confess, and the Warden's interference.

He stared at me over his plate, noodles hanging from his fork as it hovered halfway to his mouth. "Life ain't never dull with you is it, girl?"

I chuckled, pretending for a moment that things really were as light as he made it sound. "I just wanted you to know that being my friend might not be such a great thing for you—or for Madrene."

He didn't look worried as he shoved the fork into his mouth and chewed. "Don't you worry yourself about Madrene and me. The Warden's no threat to us."

I arched a brow. "You sound fairly certain of that." I hate to admit it, but for a second my trust in Antwoine wavered—just a little—as I suspected there was something he wasn't telling me.

Antwoine wiped his mouth with a paper napkin and took a drink of water. "I am. The only way she'd come after me and Madrene is if we broke one of her precious rules. Neither of us bein' Nightmares, we hardly fall under her jurisdiction anyway."

That was true. There, no need to be paranoid at all. If I'd had the good fortune to be born a succubus, the cow wouldn't be after me either. Or maybe she would, because of the prophecy.

Prophecy. Have you ever heard anything so idiotic in your life? And to think that people actually believed in it! Seriously, hadn't these people learned anything from Nostradamus? Prophecies were open to all kinds of interpretations.

"So," he said, spearing a bit of chicken. He smiled

as he spoke. "You're going to risk the King's wrath by getting two wronged lovers back together, are you?"

"I promised you I would, and I like to keep my promises." At least ones that didn't involve leaving well enough alone.

"You don't need to get in trouble just because of a promise to me."

"You don't know what I need, old man." I tried to make a joke of it, but it came out a little awkward sounding.

Antwoine gave me a pointed look, but he didn't say anything more about it.

We ate in silence for a few moments, and then I couldn't help myself. "Antwoine?"

He looked up, kind brown eyes easing the tension inside me. "What?"

"Remember that day we met at the drugstore?"

He laughed. "You ran out of there without your change 'cause you thought I was a crazy old man."

I smiled. "And you bought an iced tea with it."

He nodded, still grinning. "I did. I did. What about it?"

I stirred my fork through the shrimp and noodles left on my plate. "How did you know what I was?"

The laughter faded from his face. Even his eyes lost some of their sparkle. "I don't know. I just did—just like I knew what Madrene was the first time I saw her. It's a talent I guess."

I forced a smile, hiding my disappointment that he couldn't offer a better explanation. Then he decided to broadside me.

"But you're more than a Nightmare, Dawn."

I froze, all thoughts of digging back into my lunch suddenly abandoning me. "What am I, then?"

And then my friend shook his head with an expression of awe that made me more than a little uncomfortable. "Damned if I know, child. Damned if I know."

"Is there something you want to tell me?" Noah asked later that evening as we sat on my couch watching an episode of *Firefly*. I had the box set and the movie. Joss Whedon is a genius when it comes to dialog and character.

I choked on a piece of popcorn. Was I that transparent? And where did I start? I took a drink of diet Dr. Pepper before answering. My eyes were watering as I turned to face him. "What makes you think I'm hiding something?"

"You're quiet," was all he said in reply.

I arched a brow. "That's a bad thing?" Normally I thought maybe I talked too much.

"It's a strange thing." Notice, he didn't tell me I *didn't* talk too much.

One thing at a time. "Does it bother you that I'm not human?"

He shrugged. "I don't give it much thought."

"But when you do think of it, does it bother you?"

Noah pressed pause on the remote, freezing Nathan Fillion mid one-liner. He angled his body to face me fully. "Seems to bother you."

Wait a second, I was the one asking questions. "Well, yeah. Wouldn't you be ticked if you didn't know what you were?"

His head tilted as his lips curved. He looked so yummy against the dark brown cushions. "You're you, Doc."

I didn't share his humor. "Forget I asked. Obviously the fact that I'm half freak doesn't mean anything to you." Folding my arms over my chest, I closed myself up, feeling like a freaking idiot.

Noah reached over and tugged on a piece of my hair. "Where's this coming from?"

"Antwoine doesn't know what I am." Once the words were out there was no taking them back. I had intended to pout a little longer. I was good at pouting, especially when I felt like I was being made fun of.

His expression turned incredulous. "So?"

I sighed. "He seems to have a knack for identifying Dreamkin."

"But when you two met he called you a Nightmare."

"Apparently I'm more than that." Give me a few minutes and I'd be feeling so sorry for myself I'd be guest of honor at my own pity party.

"That surprises you?"

"Yeah." Kinda. "It doesn't surprise you?" He sure didn't sound like it did.

"You're the daughter of a god—his only half-human child. That you exist is a miracle. Why wouldn't you be something no one has ever seen before?"

When he put it like that, it sounded so simple and right—like I wasn't a freak, but something special, and that was okay.

"Maybe I just wish I was normal."

Noah laughed, "Yeah, right."

My mouth opened and nothing came out. He wasn't laughing at me to be malicious, but he certainly seemed to see me differently than I saw myself.

"If you wanted to be normal," he said, grinning to take the sting out, "you wouldn't do the work you do. If you didn't like being different, the idea of being unmade wouldn't freak you out so much."

I protested. "Being unmade would change me. I wouldn't be me anymore."

His smile turned smug and I realized my mistake. "Exactly."

Scowling at being shown so much truth about myself, I went back to petulance. "I guess it doesn't bother you, then."

Noah's smile faded, but his eyes sparkled as he reached over and pried my arms away from my chest.

He took my hands in his. "You're one of a kind. Some days I like that better than others, but I like *you*, Doc. I don't care if Antwoine knows what you are. I do."

That was quite possibly one of the nicest things anyone had ever said to me, and I was mortified when tears sprung to my eyes. "Oh." I didn't put up a fight when he pulled me close and kissed me. Sighing, I gave myself up to the sweet pressure of his lips.

I didn't protest when he pushed me onto my back on the cushions. In fact, I tugged at his shirt and pulled it up until he was forced to stop kissing me long enough to take it off. My own shirt came off next, followed by the remainder of our clothes until we were skin against skin and he was inside me, our breath mingling as our bodies undulated together. I clutched at his shoulders, feeling Noah's muscles bunch beneath my fingers as he thrust one last time. I came loudly—mindlessly—as he stiffened above me, groaning against my neck.

And in those few moments, my life was perfect.

Before I could go looking for Madrene, I had to spend some time with Verek and Hadria. The priestess sent a request for my presence shortly after I entered the Dreaming when Noah and I eventually went to bed. I really didn't want to leave Noah, but I didn't want to be rude to the one person other than my father who seemed to be on my side either. So when her carriage showed up, I climbed in. Within minutes I was in that large, shadowy cavern, told that Hadria wanted to observe my training with Verek and offer some of her own.

Of course I agreed—not that I really had a choice.

"Um, Hadria?" I asked, thinking I might as well take advantage of the situation.

The freakishly tall woman smiled sweetly. "Yes?"

I cast a quick glance at Verek, but his attention seemed focused on the shadow moving in the corner than on what I was saying. "I'm not just a Nightmare, am I?" Even though Noah insisted he knew what I was and was fine with it, I wasn't satisfied. I had this unexplainable need to break myself down to all the key components. Ever since Jackey Jenkins I'd been struck by a feeling of not knowing myself—or what I was capable of.

Hadria blinked at me—like a Himalayan cat I'd had as a kid, all great big eyes. "Why, no. You are not."

I smiled—tight lipped. "Can you tell me just what the heck I am?" Must be very careful not to use potty mouth around the adults.

She set a platter that I hadn't seen her retrieve, of fruits and cheese, onto the table. "You are a little bit of everything in this world. A little bit of all of us, and more."

And then she turned and glided away, sailing toward a doorway I hadn't noticed before.

"Thanks for the clarification," I muttered.

I heard a chuckle behind me and I turned to see Verek watching me. "What?" I demanded with a scowl.

The gorgeous big guy just shook his head. "Nothing. By the way, we're going to train with the mist again today."

"No." I shook my head violently—so much so it almost made me dizzy. "No freaking way."

But Verek only smiled. "It was Hadria's idea."

Jerk. He knew he had me now.

"Dawn—" Hadria swept back into the room with another platter of food for the table. "Am I correct in assuming you have yet to receive your mark?"

I raised my brows. "I have no idea."

Another serene smile. "You would know if you had. When you have opened yourself up to your potential and accepted what you are, you will receive the mark—the symbolic talisman of your destiny."

I looked at the tattoo on her chest. "Is that yours?"

She was still smiling—big surprise—as her fingers brushed the stylized spider. "Yes. It is the symbol of Ama, declaring me High Priestess."

So she wasn't just any priestess, but the Grand Poohbah. Nice. I turned to Verek. "Where's yours?"

The Nightmare grinned and pulled down the waist of his pants to reveal a small dagger tattoo just above and slightly left of his right hipbone. He even had muscles

there—bladelike ridges on either side of his abdomen.
I will admit—but never out loud—that my mouth went
a little dry at the sight. My cheeks burned as well. No
doubt that was the desired effect.

"The dagger is the mark of the Nightmares," Hadria
explained, seemingly unaffected by Verek's display of
golden flesh.

"So I should end up with one as well?" God, I hoped
it wasn't on my abs. I was a little squishy there.

The tall woman shrugged lightly. "Perhaps. Or, you
may develop the mark of something else. Once you receive yours we will be able to better understand where
your talents lean."

"It takes some people a long time to get their mark,"
Verek added, giving me a look that had my cheeks
warming even more, but this time because of how he
could read my insecurities. "Don't be upset if it takes a
while, especially since you're able to do so much."

He made it sound like a good thing. I think that
was the moment when the two of us officially became
friends, at least in my estimation. That was why I wiped
my slightly moist palms on my jeans, stood up straight
and said, "Let's do this."

Verek flashed me a grin so proud I had to look away.
I think I was more comfortable when he picked on me.
Still, I took some strength and confidence from that
smile as the shadow in the corner crept up the wall to

hover near the ceiling. Apparently Hadria's pet wraith didn't like the mist either.

Both Nightmare and Priestess came to me, flanking me as they each took one of my hands.

"What are you doing?" I asked, but I allowed them to twine their fingers with mine.

"Lesson number one," Verek said, glancing down at me. "Take us to the mist."

I stared at him. "I can't."

"Yes, you can." He squeezed my fingers. "Just like you do it when you open a door to this world. Think of where you want to be and then will us there."

I wanted to learn how to teleport, sure, but I thought someone would instruct me on how to do it, not just demand that I succeed right away. Talk about pressure. I didn't want to make an idiot of myself in front of Hadria, but if I didn't try I'd be a failure in more ways than one.

Sucking in a deep breath and hoping my palms weren't too clammy, I closed my eyes. I thought about the places where I normally encountered the mist and decided that the gates to the palace would be the best location. It was the one I could envision the most clearly.

I pushed everything else, especially doubt and fear, out of my mind. It wasn't easy, but I did it. When I felt ready, I pushed all the breath out of my lungs, took a firm grip on my companions' hands, and concentrated on where I wanted to go. A faint breeze stirred my hair, and when I opened my eyes we were standing in front of the Gates of Horn and Ivory.

"Excellent," Hadria praised as she released my hand. "Very impressive, Dawn."

I tried to act casual, like it was nothing, but the effect was ruined when I grinned like an idiot. "Thanks."

Even Verek looked impressed, and I realized that I had done something that Hadria couldn't do. Maybe Verek couldn't do it either. Neat.

But, as usual, my happy-times were short lived as the mist moved in like a pack of gleeful puppies. It practically rubbed against Verek and Hadria, and I imagined I could see it bristle when it set its many eyes on me.

It was so weird. It just looked like normal fog. A little on the thick side maybe, but it didn't seem the least threatening. I don't have to say that looks can be deceiving, do I?

Maybe it was my imagination, but I thought I could hear it whispering as it came toward me, gliding over the smooth stone of the drive. I stood still, letting it come to me, trying to keep my breathing mellow as it approached. Verek and Hadria watched from the sidelines. My Nightmare trainer had a hopeful look on his rugged face, and I knew he was almost as nervous as I was.

"Monster," the mist whispered. *"Strange."*

It wrapped around my legs. I could feel its cold through my jeans, but I didn't move, not even when I felt a jagged claw rake my hand. "Stop that," I said softly. "I'm no threat to you." I wasn't about to let its words get to me, not when I'd heard it all before.

"Threat," came that whispery voice that was like a thousand children whispering together.

"I'm not a threat," I repeated. I tried to keep my breathing regular and my heart rate low, but my ribs were thumping like the bass line of a dance-club jam.

The mist slithered around me, scratching and nipping as it climbed. I stiffened as it neared my face. I couldn't lose it. I couldn't get angry, no matter how much I wanted to summon my Morae blade and slice the wispy bastards to shreds.

Cool fingers threaded through my hair, tugging hard enough to bring tears to my eyes. "Stop it," I hissed.

Was that laughter I heard? My temper flared, but I set my jaw and didn't say a word. My anger and fear only fed it—made it all the more resolved that I was its enemy.

Until it laid my cheek open in three deep gashes. I screamed, which made it hurt even more. My face burned as blood gushed down my jaw and neck. I fell to my knees as the poison hit my system, gasping for air as the mist covered me, slicing and clawing and biting like a pack of hungry lions. I couldn't breathe it was wrapped around me so tight—tight enough to crack my ribs.

I couldn't fight physically anymore, but as I gasped for breath I reached out to the mist with my mind—not to hurt it, but to prove myself a non-threat. I touched something. It felt as though the mist was seeping through my skin, becoming part of me.

And then it was gone and I was lying on the stones with Hadria and Verek kneeling beside me. Verek's face was fierce and worried at the same time, but Hadria's expression was as serene as always. It was her I concentrated on.

Long, cool fingers touched my brow. "Heal yourself, Dawn," she urged, her voice soothing. "I will help you."

She began to chant in an old language I recognized but didn't really understand. It was the language of the Dreaming—a dialect older than man. The rhythm of her voice gave me something to focus on while I willed my body to knit itself back together. The first time the mist infected me, Morpheus had to use some special concoction to draw the poison out, but now that I knew what I needed, I was able to conjure up that same kind of treatment.

When I opened my eyes again I was whole, with only a slight tingling in a few places as a reminder of the mist's wrath.

"Are we done?" I asked drily.

Hadria helped me to my feet while Verek hovered close by. She chuckled. "I believe so. You will conquer the mist, Dawn, but I must tell you how impressed I am with some of your other abilities."

"Thanks." I hope I sounded more sincere than I felt. I took her hand in mine and grabbed Verek's arm. Without saying a word, I closed my eyes and willed us back to Hadria's cave, where I knew food waited. I needed to eat. And I needed to be as far away from that goddamn mist as I could get.

Verek held out a chair for me and I thanked him for his chivalry as I wearily sat. God, I felt as though I'd had the snot kicked out of me six times over. So, I was a little surprised when he leaned down and whispered near my ear, "You did good, Princess."

I snatched a piece of cheese. "Yay me."

After regaining my strength, I left my trainers and set out to do what I had originally intended to do that evening—find Madrene. I really wanted to get the hell out of there, and let myself dream and sleep like a normal woman, curled up beside my boyfriend, but that would have to wait.

Would I ever have a regular night's sleep again? It didn't matter that time in the Dreaming refreshed me like a king-sized dose of R.E.M., I simply wanted to dream like other humans, not even falling off a cliff or walking around naked would bother me so long as it was only in my sleep.

But, that would have to wait. Not long, hopefully. As soon as I found Madrene I'd have my normal sleep until the alarm went off.

Hopefully this wouldn't take long. All I wanted to do was find the succubus and make sure she wanted to see Antwoine as much as he wanted to see her. If she didn't, I wasn't about to let my friend face that kind of rejection from the woman he loved.

I had no idea where succubi spent their time—other than sexing up the dreams of human men. I certainly didn't want to walk in on one of those, so I approached my search for Madrene with a degree of caution.

I should have done this weeks ago. I was a jerk for letting crap get in the way of keeping my promise to Antwoine.

I concentrated on locating all succubi rather than just the one, because frankly, I didn't really know how to track someone I'd never met. However, I had seen the bordello before, once when I was a kid. My memory of it was squiggly, but it was good enough to bring me to the house where the girls lived. The incubi lived there as well, which I'm sure led to some interesting parties given the sexual nature of each species.

What exactly was the purpose of these dream creatures? They were there to tackle sexual issues, desires, repressed feelings. They also were there for the simple reason to give pleasure to dreamers. Is my father charitable or what?

I walked into a foyer of a building that looked like an Arabian palace. I don't know if it was my mind that made it look this way, or if this was its true appearance. Mellow stone walls welcomed me, as did silks and velvets in rich colors. In fact, it looked a bit like my bedroom in New York. Hmm. Hadria said I was a little bit of everything. I guess my decorating tastes were succubus. Could be worse, I suppose.

The air smelled of incense—soft and spicy, heady and inviting—not the cheap kind that could cover the odor of a sewer with its thick, choking sweetness. Music drifted throughout the interior, softly muted by closed doors and lush fabrics.

It was everything a sultan's harem should be. Although, I was pretty sure my father didn't use this place for his own pleasure; I hoped he didn't.

"May I help you?" came a very bored, very British-sounding voice from behind me.

I turned and found myself facing a major-domo who could have been Cary Grant's doppelganger. He didn't look impressed to see me.

"The incubi are all otherwise engaged," he told me as he flipped open a large leather-bound book. "You'll have to make an appointment."

"I'm not here for an incubus," I replied, trying not to sound as startled as I was. "I'm looking for a succubus."

He arched one dark brow, but remained otherwise expressionless. "I see."

I rolled my eyes. "No, you don't. I'm here to speak to Madrene. Is she here?"

He seemed surprised that I knew a name—surprised enough that he stopped being condescending long enough to actually look at me. I knew the moment he figured out who I was, because his expression changed big-time, even if it was only for a second. "You're the Princess."

It was hard not to puff up a bit when referred to me as royalty. "I'm Dawn. And you are?"

"Fitzhugh, Your Majesty." He actually bowed. "Forgive my impertinence. I did not expect a person such as yourself to pay a social call this evening."

Meaning most people of higher birth in the Dreaming made appointments, as he had inferred earlier. "I'm sorry. I'm afraid I'm still learning the proper way to do things." I flashed a demure smile. "Is Madrene here by any chance?"

He glanced down at the book and rifled a few pages. "She is. But I'm afraid she is with a dreamer at the moment. If you could come back . . ."

"I'll wait."

Fitzhugh appeared startled and distressed by this pronouncement. "Your Highness, this is highly irregular. It could be quite some time before Madrene is finished, and then she has another appointment this evening."

I forced a smile as I reached out and gently set my hand on top of his. "Listen, Fitz—can I call you Fitz?—I've had a really bad night. I'd appreciate it if you didn't make it any rougher. I only need a few moments of Madrene's time, so do I wait over here on this lovely sofa for you to collect her when she's done with her dreamer, or do I go looking for her myself?"

He gasped and pulled away, but I grabbed his hand in a tight grip. His wide gaze locked with mine and I knew from that familiar burning feeling behind my retinas that my eyes had gone very bright and clear with thick black spidery rims. Karatos had similar eyes and they'd scared the hell out of me, pretty as they were.

"What's it gonna be, Fitz?" Look at me being all badass. Actually I felt like I was one bad line of movie dialogue away from losing control and letting all the dark energy inside me go.

Fitzhugh must have picked up on that too, because after clearing his throat, he said, "I would be delighted to fetch Madrene for you, Your Highness. Of course her next appointment can wait a few moments. If you would follow me to the parlor, I'll have her come down."

It was that easy. I could get used to throwing my weight around, you know? For that reason alone, it was better that I didn't make a habit of intimidating my people. I didn't want to be hated any more than I already was.

"Thank you, Fitzhugh." And I meant it. "I appreciate you being so accommodating."

The doorman blinked, obviously astounded by my change in demeanor. "It is of no consequence, Your Highness."

I followed him through a dimly lit corridor. Our steps were muffled by a thick Persian-print carpet in spicy hues. Larger than life statues held sconces high above our heads, like glasses raised in greeting. One stood like a sentinel outside the door I was led to.

"Make yourself comfortable," he instructed, gesturing for me to enter. "I shall send Madrene down directly."

I thanked him again and walked through the open doorway. The parlor was decorated much like what I had seen of the rest of the place—soft plaster walls in a sand color held softly glowing lamps. The high ceiling was painted with delicate frescos and the furniture was rich in color, and so plush a body could sink into it.

I sat on an eggplant-colored sofa that was soft as velvet and three times as luxurious. The coffee table was heavy carved wood with a rough stone mosaic top. On it was a decanter of wine and two crystal glasses. Had they been there when I came in? It didn't matter. I poured myself a glass of wine, knowing it would be my favorite, and settled back against the cushions to await my succubus.

I didn't have to wait long. True to the major-domo's word, Madrene entered the room a few minutes later. At least, I assumed she was Madrene. As soon as I could lift my jaw off the floor, I would ask just to be sure.

I knew succubi were beautiful, but this woman went beyond beautiful. She was beyond sexy. This woman was nature and earthiness at its finest. She was average height, but that was the only thing average about her. Think Beyonce or Halle and then multiply that by one hundred. Her hair was thick, long and burnished with bronze. Her eyes were the color and brilliance of topaz, and her skin was unblemished café au lait.

She was in short, a goddess. And faced with such magnificence, I felt every bit the meager *half* goddess that I was.

She bowed. "Your Majesty."

"Please don't," I managed to say when I recovered from the sight of her. Her voice was just as gorgeous as her face. I might have hated her were I not so awed. "My name is Dawn. Are you Madrene?"

She nodded. "I am."

I gestured at the seat next to me on the sofa. "Will you sit? Have some wine?"

She was wary of my motives, but since I was royalty she wasn't about to refuse me. Given what my father had done to her and Antwoine, I couldn't blame her for being suspicious of anyone of my bloodline.

When she sat—barely denting the cushions, I might add—I poured her a glass of the wine and took a sip from my own.

"I won't keep you," I promised. "I've come because I have a proposition for you."

She regarded me warily with exotically slanted eyes. "What sort of proposition?"

"I'm told you might be able to give me some information about the Warden of the Nightmares."

Her perfectly smooth brow wrinkled. "Padera?"

I nodded. "Yes. I'd appreciate anything you can tell me."

Madrene shrugged. "I will tell you what I can. May I be so bold as to ask what you offer in return for this information?"

Well, wasn't she all business? "Antwoine Jones," I replied bluntly.

She started, spilling wine on the plush carpet. Her eyes were wide as silver dollars as she stared at me. "Antwoine." Her voice was hoarse. "You know Antwoine?"

"I can arrange a meeting," I went on, and she stilled. "If that's what you want."

Her cheeks were flushed, her gaze rife with disbelief. "Your father forbade us to ever see each other again."

"My father's not the one making this deal." Ohh, how arrogant and certain of myself I sounded! "I can put the two of you together again. Will you help me?"

Madrene sat in silence, her hand pressed against her mouth. What the hell was taking her so long? Either she wanted to see Antwoine or she didn't.

"You will take all the blame and punishment if my lord finds out?"

Her lord was my father. I didn't like the sound of "blame" or "punishment" but he would be a lot easier on me than he would on either of them. Besides, it was for a good cause, and Morpheus was a hypocrite.

"I will." Another promise that I hoped I could keep. I could assume all the responsibility, but whether or not my father chose to hold me to it was up to him.

But my words seemed good enough for Madrene. She nodded. "Then I will tell you what you want to know about Padera."

I hadn't realized I'd been holding my breath until her words sent it whooshing out of my lungs in one huge, relieved sigh. "Thank you."

Golden eyes glittered. "Do not thank me. Seeing Antwoine again will be thanks enough."

A little shiver ran down my spine. As gorgeous as she was, there was something hard inside this succubus—something that told me that if I didn't manage to pull off getting her and Antwoine together again, the Warden and a crazy rapist would be the least of my problems.

And I really didn't need any more problems.

Chapter Twelve

"My boobs are going to pop out of this thing."

Lola laughed as she tugged up the top of my Halloween costume. I was dressed as Wonder Woman, complete with red and gold bustier that defied the laws of nature. Thankfully the bottom was a little skirt rather than the usual panties. I won't even wear bathing suits that don't have something that covers my upper thighs.

"Damn, girl," my roommate enthused. "You look hot."

"Really?" I was, of course, uncertain. Sexy costumes weren't exactly something I had a lot of experience with. And this one was definitely sexy, with the shimmery nude pantyhose and knee-high red leather boots—not to mention the bondage-esque wrist cuffs for deflecting bullets, and thin golden lasso attached at my waist. I had to admit—I did look good with my hair all huge and teased up around the gold tiara. I had good hair.

"Noah's gonna take one look at you and know exactly what kind of treat he wants tonight."

I laughed despite the heat filling my cheeks. I had picked out this costume with Noah in mind, knowing how much he liked superheroes. Knowing that Wonder Woman was a favorite of his.

"He'll be here soon," I allowed, reaching for the false eyelashes on my dresser. "Would you mind grabbing the tube of MAC lipstick that's in the front of my purse?"

"No problem," she said with a salute and left the room as I applied glue to the edge of a fringe of lashes and adhered them just above my own. I did the same with the other side, pressing them quickly into place. I didn't wear false lashes often, but I'd done it enough that I didn't have to fuss and fool around with them.

Lola returned with the lipstick and I filled in my already lined lips with dark red. Perfect. My lips are huge, but I kinda like 'em, so I play them up when I can, and tonight the bold color looked good with my dark-rimmed, heavily lashed eyes.

I surveyed myself in the mirror. With the makeup and the full-bosom, cinched-waist illusion created by the bustier, I looked like I'd just stepped out of a comic book. I smiled. I really did look pretty darn good, if I said so myself.

It was nice to be going out, to be doing something normal. I was still feeling the stress of everything in both my worlds, but I was optimistic about the Dreaming mess, and tonight it was just me and Noah, so I was happy.

The buzzer sounded just as I walked out into the living room to slip my lipstick back into my purse. I had a little red handbag that would hold the essentials—lipstick, powder, eyelash glue, ID, and fifty bucks in case of an emergency. It wasn't like having a purse would ruin the outfit anymore than the coat I was going to have to wear over it. It was warm, but not that warm.

Lola answered the door while I rummaged through the closet for a coat. I heard her exclaim, "Holy frig!" as I pulled one off the hanger. Noah's costume must be good. I quickly stepped out of the closet, wanting to present myself in the best light as possible so he could get a load of me as I got a load of him.

My jaw dropped. "Holy frig."

Noah was Batman. And I don't mean a cheesy department store Batman. I mean Noah *was* Batman. The suit looked like it had been made to fit him—all sleek and molded and sexy as hell. Christian Bale, eat your heart out.

I couldn't see his whole face because of the mask, but I could see that he was almost as surprised by my appearance as I was by his.

"You look good, Doc," he purred in that rough, sexy voice of his. "Really good."

Lola stood between us, grinning like an idiot. "You guys totally rock the JLA. You just need Supes and the Flash and you're all set. Well, I'm gonna veg. You guys have fun!" And then she flounced off to her room, leaving us alone.

Noah moved closer, cape fluttering around his legs with the motion. "If it wasn't such a bitch getting into this getup I'd say screw it and we could spend the night in."

I admit I shivered as though his voice had managed to caress my spine. In costume we were the same height, but somehow he managed to make me feel feminine and delicate, despite my Amazon façade.

"My costume feels cheap compared to yours." Now, why the hell did I say that? Granted, it was true, but ridiculous all the same.

Noah lifted a gloved finger and ran it along the tight valley of my cleavage. I shivered again, damn him. "I wouldn't mind feeling what your costume feels." Then he grinned. "You know you're fulfilling a major fantasy for me."

I arched a brow. "Really?" As if I hadn't known.

Another step closer, and this time his arms came around me, pulling me tight against him. Any tighter and my boobs really were going to spill out. Strangely enough, I suddenly didn't care. I was tingly and warm and feeling very much in character.

His gaze fell to my lips, then my chest, before rising to meet mine once more. "Oh, yeah. Leave it on for me later?"

I reached up and ran my fingers along the smooth skin of his freshly shaved jaw. "Only if you promise to leave on the mask."

He grinned. "Will it ruin your lipstick if I kiss you?"

I nodded glumly. "Uh, yeah."

He leaned in and pressed his lips to the flesh just below my collarbone instead, raising those familiar goose bumps on my skin. "I'll have to make do with other parts." And then he kissed my shoulder, and up to my throat.

When he was done, my knees were wobbly and I could care less about the damn party.

He helped me with my coat and I yelled good-bye to Lola as I buttoned it. Fudge lifted his head from the couch long enough to yawn in my direction and then went back to sleep.

Noah had brought his car—an old Impala—and for that I was grateful. This outfit wasn't made to be worn on the back of a motorcycle in October. The Impala was a classic, apparently. Black, shiny with a completely rebuilt engine. I nodded my approval, but really I didn't care. It looked hot and had plenty of leg room, and that was really all that mattered to me.

The party was at Elly and Matt's in Brooklyn. I'd met the two of them at a showing of Noah's work when we first started seeing each other. I didn't remember much about them except that they had seemed nice. They obviously were quite well off, given their neighborhood. They lived on a lovely tree-lined street in a tall, dark, brick town house. I could see people through the windows, dressed in various costumes, drinking wine amid upscale décor.

We had to park down the street because there wasn't any space in front of the house. I was a little slower than usual in the big boots, but Noah held my hand and didn't complain.

Matt answered the door when we rang. He was dressed as a salt shaker and had a plastic Uzi in his hand. Matt was an average-sized guy, and somehow he managed to look both cute and intimidating.

I gave him a quizzical look as I stepped inside and began unbuttoning my coat. "A salt with a deadly weapon?"

He laughed. "Good guess—whoa!" He gave me a once over as I handed him my coat. "Hello, Princess!"

I froze, but just for a second. There was no way Matt could know what I was. And I was dressed as Wonder Woman, aka Princess Diana.

Noah snapped his fingers in front of his friend's face. "Put your tongue back in your mouth, man."

Matt had obviously had a couple of drinks, so rather than apologize he just flashed a chastised grin. "You look great, Dawn." Then to Noah, "Man, you know Wonder Woman can totally kick Batman's ass."

Noah's lips curved as he flashed me an appreciative gaze. "I wouldn't put up a fight."

We laughed and Matt shooed us off to join the party while he took care of my coat and purse. I knew he'd been joking, but his words stuck with me for a while. In this world I couldn't kick Noah's ass, no way, but in the Dreaming . . . Did that bother him? And there had been times when I'd felt a surge of power in this realm. What if I was capable of doing some of that stuff here? Would Noah still be okay with it? Or would that part of him that needed to be strong and in control hate feeling weak?

It wasn't something I ever wanted to test.

Noah introduced me around. I met a Supergirl, and a Xena, but no other Wonder Women were in attendance, which was good. I got a lot of comments on my costume—mostly from guys—which made me both confident and very self-conscious, depending on the way it was delivered.

We'd been there a couple of hours when I felt familiar hands—encased in gloves—settle on my hips. "Let's go," Noah whispered in my ear.

I shivered—again—and nodded.

Matt gave me an enthusiastic hug good-bye at the

door, and then told Noah he was a lucky man. We were still laughing when we hit the sidewalk.

The drive home was quiet, but strangely comfortable despite the sexual tension between us. We both knew what was going to happen. And once we reached Noah's apartment, we headed straight for the bedroom. We left as much of our costumes on as we could, and we bounced back and forth between serious playacting and laughing our asses off. It was good. Very good.

Afterward, when the costumes were all gone, and I had washed off my makeup, we curled up in bed and talked. I felt soft and warm and totally relaxed.

In other words, I never saw it coming.

"I have to ask you something," Noah said quietly— too quietly.

I lifted my head from his chest and looked down at him, a sudden chill settling around my heart. Did he know I was still trying to get Phil the rapist? "What?"

He kept his dark gaze locked on mine. "Have you ever altered my dreams?"

I hadn't been expecting that. Quite frankly, I wasn't sure how to take it either. "Excuse me?"

His fingers trailed down my arm—a gentle caress. "You've changed Amanda's dreams to help her heal. You made the rapist want to confess, and neither of them knows that you were there."

I pulled away, lifting myself up on my arm so I could put a little distance between us. "You think I've played with your head?" Fuck around.

"No." To his credit he met my gaze and there was nothing but honesty in his eyes. "I want to know if you've ever altered my dreams."

"No," I replied hotly. "I haven't—not without your consent. Jesus, Noah. What do you think I am?" I moved to get out of bed but he stopped me.

"Don't get mad."

"I'm not mad!" I tried to jerk my arm free of his hold, but he was too strong. And when I felt the burning in my eyes, I stopped, shaken. I didn't want to test my theory about having powers in this world like this. "I'm hurt."

He leaned up on his elbow, tugging on my arm to bring me closer. "Look at me." I did—reluctantly. "Doc, I know how much you want to help people—to fix them. I'm not asking this to piss you off. I just want to know if you've tried to fix me."

"I've never done anything to your dreams," I told him petulantly. "You asked me to stay out of them unless invited and I have."

His face relaxed. "Okay."

He sounded so relieved that my feelings bruised a little deeper. But when he hauled me back into his arms, and down onto the bed with him, I didn't fight, even though he didn't apologize for asking. It couldn't be easy being like he was and being with a person like me. Really, if I were less scrupulous, I could find out every secret he had just by invading his dreams, and he'd never know I was there.

I suppose I should be relieved that he trusted me when I said I would never do such a thing. I should be glad that he believed me. And I was.

But part of me wondered—and not for the first time—what it was that he kept hidden in his dreams.

And why he was so dead against me finding out.

To say that I was tempted to waltz right into Noah's dreams and demand to know what all the fuss was about would be an understatement. I stayed away for a long time that night, watching him sleep and fighting the temptation to violate his trust.

Noah hadn't opened his dreams to me, and I really didn't want to go knocking on his door, so to speak. Besides, I had work to do.

Originally I had thought that Morpheus had taken away Antwoine's ability to dream, but that was basically murder. What my father had done was lock Antwoine away in his own little corner of the Dreaming, much like I had done to myself after mangling Jackey Jenkins.

Antwoine was able to dream, though, and that's how I would find him. All I had to do was reach out and find his signature. But first, I had to collect Madrene.

This time I didn't go into the house, but rather waited in the garden toward the back. Even though it was dark, I could see each bright bloom in the walled area. The air was thick with the smell of jasmine and cinnamon and I breathed deep as I sat on a low stone bench and watched the house for signs of Madrene. Almost every window glowed with soft light—like from a candle or lamp. Some rooms I could see into, but others were shrouded with gauzy curtains that kept me from spying. That was just as well. I had no desire to play voyeur.

I didn't have to wait long before I heard the soft creak of a door. And then the garden gate swung open and Madrene drifted into the garden. She was so graceful I had to wonder if her feet even touched the ground.

I eyed her white silk gown—the bottom foot of which was a swirl of hand-painted butterflies—with envy. Even if I could afford such a gorgeous thing, I'd never do it justice. "You are so gorgeous," I said before I could stop myself. "I love that dress."

She smiled. "Thank you. I like yours as well."

Confused, I looked down. I had been wearing jeans and a T-shirt, but somehow that had changed. Now I was dressed in a gown very much like hers, only mine was violet and painted with flowers. "What the—?"

The darker woman chuckled as she walked toward me. "A succubus who can't identify desire when she sees it can't do her job."

"I thought sexual desire was your thing." I towered over her, but she had so much presence I actually felt small next to her. Interesting.

One mocha shoulder shrugged. Her skin looked as smooth and supple as her gown. "It's the most common, but to be good at my job I've studied desire of all types."

I suppressed a shudder. I could only imagine the freaky things she'd seen and done. "I'd never be able to do what you do." I meant that sincerely and not as a put-down. I really admired anyone who could separate themselves emotionally. I wish I could.

She looked surprised. "You don't know much about my kind, do you?"

"No. Sorry." Why did I get the feeling that I was about to learn more than I wanted to know?

A sly smile curved berry-red lips. "There is very little that isn't 'pleasant' for us, as you put it. We feed on desire—or live on it, if that terminology makes you more comfortable. Everything else is muted, if not eliminated in the face of the dreamer's desire."

I stared at her, blinking slowly. "So, if a dreamer punches you in the face, it won't hurt you because his desire overpowers your feelings?"

"Or hers," she amended with a cheeky grin. "We service women as well."

Of course she did. A lesbian would hardly have any

use for an incubus and his talents. Huh. Learn something new every day. Who would have thought my father had such a kinky side? He had created this world and everything in it, after all.

When I thought of that, it made my head swim. My father was a god. A freaking *god*.

"We should go. He's probably wondering where we are," I said, meaning Antwoine, of course. "Ready?"

She smoothed her long, delicate hands over her hips. Not an undergarment, line, or bulge to be seen. "Do I look acceptable?"

My eyes widened—a lot. "Uh, yes."

"You think he'll be pleased?"

"You do know that he's aged since you last saw him?" I couldn't believe she was concerned about how he would see her when she was undoubtedly as perfect now as she had been then.

"He's still my Antwoine," she replied with a bit of bite.

I smiled. "All right, then. I don't think he'll find you lacking, so don't worry."

She smiled back—a little shakily I noticed—and offered me her hand. "I'm ready. Take me to him, please."

I took her warm fingers in mine, thought of Antwoine, and willed us to where he was—just like I had done with Verek and Hadria the other night. One minute we were in the garden at night and the next we were standing on a walkway leading to a large white house with a huge front porch complete with old-fashioned swing. The full glory of a midday summer sun shone down upon us. Birds sang in thick, tall trees and the air smelled of flowers, fresh-cut grass, and baking apple pie.

Madrene turned a face lit with wonder toward me. "You really aren't like the rest of us."

I think she meant it as a compliment, so I tried really hard not to wince as I released her hand. "I know."

She actually knelt before me. Before I knew what she was doing, she had lifted her skirt and gracefully sank to her knees on the stones, her head bowed. "Thank you, Your Highness. I am forever in your debt."

"Oh my God, please get up." I would have helped her, but I was scared I'd yank her slender form to her feet and hurt her in some way. "I really wish you wouldn't do that. My name is Dawn."

When she stood, she caught both of my clenched fists in her soft hands. She kissed my knuckles, and despite the redness of her lips, left no trace of cosmetic behind. Her lips were naturally that red. Can I hate her now?

"Dawn," she repeated. My name sounded exotic on her lips. "I can never repay you . . ."

"Madrene?" Antwoine's anxious tone cut her off, and had us both looking toward the porch.

I blinked. Hell, I *gaped*. I might have even gasped.

There, on the white-washed porch stood a man who sounded like my Antwoine, but that was where the similarities ended.

This Antwoine was young—maybe in his thirties. He still wasn't all that tall, but he was fit and muscular, wearing khaki trousers and a white shirt open at the throat. He looked like a cross between Denzil Washington and a young Morgan Freeman with a little Sydney Poitier thrown in. He looked gorgeous—and smart and classy. Damn. This was how Madrene saw him. How he saw himself.

Madrene's big doe eyes filled with tears as she dropped my hands like hot potatoes. "Antwoine!" And then she ran to him, and he was down those steps in one leap, catching her up in his arms and swinging her around like they were in a phone company commercial.

When I realized they were both crying I knew it was time to leave. This was private. Smiling, and yes, a little teary myself, I turned to go.

"Dawn."

I glanced over my shoulder at Antwoine's voice. He looked so young as he smiled at me, tears trickling down his cheeks. "Thank you."

I nodded, throat too choked up to speak, and then took myself away from the happy scene. I went looking for Noah. We had a system where if we hadn't agreed to meet in his dreams I'd announce myself first. For lack of a better way, I actually climbed a set of steps to a heavy oak door complete with gothic gargoyle-head knocker. He answered almost immediately, and my heart soared at the smile on his face.

"Hey, Doc." Black eyes sparkled, and I understood the power Madrene got from being the object of desire. "Nice dress."

A little while later, I felt the familiar buzzing of someone from the Dreaming "calling." Would I ever develop the ability to suss out who wanted to talk to me? "Dream Waiting" would be much appreciated.

I stumbled upon my friend Julie's dream and went in. She was dreaming about being in a Starbucks trying to order a chai latte, but she was naked and had no money. I tried not to look. And I didn't give her money. I know, I'm a bad friend, but I wasn't here to call attention to myself. I was here so whoever was paging me would have to talk to me in a "public" place. Having been ambushed by Karatos in the past, and knowing that there were those out to get me, made me a little more cautious about answering unfamiliar summons.

I sat at a table in the far corner where Julie couldn't see me as she patted her naked thighs and cursed herself for not having brought a purse. Within a few seconds, I was joined by a guy in tight jeans, black boots, and a black sweater. Verek. The Nightmare was every bit as gorgeous as he was intimidating.

"What's up?" I asked as he slid into the chair opposite me.

"I need to talk to you," he replied, glancing around, as though making sure we were alone. "You need to be careful."

"Of what?" Did he know about Antwoine and Madrene? No, that was impossible. How could he?

Seemingly satisfied that we weren't being watched, he turned his pale gaze to mine. "Of the Warden."

I hadn't seen or heard of her since she told me that she'd undone what I did to Durdan. I had been kinda hoping she'd forgotten about me. "I haven't done anything for her to ride my ass for." Okay, so maybe that was a lie, but I really hadn't broken any rules.

Verek leaned his large forearms on the table. "Dawn, she hates you almost as much as she resents Morpheus. She'll do whatever necessary to destroy you—even set you up."

I frowned, trying to ignore the sick churning in my stomach. "How do you know this?"

He didn't flinch, didn't hesitate. "Because I've been spying on you for her."

If he had punched me in the face I would have been less surprised. "You bastard."

He shushed me, glancing around again. "I'm here now. Doesn't that tell you something?"

"Yeah, that you're a two-faced, lying jerk!" I fought to keep my voice low. "I thought you were loyal to my father!"

"I am." He scowled. "And to you. That's why I'm here."

"To spy?"

"To ask you to be careful. Until I can find out what she is up to, you're not safe."

"Have you told my father about this?"

He shook his head. "Not without concrete proof. The Warden hasn't asked me to do anything wrong, just sneaky."

"She can't hurt me," I insisted. "I can't die in this world. All she can do is push to have me unmade, and the Council won't do that without reason."

He stared at me—hard. "That's what I'm trying to tell you—she's looking to give them a reason."

"But why?" It came out whinier than I thought. "I'm nothing to her."

Verek looked as though he'd like to argue that, but instead he said, "If she has you unmade, you won't be of both worlds anymore. You won't be a threat. All of those who think you might destroy us will be relieved, and all of us who believe you are the herald of change will be proven wrong."

I blinked. "Herald of change?"

He sighed. "The one that will bring about the change necessary to save our world."

Oh yeah, Hadria's prophecy.

Verek ran a hand over his jaw. "Dawn, I'm afraid the Warden might try to harm you. Will you just promise me that you'll be careful?"

He sounded like Noah. Gah. What was the good of being something special if no one thought you could take care of yourself?

But this was Verek. He trained me. He knew more about me than I did at times, and he had never given me reason to doubt him. Even now, I could tell that he had taken a big chance coming to see me like this. His trust in me might well get him in some very serious trouble with his boss. The least I could do is listen.

"I promise," I replied. "I'll be careful." And I would be. The Warden couldn't enter the human realm, but that didn't mean she couldn't get to me if she wanted. The woman had power.

Verek was visibly relieved. "Thank you."

"Dawn?" came a surprised voice. "What are you doing here?"

I looked up to see Julie coming toward me. She was dressed now and carrying a paper cup that had to be at least a foot tall. I smiled despite myself. Even in dreams the girl liked her coffee—and a lot of it.

"I . . ." I glanced at Verek, but he was gone. Vanished. He really was a jerk. "I'm waiting for you."

My friend grinned. "Yay." And then she sat down beside me and started talking about things that I'm sure made sense to her on some level, but were one step up from gibberish to me. Sometimes dreams were just that—dreams. Nothing dark and scary, no big problem that needed solving—just the human brain dancing around, cleaning out its closet, trying to figure out what to keep and what to donate to Goodwill.

The fact that Julie didn't need my help with anything, or wasn't declaring me a prophet or the destroyer of worlds, was nice. She didn't tell me to be careful. She didn't tell me to watch my step. She told me about an article she'd read on bacon being good for your skin, something that I'm pretty sure was wishful thinking. And I sat back in my chair, summoned up a chai latte of my own, and listened to my friend talk with a smile on my face.

Sure, it wasn't my idea of the perfect dream, but it was a pretty damn good one all the same.

I woke up to find Noah sitting in a chair, his bare feet propped up on the bed. He had a sketch pad in one hand, a pencil in the other, and a serious expression on his face. His hair was a mess and he needed a shave. His T-shirt was wrinkled and his paint-splattered jeans were baggy with holes in the knees. In short, he looked undeniably sexy.

"You are *not* drawing me." It was more of a warning than a command.

He made a face at me over the top of the pad. "Yeah, I am. And I'm almost done, so hold still."

So I lay there in the mussed sheets, enjoying the watery sunlight coming through the huge windows as it bathed me in warmth. I could curl up here and sleep all day, like a fat contented cat.

"That's quite a smile," Noah commented when he finally put the pad down. He pivoted out of the chair to join me on the bed. "Did you sleep well?"

I nodded. "I did."

He eyed me with mock suspicion. "Good dreams?"

I chuckled, thinking of Julie and her naked Starbucks run. "Yeah. They were."

"Hmm." He ran a finger down my bare arm. "Should I be jealous that I wasn't part of them?"

"No. It was just silly stuff." Unless you included the warning from Verek, of course, but I wasn't going to worry about that right now. I would take his advice and be careful, but I wasn't going to cower in fear from the Warden. "Julie was in it."

He smiled. "The two of you weren't pillow-fighting in your panties were you?"

I rolled my eyes. He was such a guy sometimes. "No, but she was naked."

Dark eyebrows shot up as his gaze lit up. "You dirty girl." He propped himself up on his elbow. "Tell me all about it."

"We were at Starbucks," I replied with a laugh. "Getting lattes."

"Were they *sexy* lattes?"

I couldn't help it. Who wouldn't burst out laughing in the face of such blatant foolishness? He laughed too, and we locked gazes, grinning at each other long after the laughter faded.

It was then that I felt the pinch in my heart—a sudden sharpness that made it difficult to breath, and made Noah suddenly all the more beautiful to my eyes. It was the moment I realized that I wasn't *falling* in love with him, but that I had already fallen.

I opened my mouth, desperate to say something, to confess to this newfound revelation before it consumed me. Unfortunately, my cell phone chose that exact time to ring. I rolled and lunged for it, not caring if I mooned him in the process.

"Hello?"

"Dawnie?"

"Hi, Ivy." It was my oldest sister. "What's up?"

I felt Noah ease off the bed. "I'm going to make coffee," he murmured, and gave my arm a pat. I flashed him a quick glance and a nod.

"I just wanted to tell you that the specialist went to see Mom today."

"And?" Ivy was the queen of the dramatic pause.

"Oh, Dawnie! She actually *moved*!"

"What?" This wasn't fear I felt—not of Mom waking up. No, this was surprise, and okay; yes, there was some fear as well. Who the hell was this guy that he could actually break through my father's spell? No human could do that. He had to be a conman or something.

"She moved her finger."

I bet she did. Probably trying to flip him the bird. "Ivy, that might have just been involuntary." The moment I spoke I knew I should have kept my mouth shut.

"You weren't there," my sister retorted hotly. "I know what I saw. He got a reaction out of her, Dawn. Why can't you believe that?"

"Because he's seen her what, twice? And now I'm to believe he's done what no one else has ever been able to do?" Not even me? Oh, that was a huge and unpleasant realization to have at such a moment. I didn't want to believe in this guy because believing in him would be admitting that he had some greater pull than my mother's favored child—me. And if there was a human with that kind of power, not only over dreams, but over my mother, I would do one better than believe in him—I'd be downright scared.

"He's a miracle worker," my sister practically sighed.

"He's something," I muttered. I wasn't going to freak out until I talked to my father about this. If this guy really had power then Morpheus would know—and he would know what to do about him. I hoped. Or maybe this was one more step toward usurping my father's power. One more way to weaken him.

So much for my good day.

"I thought you'd be happy about this."

I was having a hard enough time holding it together without Ivy getting petulant and guilt-trippy on me. I promised myself that I wouldn't freak out until it was necessary and I meant to keep that promise. "I am, Ives. Really." It was a big fat lie, but it sounded true and that was all that mattered.

She obviously believed me, and for that I was thankful. We talked for a few minutes longer about mom before turning the conversation over to more mundane things, like the rest of the family, the kids and finally her twenty questions about Noah. Every time we spoke she made a point of trying to find out as much about him as she could.

Noah returned with coffee during this point in the conversation, so I sat there and answered questions about him as he listened—and sometimes tried not to laugh at my answers.

Finally, I said good-bye and hung up.

"Your sister, I take it?" Noah said.

I rolled my eyes—a bad habit I seemed to be developing as of late. "Yeah. She wanted to talk about Mom. I'm a little worried this guy might actually be able to wake her up."

He frowned and took a drink of coffee. "I thought that was impossible."

"It *should* be."

"You have doubts?"

"I'm proof that the impossible can happen."

He grinned at me. "Yes, you are."

I drank my coffee and we sat in silence for a moment. I felt better with him beside me—grounded and strong.

It was Noah who broke the silence. "Do you resent her—your mother?"

"All the frigging time." I sighed. "I know she has a right to a happy life, and it wasn't like any of us were children . . . it hasn't been easy for her, but sometimes I wish it was a little more difficult."

Noah dipped his head, in what I assumed was a nod. "I used to have a lot of resentment toward my mother. I still do."

This was new. My head whipped around to face him. "Really? Why?"

"Because she let him abuse her. Because if she had left sooner I wouldn't have had my arm broken in two places." He smiled grimly. "It's one thing letting someone wail on you, it's another when it's your kid. At least it should be."

"At least she left then."

He gave me a look that made me feel like I had entirely missed the point. "It wasn't the first time he hit me, Doc. It was just the first time he'd done something people would notice."

I swallowed. "How old were you?"

"Fourteen when we left."

"I'm feeling a little resentful toward your mother as well."

He shrugged. "She was scared. She did the best she could. Looking back I think she got to the point that it was normal for her. If you didn't bleed it wasn't that bad, y'know?"

No, I didn't. Thank God I didn't know about that at all. "Sucks seeing them as human, doesn't it? When you realize that all those choices we judged them for must have been so hard to make."

He smiled. "I love it when you're insightful."

Setting my coffee on the bedside table, I held out my arms, letting the sheets drop so he caught an eyeful of nakedness. "Come show me."

And he did.

Chapter Thirteen

Given the twists and turns my life has taken since facing up to the reality of who and what I am, you would think I was beyond false hope. Unfortunately, I've always had the propensity to become an exuberant optimist the moment things look even remotely up.

And this was the misfortune I fell into the next day. The sun was shining as I made my way to work, Venti low-fat latte in hand. Traffic seemed less obnoxious, fewer horns blared. I didn't bump shoulders with more than half a dozen pedestrians because the sidewalks just didn't seem to be that crowded despite the lovely weather and time of morning. My hair looked good, my skin was flawless—not a pimple or funky tattoo to be found—and my lip gloss matched the swirls of red in my blouse. I felt great after a night of great sex with my fabulous boyfriend. I had reunited long lost lovers, and my case load for the day was busy—clients at last!

I should have known the axe was going to fall—or at least take a swing.

My first two appointments went well. Dream diaries, discussion, and everything stayed fairly calm. No breakdowns, which was good. I wasn't one of those therapists who thought a client had to burst into tears in order to have a breakthrough.

I was feeling pretty good when lunch rolled around. Even better when I found out Noah was waiting for me. But one look at his face when he came into the office— all casual and delicious in a black leather coat, crisp white shirt, and faded jeans—and I knew something was up.

"You're not here to whisk me away to a romantic lunch are you?" I tried not to sound defeated, really.

He smiled crookedly. "Sure I am. I don't wear two-hundred-dollar shirts for just anyone, Doc."

I blinked. To me, that was a lot to pay for a shirt. Then again, Noah was one of those people who liked to have a few good items that lasted, while I liked to change my style and wardrobe with the seasons. That was why he shopped at Armani and Gucci and I shopped wherever the sales were.

"But lunch isn't the only reason you're here?" I was a dog with a bone, and not about to let go.

He shook his head, stuffing his hands into the pockets of his jeans. "No. Can we talk?"

I gestured to the sofa, and after telling Bonnie I didn't want to be disturbed, *and* suffering through the bawdy wink she gave me, I joined him.

"What's up?" I was nervous. Even though things were good, I half expected the "it's not you, it's me" conversation. So much for optimism.

Noah leaned his forearms on his thighs and linked his fingers. A lock of inky hair fell over his forehead as he turned his dark gaze to me. "I had a strange dream last night."

I flashed a cheeky grin, relief washing over me. No gentle breakup just yet. "It wasn't that weird. Surely you've done those things with other women."

Noah has this way of looking at a person—totally expressionless—and yet the look says very clearly that he got the joke, but it wasn't funny. He gave me that look now. "Hundreds, but that's not what I meant."

Hundreds? He had so better be kidding. "What do you mean, slut boy?"

He started a little, then grinned. "Slut boy. I've never been called that before." He shrugged, going blank again. "I think I met the Warden."

Well, that certainly killed any humor I had toward

the situation. "What?" It was like Karatos all over again. I remembered the day Noah told me he thought his dreams were trying to kill him and how the world suddenly seemed off kilter.

"There was this woman—tall and severe. Red hair." He rubbed a hand over his jaw. "She reeked of power—like you do sometimes."

I'm pretty sure he only thought that because I was his girlfriend and the only Dreamkin he knew on a personal basis. "Did she say anything to you?" My heart was thumping heavily, and I felt something like a cool touch at the back of my neck—the feeling of my blood running cold.

"Yeah." He frowned, and met my gaze with some hesitation. I didn't like it when Noah hesitated. It generally meant bad things. "She said I was your weakness. She said if I cared about you, I should break it off because she had no problem using me to get to you."

Anger swept over me—and fear. "Bitch." My right eye twitched. A prickling feeling not unlike the burn of tears started behind my retinas, but it wasn't tears that smoldered there. A not so gentle reminder of what a freak I was and why the Warden despised me in the first place.

Noah was remarkably calm for someone who had just been threatened. "You have to tell Morpheus. Threatening you has to be against some rule."

Noah was right. Threatening a member of the royal family should be against the law. Not only that, but she had threatened the safety of a dreamer—Noah. She had to know she was pissing all over her precious rules. So why had she done it? Because she knew going after someone close to me was the easiest way to provoke me.

Karatos had done the same thing. He had killed one of my clients, and tried to possess Noah. I'd be damned if I'd let the Warden fuck with him as well.

Slowly, I turned my head as I rose to my feet. My knees felt wobbly. "Did she say anything else?"

Noah raised a brow at my stiff tone. "She said I was 'one of them.' Whatever that means."

Maybe I should find out. Out of habit, I moved toward the bathroom. My high emotions made my movements short and jerky—like my legs were asleep.

He followed me. "Where are you going?"

I flung open the bathroom door and ripped open a portal slick as snot. "I'm going to have a chat with the Warden."

"Are you nuts?" Noah demanded. "Dawn, that's what she wants. She knew coming to me would push your buttons. She's a bully, remember?"

I whirled around. I should wonder how he felt about all of this. Hadn't Padera pushed his buttons as well by trying to make him a victim and playing on his baggage? "It's about time I stood up to her."

He stared at me. "Your eyes. They look like they do in my dreams." Then he blinked. "You're not supposed to be able to do that here, are you?"

My jaw tightened. "I'm not supposed to be able to do a lot of things." I turned then, all melodramatic and pissed off and stepped through the portal. But instead of taking me to the Warden, I ended up in Morpheus's study. He was there with Verek, and the two of them looked up at my entrance. Damn my father for picking up on my intentions.

"Where's the Warden?" I demanded, stepping through, fists clenched at my sides.

My father looked mildly concerned, an expression that would have worried me once upon a time because he was normally good at hiding his emotions. "What's happened?"

"She threatened Noah." My jaw was clenched so tight it was beginning to ache. "Where is she?"

Verek stepped forward. "Dawn, you don't want to confront her."

I was freaking sick of people dictating my life. Fury ripped through me. I unleashed it unthinkingly, letting the full torrent of emotion sweep the Nightmare up and toss him across the room. He hit the wall like a rag doll. "You have no idea what I want," I informed him, my eyes feeling like they were on fire.

Verek didn't say anything as he picked himself off

the floor. He was a big guy and I'd tossed him like he was nothing.

"Dawn." Morpheus touched my shoulder. My first thought was to toss him as well, but his touch took all of that anger away, calming me. I had to get a grip.

"I'm sorry," I muttered, suddenly drained. "Verek, are you all right?"

White teeth flashed in his tanned face. "That was fun, Princess. Next time it's your turn." It sounded more seductive than a threat like that should, but I didn't have the time or the inclination to be concerned with that right now. I turned to my father.

"I won't let her hurt Noah," I told him. "If she touches him I'll kill her." Only I don't think I could kill her, not really. People didn't die in this world, they just got remade into something else.

"You're not killing anybody," came a familiar voice from behind me.

Morpheus and Verek turned toward the portal I'd left open as I closed my eyes. *Oh shit*. Noah had come through. Again. And this time, I knew it was against the law.

I turned. "You shouldn't be here," I told him, my anger focusing on him now. Bringing him into this world was what got me into this mess. "If the Warden found out—"

"She'd do nothing," my father cut me off, staring at

Noah with frank curiosity. "You shouldn't have left the portal open, but Mr. Clarke shouldn't have been able to see it let alone come through on his own." Huh, and here I'd been taking all this trouble to hide my portals. My boyfriend was turning out to be almost as surprising as I was.

That was a good thing, right? I mean it put us on slightly more equal footing. So why did it bother me?

My father's reddish brown brows drew together as he circled Noah like he was sizing up a new car. "How did you come through, Mr. Clarke?"

Noah shrugged, watching him warily. "I walked."

"Interesting." My father shot a glance at Verek. "What do you think?"

Verek came forward to stand next to me—a little too close. His expression was less curious and more on guard, as though Noah might be some kind of a threat. "It could be due to Dawn's unusual abilities," he suggested. "Her ability to cross between worlds extends to any who stumble upon the door. It doesn't explain how he saw the entrance."

Morpheus scratched his jaw. "The first time Dawn brought him through, just like she took Karatos out of this world." His pale gaze met mine. "But this is different. Is it because of the portal, or because of him? This is the first time a human has ever simply walked into our world."

Oh. Shit. Noah and I stared at each other. And the surprises keep coming. I glanced at Morpheus. "The Warden called Noah 'one of them.' Does that tell you anything?"

Now it was my father and Verek who exchanged a glance. "For the last few decades, there have been incidents of humans crossing the veil," my father explained. "People who could interact with our world in ways that shouldn't have been possible. At the same time there have been Dreamkin who have been able to interact with the human realm in the same way."

I thought of Karatos and his plan to cross over. He wanted to be one of those Dreamkin. He wanted to terrorize the "real" world.

The Warden had mentioned strange occurrences—occurrences she blamed on me. "It's because of me, isn't it?" I searched my father's face for the truth. "I'm not supposed to exist, that's why this other stuff is happening."

Morpheus smiled gently as he approached and wrapped his strong arms around me. I couldn't look at him. I couldn't look at Noah either. I didn't want him to see the fear in my eyes.

"My dear girl, these anomalies started happening long before your birth." He stroked my back and I clung to him like a child. "In fact, I think your birth was the result of this phenomenon, not the cause."

When I lifted my head, he was all feigned surprise. "What? You think your mother was the first human I had a relationship with? No. But the first that gave me the gift of a child." The way he said it made me feel like something special rather than something wrong. A gift, not a mistake.

"The people who are angry with you, they blame me, though. Don't they?"

He nodded. "I'm afraid so. But Mr. Clarke has given us something new to explore. Of course, his proximity to you doesn't help, but perhaps we can test this new theory in other ways."

I frowned. "What new theory?"

He released me. "That there are those who have the power to pass the barriers between your worlds." He smiled again as he lightly touched my hair. "You might not be so alone after all, little one."

Other freaks like me. I didn't know if that would prove to be a good thing or bad, but right now I was pretty damn glad to hear that whatever was happening was not my fault.

"It doesn't change anything. If they can't blame me, they can still blame you."

My father squeezed my shoulder. I could feel strength and love pouring into me through his fingertips. "You let me worry about them."

From the light in his eyes and the tightness of his

jaw, I wouldn't want to be one of "them" for anything. Morpheus was good to me, but he wasn't known for being a pushover.

He turned me toward Noah and gave me a gentle shove. "The two of you go now. No one will know of this visit. And I'll have a chat with the Warden, I promise you."

That made me smile. Wish I could be there for that. "Thank you."

Morpheus merely smiled. He and Noah exchanged brief nods and then I let Noah exit through the portal ahead of me. Did I feel any better as I walked through to my office once more? I don't know. I felt different, that was for sure.

What was up with tossing Verek around? And why had Morpheus never mentioned this "thinning" between the worlds before? What did it all mean? I was more confused now than ever. I knew myself less than ever before.

But I knew this: Noah was in danger because of me. The fact that he was special in his own right only added to the danger. Karatos had targeted him, and now the Warden. And after the Warden—if we made it—there would be someone else waiting. Melodramatic? Maybe, but I also knew it was true.

"I don't think we should see each other anymore," I blurted.

Noah scowled deeply, a sure sign that he was truly disgusted. "That's the stupidest thing I've ever heard you say." He made it sound like he'd heard me say plenty.

I smiled sadly. "Being with me isn't safe for you." No one had noticed his unique abilities until I came into his life. What if being with me somehow magnified what he was? Karatos had insinuated there was more to Noah than met the eye and I'd ignored it. What if Noah knew more than he let on? What if Noah was only using me . . . ?

Okay, that was enough of that crap. I was so not going there.

He shrugged—still frowning. "I'm not safe crossing the street in this city. Hell, I could fall on a paintbrush and impale myself."

I smiled despite the pressure in my chest, the pain in my heart. I had to protect him. I'd never forgive myself if something awful happened to him. "Now you're being an idiot."

"And so are you."

"No." My voice was as firm as my resolve. "I know you say the fact that I'm not totally human doesn't bother you, but it does bother me, Noah. It bothers me that you might suffer because of me. And it bothers me that you walked into what could have been a dangerous situation because you were worried about me. I don't need your protection."

He stiffened. "And I don't need yours."

My heart just about broke as I looked at him. "Yeah," I whispered. "In the Dreaming, you do." And I couldn't guarantee that I could keep him safe.

The hurt on his face broke my heart—not just because of how stark it was, but because he actually allowed me to see it. "Right."

I didn't try to stop him when he turned on his heel and moved toward the door. I wanted to, I really did, but I made myself stand there and watch as he walked out of my office and potentially out of my life.

As soon as I was sure he was gone I let the tears come.

Later that week Antwoine called me at work and asked me out to lunch. I immediately jumped at the offer, being eager to hear all about his reunion with the love of his life.

And to be honest, I needed a distraction that training and learning with Hadria and Verek couldn't give me. I needed something in this world to keep my thoughts off Noah. It had been three days since I last saw or heard from him. Several times I'd been tempted to call and apologize for being an idiot, but I didn't. Call me a martyr, but the hard truth was that not only was Noah safer away from me, but the Warden has less to use against me with us broken up.

I refused to think about whether or not we'd ever get back together. One thing at a time.

I met Antwoine at a little soup-and-sandwich place not far from work. I had a craving for a chicken Caesar salad, and this place made the best. I paired it with creamy tomato soup with Asiago croutons—yum. Antwoine ordered black bean chili and a smoked turkey on honey wheat—in case you're interested.

We sat at a table in the back, where we could talk without worrying about anyone hearing if we started talking about "crazy" stuff like walking into dreams and succubi.

Antwoine looked good—well rested and relaxed. I had a pretty good idea what had brought on this new look and did not want to know. I could only assume that Madrene was very good at her job. He looked happy, and that was enough for me.

But when he looked at me after several minutes of small talk, I saw the hesitation in his chocolaty gaze. Hesitation and contrition—not a good combination in my experience.

"What's up, Antwoine?" I took a sip of my water and tried to calm the fluttering in my stomach. I'd know if my father had found out about the part I'd played in getting Antwoine and Madrene back together.

"Madrene had a visitor yesterday."

I set my water bottle aside. "From whom?" I refused

to let my mind run through the possibilities. Better to remain calm until he told me. But I had a pretty strong suspicion who the visitor was.

He shook his head, the watery sunlight coming through the window caught the gray in his hair. "She's gonna be so mad at me for telling you." His gaze locked with mine, "but you know I can't let her do something that might get her in trouble."

He sounded like Noah. I smiled slightly. "I know. What happened?"

Antwoine sighed, as though I had lifted a great weight off of his shoulders. His forearms rested on the table as he leaned forward over his food to fill me in.

"It was the Warden. She wanted to talk to Madrene about you."

A chill settled over me. Not enough to make my teeth chatter, but I shivered. I had such a hate-on for that woman, but I was still smart enough—for the time being—to be a little afraid. "What did Madrene tell her?"

Antwoine hesitated, but only for a second. "Nothing of importance that I could tell. In fact, I think they argued about what the Warden's been doing. I heard Madrene tell Padera she was disappointed in her. The Warden didn't like hearing that."

I frowned. "Why would the Warden care what Madrene thought of her?"

He shifted in his chair, looking down at the table as his slightly arthritic fingers toyed with the silverware. "Well, that's the part I felt I needed to tell you. Remember I said that Padera had grown up with the succubi?"

"Sure. You thought Madrene might be able to tell me about her." The succubus hadn't told me a damn thing, by the way.

Antwoine looked as though someone had put a plate of live worms in front of him. "I'm not sure how reliable Madrene's information will be."

I was shocked to hear such doubt come from his lips. "Why?"

"Because Padera is Madrene's daughter."

Chapter Fourteen

"You have to be fucking joking."

Antwoine flinched despite my best attempts to keep my voice at a moderate level. New York might be a "do your own thing" city, but people tended to frown upon screaming obscenities in public.

"I didn't know," he insisted, holding his hands out in supplication. "Child, you have got to believe me."

"Do I?" I demanded, angrier than I could have ever imagined. "You admit that you hate my father. He locked you up in a private cell, and now I'm to believe that it's just a coincidence that your girlfriend is the mother of the bitch who is trying to have me unmade?" Really, it sounded like something off a bad paranormal soap opera.

"It's true."

I might not be able to ignore the pleading in his tone, but I could at least distrust it.

"I knew that Madrene had a daughter, but I never met the girl. Madrene said she wouldn't understand her mother falling in love with a human."

Okay, so that I could believe. "Oh, Antwoine." I sighed and shook my head. I was disappointed, but the anger had disappeared as fast as it had come. Maybe Antwoine was a great liar, but there was no way anyone could fake the distress etched in every line of his open face. If I was going to be mad at anyone, it was Madrene for not telling me the truth when I asked her for information. She'd put me off because she wanted to see Antwoine. Would she have ever confessed?

Probably not. And that didn't bode well for me ever trusting her again. God, what if Madrene supported her daughter against me and Morpheus? It would make sense. The succubus's dislike of my father might be what had bred Padera's own hatred.

I gave Antwoine a sympathetic look. "I'm going to have to tell Morpheus."

He nodded, defeated. "I know." Then he reached across the table and placed his hand on top of mine. "Don't be too angry at her, Dawn. She's just trying to protect her daughter and make the most of what time we have left."

I could care less about her kid, but appealing to my romantic nature was effective. "I'll try." It was the best promise I could make.

We passed the rest of our lunch uneventfully and quickly. We hugged when we parted company, and I could feel turmoil surrounding him. Was he worried Morpheus would separate him and Madrene for good? Or was he too having doubts about the woman he loved? I had no idea, and quite frankly Antwoine's love life was the least of my concerns.

What the hell was I going to do about the pain in my ass that was the Warden?

I had made my mind up on that particular issue by the time I got back to my office. Unfortunately, I had to wait until after my next two appointments before I could act. That was probably just as well; it kept me from being too impulsive. And since my impulses tended to turn my eyes into a freaky state and gave me the ability to toss huge Nightmares across rooms, it was probably good that I had time to stew.

When I finally had some free time, I went into the bathroom and locked myself in as usual. Then I opened a portal, stepped through and closed it behind me. Paranoia dies hard, and despite being told that no one could see my portals, I wasn't going to risk Bonnie having some weird abilities as well. Shit, it was beginning to seem like almost everyone did.

Since I'd met the Warden before it was easy for me to track her—you know the drill. This time my father didn't pick up on my intent since I managed to keep my emotions at a less noticeable level.

I could have "called" the Warden, let her know I wanted to see her, but since she showed me no consideration whatsoever, I decided to return the favor.

I found myself just on the outside of a small wrought iron gate that surrounded a small English garden and quaint stone cottage. It was tranquil and peaceful. The Bitch Warden lived here?

I followed the walk through the gate and made my way up three shallow steps to the front door. It was heavy oak, old and scarred but undeniably sturdy. The knocker was an iron dagger that matched Verek's tattoo—the symbol of the Nightmares. I clapped it against the door.

And waited.

I didn't have to wait long, although it was longer than I wanted. No doubt she knew that. Still, I was surprised at just how little fear I felt when she finally opened the door. Mostly I was just annoyed.

And now here we were, just me and her. And I was definitely bigger.

"Hello, Princess," the Warden said with a smirk. "You wanted to see me?"

What would her reaction be if I punched her in the mouth?

Honestly. Would she screech like a crow, or would she come out fighting like a rat? I picked the rat. I didn't trust rats, so I kept my fists balled tightly at my sides.

"I think you and I need to talk," I told her, my jaw clenched.

"Oh?" She made no move to step out of the doorway and let me inside. "About?"

"About the fact that you want me unmade for endangering a dreamer, yet you threatened that same person."

Her pale cheeks flushed with pleasure. "Noah squealed on me. I thought he would. Really, Dawn. How can you date a guy who has to hide behind you?"

She was baiting me. I didn't rise to it. Had Noah? Had she said as much to him? "Leave Noah alone. He's nothing to you."

"He's another one of those disgusting anomalies that threatens our world. He's almost as much a threat to this world as you are."

I arched a brow. "Hmm. Sounds like you're losing sight of your job description. You're a Nightmare. You're supposed to protect dreamers."

She flushed as only redheads can. "My job is to protect this world."

Now I was smug. "No, your job is to protect dreamers first. I know this because I've been learning the rules with Hadria and Verek. But maybe you're right. We could always ask Morpheus for clarification."

Twin splotches of crimson marred her cheeks as her eyes glittered like onyx-trimmed jade. "He'd no doubt like to hear that you went against his ruling and re-united Madrene and her lover."

I smiled, because I had every intention of telling him that myself. "You call your mother, Madrene?"

That drained the color from her face.

"Morpheus would probably be very interested in what you said to your mommy about me. Almost as interested as he was that you threatened Noah."

For a second—an extremely satisfying second—she looked scared. But then it was gone, and her usual snide arrogance returned. "Be careful what games you play, Little Dawn, you might get hurt."

I straightened. "Don't threaten me."

One shoulder lifted. Were she human I would swear she was French, she was just that good at saying so much with a casual shrug. Every time she did it, I felt waves of disinterest wash over me. "I was merely voic-ing my concern."

I scowled despite my best efforts to remain as cool as my opponent. "Why do you hate me so much?"

Padera didn't look the least bit surprised by the ques-tion. "I hate who you are. I hate what you are. I hate what you've done to our world."

"I haven't done anything." Whine much? I made my voice firm. "The anomalies started before I was born."

"But you're the worst one of all. Don't you see?" There was a passion to her voice that made me uneasy—like when I dealt with a client who I knew was on the verge of a psychotic break. "You're going to be the end of us all."

"That's a little melodramatic, don't you think?"

The Warden's lips thinned. "If you cared about this world, you'd let them unmake you, turn you totally human."

"If you cared about this world, you wouldn't conspire against your king."

She laughed then, but didn't bother to deny my accusation either. "Don't you wonder why Noah won't let you into his dreams?"

Rage bubbled in my veins at the thought of her invading Noah's dreams, his private thoughts without his consent. Not only that, but she knew things about him that I didn't and probably never would. It didn't matter that she had taken those things from him, she still knew what he would never share with me. "If he wanted me to know, he'd tell me."

Her smile was oily and crimson. So smug and pointed—like a dagger about to plunge into its mark. "I know what he's hiding from you, and I can't wait for you to find out what he really is."

That's when it happened—when I found out what her reaction would be if I punched her in the mouth. It felt good, the way her lip split beneath my knuckles. I even kinda liked the way her teeth tore into my skin.

She staggered backward, hand at her mouth to staunch the flow of blood. "Did I break any rules by doing that?" I asked sweetly.

The Warden started to smile, winced, and stopped. But there was a gleam of triumph in her gaze that told me to go for the eyes next time I took a swing. "I will make you pay for that."

I smirked. "Whatever the price, it will be worth it."

Some of the gleam left her eyes. "We shall see about that, *Princess*." Sneers weren't attractive on a good face, on a bloody one they were definitely cringe-inducing. "You have no idea what I am capable of."

Another threat. My palms itched, and I wanted to smack her again. "If you hurt anyone I care about—"

She lunged forward, but stopped just shy of actually attacking me. My fists came up, but that was the only response I had time for. "If I hurt anyone, Your Highness, it will be *you*."

I felt the grin tugging at my lips with disbelief. How could I smile at a time like this? The bitch was threatening me! "Go for it. I'd love to plead self-defense after kicking your ass." Okay, this was dark Dawn talking. I could feel her twitching and dancing on the balls of her feet. She wanted to let it all out and come down in all her glory on the Warden. I held her back. I didn't know what I was capable of, and to be honest, part of me didn't want to find out.

Pale eyes were hard as they gazed into mine. "You have no idea the pain I can bring you."

This was what it felt like to go to war—not just to defend myself against an attack, or fight back like I had with Karatos. I was engaging in battle with a foe who could probably kick my ass six ways from Sunday and I wanted it more than I wanted the entire MAC spring line.

"You might be surprised at what I can do," the dark side of me said with a grin. "Keep pushing and you'll find out."

Her face was a mask of fury in the face of my insolence. "I will be the end of you," she promised. And then she slammed the door in my face.

Instead of being filled with fear or regret, I was filled with elation—and a sense of . . . bloodlust. It was like going into a game, determined to win.

"Not"—I murmured with a smile as I turned to go—"if I end you first."

My mother looked like crap.

I watched as she poured tea for both of us. She looked more delicate than usual, but without the glamour she normally exuded. She was pale, and she looked tired. Oh, she was still dressed to the nines in a plum sweater and chocolate pants with Prada shoes and Chanel jewelry, but I could see the signs.

"How are you holding up?" I asked dumbly, as though the answer wasn't sitting across the table from me.

"All right," she replied, but even her voice sounded wary. "The pull from the human world is very strong." She smiled but there wasn't much humor in that. "I suppose you're happy that I may have to face my sins."

I would have thought that too. "Not like this, not being forced against your will."

She looked surprised as she set the teapot back on its tray. She paused for a second before speaking. "Part of me thinks I should let this doctor bring me back and say good-bye properly, but I'm scared."

I picked up a little tuna sandwich and nibbled on the corner. "You think if this guy can wake you up, he can also stop you from returning here?" It's what I'd be afraid of.

She nodded. "That makes me awful, doesn't it?"

I shrugged, surprised at just how charitable my feelings toward her had become. "Your life is here." Now I smiled without humor. "At least you know which world you want as your own."

A thin hand closed over mine. Frail she might be, but she was still warm and surprisingly strong. "I have to choose, Dawn. You don't. You can belong to both."

I chuckled drily. But couldn't it also be said that I

didn't truly belong in either? Really, I don't think the majority of people in either world would accept me for what I was. "I'm not sure my balance is that good."

"If anyone can do it, it's you. You always did whatever you set your mind to."

I didn't remember being like that at all, but I didn't argue. I really wanted her to be right. I didn't want to have to choose.

Instead, I changed the subject. "Morpheus must be going nuts over all of this."

Mom rolled her eyes. "You don't know the half of it. He's bound and determined to keep me here. If not for him I might have already given up."

If not for him she wouldn't be here, but I didn't say anything. I resented my mother for so long for leaving us, but part of me could understand the allure of a man who wanted you just as you were. I had hoped Noah might be that man for me, but right now I just didn't see how that was possible when there always seemed to be someone from the Dreaming gunning for me and using him to do it.

And someone insinuating that he was hiding something from me—something that could change how I felt about him.

I took a sugar cookie from the plate before me—my grandmother's recipe—and drank my tea. We made a little small talk, and then Mom got down to business.

"I have a favor I need to ask of you, Dawnie."

I set my cup and saucer on the floral-print tablecloth and folded my hands in my lap. Composed, ready, and putting on a good face. "What?"

She held her cup and saucer in her lap, toying with the handle of the cup to turn it one way and then the other. It reminded me of my grandmother telling me how to turn the cup before she read my tea leaves. "If they wake me up, I want you to look after your father. He's not going to accept my being gone easily."

"You make it sound like you're dying." It was a lame-ass attempt at humor.

Her gaze locked with mine. "He'll feel like I have."

God. Throat tight, I nodded. "I'll look after him." Really, what was I going to do? Hold his hand? I hated to think of what he might do if she was gone—how grief might make him react. Grief always made gods unstable, irrational, and downright dangerous. I know this because I took a class in mythology in university.

Then the lightbulb went off. Was this another plot by my father's enemies? Getting rid of Mom would put Morpheus on edge, make him vulnerable and angry. It wasn't as though they could stop her from entering the Dreaming—could they? She'd be able to return, but it wouldn't be the same. Morpheus wouldn't be her whole world anymore. That would seriously piss him off, and he'd be primed for whatever his enemies had planned for him.

Not only primed, but if they provoked him, he'd give them exactly what they want willingly. Oh, shit.

"I'll help him," I reiterated. "I'll do whatever I can for him." And silently I prayed to whatever gods from whatever worlds might be listening that I would be able to hold him together—and along with him, this world.

But mostly I prayed that Mom simply wouldn't wake up.

She squeezed my hand. "Look after yourself as well. They'll try to get to him through you if they can."

"I think they already have."

Mom cocked a brow. "The Warden?" At my nod she made a face. "I've never trusted that woman. Don't turn your back on her, Dawn."

"I won't."

"Don't turn her back on who?" came Morpheus's voice from just behind me. I hated when he just appeared like that.

"The Warden," I replied when he leaned in to kiss my cheek.

"What's she done now?" He took a seat beside my mother, kissed her cheek, and took her hand in his in one swift motion. He was smooth, my father.

"Tried to blackmail me." I might as well come clean and tell him everything now. That way the Warden wouldn't have a leg to stand on. Of course, both of my legs might be broken by the time my father was done with me.

Morpheus frowned as he sat down beside Mom. He snatched a cookie with his free hand and bit in. "She's looking to lose her position over this. What's this blackmail you mentioned?"

I took a deep breath. "She threatened to tell you that I reunited Antwoine and Madrene in payment for Antwoine's help with Karatos."

He took it better than I thought he would. He brought his fist down on the table and smashed it completely, and then of course, rebuilt it exactly as it was, right down to my half-empty cup of tea.

I sat very still, as did my mother, waiting to see what he'd do next.

"My apologies," he said very softly. He looked angry and a little foolish at the same time. "I shouldn't have reacted like that. I don't approve of your actions, Dawn. You should have come to me first, but Antwoine helped you defeat Karatos and assisted in bringing you back to me, so allowing him time with Madrene is a reasonable price."

I was mid-sigh when he continued: "So long as their relationship doesn't interfere with her other duties, I have no problem with them continuing to see each other—but Antwoine stays where he is."

So Antwoine remained a prisoner within the Dreaming but he got his girl. "He's an old man, Morpheus." And why did I have the feeling like there was more going on than he wanted to tell me? It was like a scavenger hunt being in this world, trying to find all the missing information. All this doubt and secrecy wore me out.

"He's an anomaly," he replied. "And a dangerous one."

I choked on laughter. "Antwoine, dangerous?"

My father didn't share my humor. "Someday, perhaps, your friend will tell you the whole truth about why he is in that prison I made for him. It's not just about his relationship with Madrene, or that he attacked me."

"Are you telling me I shouldn't trust him?" My chin actually quivered as I asked the question, because I had enough doubts where Antwoine was concerned.

"Of course not. He's proven himself a friend to you. But I'd ask that you take what he tells you about me and the circumstances of his banishment with a very large grain of salt and allow me to distrust him for both of us."

Fair enough, but I was still unsettled. I didn't like thinking Antwoine kept things from me, that my friend might not be what I thought him to be.

"Was her threat the reason you decided to confess to me now?"

I had no trouble meeting his gaze, because I would feel way worse if I didn't tell him and the whole thing blew up in my face. "Partially. Mostly I decided to tell you because Antwoine just found out that Madrene is Padera's mother." Which, of course, was weird because Padera was so white and Madrene wasn't.

My mother's jaw dropped. "She is?"

Morpheus glanced at her as he shifted in his chair. "Yes," he replied.

Mom's mouth thinned. "I see."

My gaze went back and forth between them. WTF? "The Warden apparently came to Madrene and started asking about me." I took another bite of cookie. God, it was good. "Madrene lied to me. She said she'd tell me about Padera but she never did. Now I know why."

"You don't know all of it." My mother's cheeks were brightly flushed as she turned her angry gaze away from Morpheus. "Tell her."

I stared at them both again. "Tell me what?"

"Maggie . . ." My father's voice held a note of warning, but Mom was obviously too pissed off to care.

Mom fiddled with a napkin. "You never told me who her mother was."

"Should he have?" I asked, not liking the suspicion that was forming in the back of my mind.

My mother looked at me with a gaze so intense I felt like a butterfly pinned to a board. "Perhaps, Dawnie, your father hates this Antwoine person because he stole away your father's lover."

My mouth fell open. Morpheus cursed and refused to meet my gaze—he was too busy glaring at my mother, who was still looking at me.

I couldn't find the words. All I could say was, "You and Madrene?"

"Yes," Mom replied. "Your father and Madrene were lovers for many years before he met me. Antwoine came between them, didn't he, Morpheus?" The look she shot my father could have sliced a car in half.

There was only one reason Mom would be this angry. *You never told me who her mother was.* Shit on a stick. "Do you mean . . ." Oh God, I couldn't even say it.

My father did it for me. "Yes, Dawn. The Warden—Padera—is your half sister."

Chapter Fifteen

"Did you know?" I demanded of Verek as I gazed down the rock cliff he was climbing.

His head lifted. His brow shone with sweat and his cheeks were flushed. He looked pretty good for having climbed almost to the top of a humungous mountain. His fingers gripped jutting rock, muscles in his big arms straining as he pulled his weight up. "Know about what?"

"That Padera is my freaking sister."

He reached the top and hauled himself up onto the rough stone at my feet. "I knew," he said as he straightened to his full height.

I stood there, watching in spiraling frustration as he wiped his brow with his forearm. As sweaty as he was, he didn't stink. "Why didn't you tell me?"

He shot me a dry glance. "Would it have changed anything?"

"Of course it would have!" Wouldn't it? I mean, she obviously knew we were related and it hadn't stopped her from wanting me long gone.

"No, it wouldn't," he argued as he brushed past me. He smelled like warm, damp male. Very nice, I'm embarrassed to admit. "It still doesn't, but now you'll feel guilty for hating her."

"I don't *hate* her," I insisted. He shot me another look and I rolled my eyes. "Okay, so I hate her." And he was right, I felt guilty for it—not because she didn't deserve it, but because it went against everything I believed to hate a sibling.

Verek chuckled, the low rumble seeming to come from his toes. "Don't worry, Princess. I'll help you relieve all that frustration."

I just bet he could. "I feel like sparring," I said. "Are you up for that?"

He offered me his hand. "Lead on."

I wrapped my fingers around his much larger ones and "wished" us to another location where we sometimes trained. Verek had it set up like the kind of gym you'd see on TV. I think he's watched *Rocky* one too many times.

I had put myself into yoga pants and a T-shirt, so I was ready to go. When I turned around, Verek was standing there in a pair of tight shorts and nothing else.

Good lord, he was going all UFC on me.

I was a Nightmare too, why didn't I have washboard abs? All right, so I really wouldn't want to have a stomach that ropey, but a little definition might be nice. I guess it was because in most mythologies, the men were who had all the muscles and the women were soft and curvy. I was definitely soft, and very curvy.

"Come on," Verek called, "get in the ring. Let's get started."

Gingerly, I climbed the steps leading up to the ropes and slipped between the top two. The mat was cool beneath my toes.

"I know you've learned some martial arts already," he said, "so I thought we'd build on that."

I raised a brow. "We're going to *wrestle*?"

He grinned—a wolf with sparkling white teeth. "No, Princess. You want to fight, and we're going to *fight*." And then he dropped to the mat in a crouch and knocked my feet out from under me with one swift kick.

"Gowf!" I hit the mat hard, the air rushing from my lungs. Next thing I knew Verek had me bent like a pretzel and was trying to explain what the hold was called and why I couldn't get out of it. I'm sure it made a lot of sense, but I couldn't hear him very well over the roaring in my ears.

"Now, get out of it." Of all the things for me to finally hear, that wasn't what my ears strained for.

"I can't." I gasped for air. "You're stronger than me."

He bent down. I could smell the heat of his skin. "Princess, this is your world. Kick my ass."

"How in the hell am I supposed to do that?"

"Try." That was all he said, and obviously all he was going to say. He simply went silent and continued to hold me in this damn crazy position.

OK, get out of it. If I didn't get out of it soon my head was probably going to explode, or I was going to pop a disc. I closed my eyes, concentrated on drawing as deep and as soothing breaths as I could, and then I focused all of my senses inward. Verek was right. In theory I should be able to at least match him. He was bigger, but I was Morpheus's daughter, and therefore something of a Wonder Woman in this world.

And here I was without my lasso.

I moved one arm, so that it was braced tighter between our bodies, and then pushed, not just with the arm, but with one leg as well. Verek's weight shifted as he sought to remain in control and I took that opportunity to use his posture against him. The result had me straddling him, spitting hair out of my mouth as I pinned his arm behind his back.

"How was that?" I asked gleefully.

"Perfect," he replied in a gruntlike tone. "But you

should know better than to gloat." And the next thing I knew I was on my back with my legs over his shoulders and my hands locked behind my back, held in one of his.

Good thing my face was already red or he would have seen the scarlet blush flood my cheeks. Did he not realize how sexual this position was?

"Now what are you going to do?" he taunted.

I didn't think, I simply reacted. I locked my thighs around his neck, and squeezed while lifting my weight onto my shoulders. I pushed up and forward, using my abs to stabilize the movement. I was going to be sore later, but it would be worth it. I sailed into the air, up and over.

And landed practically sitting on Verek's face. Dear God. I rolled to the side and onto the mat as fast as I could.

He rose easily into a sitting position with a big-ass grin on his face. "That was interesting."

"Shut up." Yes, that was the most intelligent thing I could think to say.

He dove for me. He was so fast I couldn't even react. I cursed myself for being such an idiot as he pinned me once more, one of his big legs over mine as he held my hands above my head.

I could feel every hot, solid inch of him against me. Those washboard abs felt like rough silk against my stomach. And against my thigh . . . well, that was hard too. My gaze locked with his, and I knew with total certainty that if I gave the slightest indication that it would be welcome, Verek was going to kiss me.

When the hell had this happened? I had no idea he was attracted to me. I thought he respected me, but found me somewhat annoying or frustrating. I certainly hadn't expected this turn of events.

Worse, I wouldn't have expected my reaction. Verek was gorgeous—scarily so. In the human world he'd be an action star or a model—and he wouldn't even know I was alive. Of course I wanted him to kiss me. I might even be curious as to what it would be like to have sex with him. He was everything most women dreamed about, read about. He was a romance hero come to life, right down to his annoying tendency to think he was right all the time.

But he wasn't Noah, and that was the problem. My body responded to Verek like any straight woman's would, but my heart wasn't in it. My heart belonged to Noah, and that meant the rest of me did too. Truthfully, I didn't regret it one bit.

So, I can honestly say that I enjoyed jerking my head up to give him the head butt to end all head butts. He rolled off me with a groan, clutching his bleeding nose. He sat up and glared at me over the top of his hand. Blood seeped through his fingers. "No fair," he bitched. "You distracted me with your feminine wiles."

I always wanted to guffaw, and now that I finally had the opportunity, I took it. "And I suppose it wasn't your intent to distract me with Captain Love Rocket?"

He grinned. "You noticed."

Then he snapped his nose back into place and I winced at the sound it made. He took his hand away. The bleeding had already stopped. He held out his hand. "Good job."

I accepted the handshake. "Thanks. You too."

I should have known better than to trust him. The second his fingers closed around mine, he yanked me forward and I fell against his naked chest with a gasp.

Strong fingers—not the bloody ones, though—held my chin as unyielding lips smoldered against mine. It was like kissing an inferno—a big, sexy, yummy one.

He thrust me aside as fast as he had grabbed me. I felt his fingers wipe away a smudge of wetness on my upper lip. I think it was blood. Was it wrong of me to find that kind of hot?

"Just a little something for you to think about, Princess," he murmured, oh-so arrogantly as he slowly rose to his feet. "If you decide you want to play again sometime, give me a shout."

I sat in the middle of the ring and watched like an idiot as he walked away. My mind reeled. What the hell had just happened? Was this real or had I dreamed the whole thing? And could my life get any weirder or more unbalanced?

The answer was yes, it could. And that also gave me the answer to Verek's offer as well. I was tempted to play with him, of course, but not tempted enough, although that darker side of my nature—or maybe she was simply the Dreamkin side—wanted to chase after him and run him to ground like a lion after prey.

There was only one person I was willing to risk losing myself to, only one person worth the odds, and that was Noah.

I hoped I hadn't already outplayed my luck with him.

I met Antwoine for lunch the next day. I needed something to take the taste of Verek out of my mouth. Crass? Yes, but it was true. Probably it was because he was Dreamkin, but a part of me liked what he did to me and wanted to experience it again.

On my way to meet Antwoine, I called Noah's cell. I was walking up Madison, the roar of the city buzzing around me making it hard to hear when his voice mail picked up on the other end. Screening his calls? Maybe, but more likely he was working.

I didn't bother leaving a message. I had no idea what to say that wouldn't make me sound like an idiot, so I disconnected and shoved my phone in the side pocket of my bag. If I got the courage up I'd try again later.

What the hell had I been thinking, breaking up with him? We were stronger together than we were apart. Anyone with a brain would know that I only dumped him because I was afraid for him, and they'd go after him anyway. Only now, with his pride bruised, I wouldn't know about it until it was too late.

Verek had made me realize how much I missed Noah. Verek also made me realize that there was little difference between grappling and foreplay. I was going to have to see if Noah had any mixed martial arts experience.

I ducked into the little restaurant and was just sitting down in my favorite booth when Antwoine arrived.

"This is getting to be a regular habit," he remarked, sliding in across from me. "You and I meeting for lunch."

I returned his smile, but it felt a little strained on my lips. "Thanks for meeting me on such short notice."

"I figured it had to be important." When he looked at me so full of warmth and concern I couldn't think the worst of him, I just couldn't. "What's wrong, little Dawn?"

The waiter took that moment to show up and ask if we wanted drinks, so I ordered a diet Coke. We knew what we wanted to eat as well, so we ordered our soup and sandwiches too.

When we were alone again, I turned to my friend. "A couple of things. Firstly, Morpheus isn't going to interfere with you and Madrene."

To say Antwoine was surprised was an understatement. "Really?"

I nodded. "Provided Madrene doesn't shirk her succubus duties, he doesn't care how much time you spend together." I'm not sure that last part was completely true, but what the hell.

"Well, I'll be," he murmured. "I wasn't expectin' that."

I placed my napkin over my lap, smoothing it so I didn't have to look at him. "Antwoine, I know that Morpheus and Madrene were once together. Padera is my half sister." Only once the words were out did I look up.

The older man sat across from me, noticeably pale. "Well," he rasped. "I can't say that I was expectin' that either."

I believed him. "That's the bad blood between you, isn't it? You took Madrene away."

He nodded slowly. I watched as some color bled back into his cheeks. "That's a bit of it, but Padera was already grown by the time I came along. Madrene wouldn't have gotten involved with me, though, if she was happy."

That was true. Just like my mother wouldn't have

left her family if she had been happy where she was.

"Antwoine . . ." God, how did I do this? I scooted closer to the table. "I need to know if you or Madrene are in league with the Warden."

He frowned. "You mean, are either me or Madrene out to get you and your daddy?"

I held his gaze without flinching. "Yes." I had to know that it really had been a coincidence that he and I met that day in Duane Reade. That he hadn't been conspiring against me all these weeks.

He smiled. "Dawn, if I wanted to get to Morpheus, I wouldn't use you to do it. I don't play like that. You're my friend."

I believed him. I admit that I really wanted to believe that he cared about me, that I wasn't just a way to my father. "I had to ask."

"Of course you did. And you're smart to be suspicious."

He didn't speak for Madrene and that unsettled me a little. But like he said, I was right to be suspicious. If Antwoine trusted the succubus, then I would as well. After all, Antwoine had said that Madrene had argued with her daughter about me, so maybe the succubus was on my side.

"You know that if you ever do try to get revenge on my father I'll have to stop you." Now what the hell made me say that?

Again the kind smile. "I know. Someday you and I might find ourselves at odds, child, but not today. Not any day soon. I hope never."

I swallowed. "I hope that too."

He patted my hand. "Don't you fret over things there's no point in fretting over. Tell me how you and young Noah are doing."

Talk about fretting. I sighed and told him what had happened. Antwoine sat and nodded, not saying anything as I verbally vomited all over the place. I kept talking even after the food arrived.

Afterward, Antwoine flashed another of his smiles and spooned a cheesy crouton out of his tomato soup. "That's love, child. You got to work things out, and sometimes it's not easy."

Well, that was simple. Wasn't it? I guess if Antwoine and Madrene could find a way when they were from two different worlds, if my mother and father could do it, then Noah and I eventually could. At least we had the benefit of being from the same dimension.

I just couldn't bear the thought of something happening to him because of me. When I thought of what Karatos had done to him, how the Terror had robbed him of his ability to dream . . . it made me feel sick. But it was even worse thinking that I might never see him again.

I felt much better about things when Antwoine and I parted company. I walked back to the office, grabbing a coffee on the way. Yes, I drink way too much of the stuff, so sue me. I don't smoke and I gave up potato chips a year ago. Other than makeup it is my one vice and I like it. So there.

Inside my pretty little space, I hung up my coat and took my phone from my purse once more. Before I could chicken out, I speed-dialed Noah's number and bounced on the balls of my feet waiting for someone to pick up.

It was his voice mail again, "This is Noah. Leave a message, I'll get back to you."

"Hi," I said hesitantly. God, I felt like such a jerk. "It's me. I'd like to talk. Give me a call if you'd like that too." Then I hit End before I could say anything that might make me sound even more lame. Although, I'm sure saying I was sorry would have been a good thing.

I set the phone on my desk and sat down to go over the afternoon's three files. At least I'd have plenty to keep me busy and keep me from fretting.

I checked my phone every fifteen minutes, just in case something was wrong with it. Nothing was. Maybe Noah was just busy, I thought as I left work for the day.

But by the time I went to bed that night, I realized that the man I wanted most in my life had no intention of calling me back.

I dreamed that I was on a beautiful carousel, lazily spinning around and around on an antique lacquered horse while calliope music played in the background. It was wonderful. I felt alive and free. The only problem was that I could pick one of two places to get off, and I didn't know which one to pick.

I was just about to make my decision when the music slowed to a droning, creepy melody and finally stopped—as did the carousel.

And then the lights went off on the ride. Without the brightness, I was able to make out surroundings that I hadn't seen before. Or maybe they just hadn't been there before. Regardless, I found myself in an amusement park—one that was obviously closed.

I eased off the wooden horse, unease tracing a light finger down my spine. There was something not right about this dream, but I couldn't quite put my finger on it. Slowly, I stepped down from the turnstile and turned in the direction of the midway, where the lights were brightest.

Discarded gum and tickets littered the pavement, along with pieces of popcorn, straws, and smushed french fries. The smell of cotton candy hung thick and sweet upon the air along with the tinny smell of machinery and the stale odor of cigarette smoke.

Every step I took was cautious. I waited for something to happen, for someone like Freddy Krueger or Leatherface to jump out and disembowel me. I didn't call out like the stupid girls in horror movies did. I knew something was out there waiting for me. I just didn't know how much of a threat it was.

"A woman like you should know better than to be out alone at night."

I froze, the sole of my shoe landing squarely in a wad of pink bubblegum. I knew that voice, and it wasn't one I ever hoped to hear again. I didn't want to turn and face him, but this was just a dream. It wasn't real. It couldn't be.

I scraped my shoe against the pavement as I turned. Standing beneath the harsh glow of a lamp was Phil Durdan. He was dressed in jeans, boots, and a sweater. He looked like any old Average Joe with nondescript features. The only thing remotely standoutish about him was the old tarnished medallion hanging around his neck.

My smart-ass reply died on my lips the moment I looked into his eyes. This was no Dreamkin. It really was Phil. But this wasn't his dream. It was mine.

And when I tried to push him out, he wouldn't budge. He only smiled. "Not used to people walking into *your* dreams, are you?"

It was a good dig, and were he a normal person I wouldn't begrudge him for it. But he wasn't normal, he was a sociopath and he scared the hell out of me. "No, I'm not. I don't suppose you'd like to tell me how you did it?"

He laughed. "And let you ruin everything? I don't think so." His laughter faded. "You put me in jail."

"The fact you're a serial rapist put you in jail, Phil." I kept my tone casual, non-threatening, just like I would with any potentially dangerous client.

"You destroyed my life!"

I didn't flinch. "You've ruined a few yourself." I thought of Amanda and the bandage on her scalp—and the tingle of fear that had been growing at the base of my spine turned into something angrier. Durdan was a monster, and somehow he had gotten into my dream where I should be all-powerful and wasn't.

That meant someone had helped him.

Three guesses as to who his mysterious benefactor was. Hmmm. The Warden maybe? My psycho half sister who thought of herself as the defender of all and me as the destroyer of worlds. Again with the paranormal soap opera.

"She must really hate me," I muttered out loud.

"She does," Phil agreed, not bothering to pretend that Padera wasn't the one who made this possible. "She told me to make sure you didn't survive. And she told me to do whatever I wanted to you."

There was a hungry, angry gleam in his eye that I didn't like. I backed up a step. "I can't die in this world, Phil."

He shrugged. "But you can suffer." And then he

smiled. "And I'm pretty confident that by the time I'm done, you'll wish you were dead."

What a charmer. "You can suffer too." As soon as I said the words I had a flood of confidence wash over me. I had the power here. Not him. This was my world.

Huh. *My* world.

Phil smiled. "I'm not afraid."

He should be. Shouldn't he? If I defended myself against him, would it fall under the category of me harming a dreamer, or would it be self-defense? And would anyone believe the Warden—my half-fucking-sister—put him up to it?

Given my luck, probably not. Right now that was the least of my concern. Keeping Phil from doing all the damage he could was top priority.

I began backing away. Then, I turned and ran. As my legs ate up the ground beneath me I focused on pushing myself out of the dream. I tried to wake up and that didn't work. I tried to teleport somewhere else. That didn't work either.

And then I hit the fence—literally. Easily twenty feet high, it was steel mesh topped with barbed wire. There was no way I was going over it. And a padlock the size of my head ensured that I couldn't go through the gate.

The Warden had really thought this through. I couldn't get out in the usual ways. But could I bend the dream to my will?

I heard Phil come up behind me. "This would go a lot easier if you don't fight."

I turned as my heart slammed against my ribs. "That's not going to happen, Phil."

He looked resigned. "I didn't think so."

When he came at me I was ready. This time I side-stepped out of his path, and deflected his oncoming blow with one of the aikido moves Noah had taught me. Phil stumbled, but didn't fall. And he managed to avoid my foot as I tried to kick him.

"I know I said it would be easier," he said as he straightened, his face flushed. "But I actually like it better when they fight."

"I bet you do," I replied. My adrenaline was pumping now, along with anger, which had thankfully replaced fear as my dominant emotion. I was no good when I was scared, but anger worked for me. It would keep me fighting until I gained control.

He came at me again. This time he managed to land a blow to my stomach, but got my elbow to his jaw, so we were pretty even. But then he grabbed the waist of my jeans and hauled me close. He kicked my feet out from under me as I struggled and I fell. My head hit something solid—not hard enough to make me bleed, but hard enough that I saw stars. It was an old coffee table.

I looked around, half dazed and trying to shake it off

as I attempted to roll to my feet. We were in the doll shop I'd seen in Phil's dreams. He was the one in control.

He jumped on top of me and slammed me back to the floor. At least he hadn't thought to change my clothes, and I was thankful for that as I blocked another punch. In jeans and a T-shirt, I wouldn't be easy to rape. I was pretty certain that a very brutal assault was part of the "whatever" promised to him by the Warden.

I wasn't going to make that easy for him. I was going to punch and kick him with all I had. In fact, I rather liked the idea of possibly stuffing my heel in his mouth.

He punched me again in the face—the same place as before. Pain raced up the side of my head, making the edges of my vision darken. And then he punched me in the eye. If he kept pounding on me like this, I was going to pass out, and then he could do whatever he wanted.

I couldn't let that happen.

As soon as that realization hit me, something else did too—and it wasn't Phil. It was the telltale burning in my eyes. The Nightmare part of me was coming to life, and she was so pissed it wasn't funny.

It was about damn time.

I smashed my head into his face, knocking him sideways. As he fell to the floor, my gaze landed on the medallion around his neck. Up close it looked familiar—eerily so. It was an object of the Dreaming, marked with two crescent moons back to back. I didn't know what it meant, but it wasn't much of a leap to assume that was what gave Phil power in this realm.

Power coursed through my veins and lit my soul with a terrible glee. Now it was me on top. Me pummeling my victim with brutal jabs. Phil landed a few good ones of his own, but when it seemed that he might recover some of his strength, I wrapped my hand around the medallion and squeezed.

It shattered beneath my fingers. I probably could have crushed diamonds at that moment. Reaching down, I grabbed his chin with one stiff and bloody hand, forcing him to look at me with his swollen eyes.

"Hey, Phil." My voice was thick because of my battered jaw. It didn't want to work quite right. Maybe he had broken it. I could fix it later.

He looked at me, and frowned when he saw the color of my eyes—pale aqua with thick, black spidery rims. "What the fuck?"

Only one side of my mouth smiled. "What's your worst nightmare?"

I saw it like a picture in my mind, as though he'd flipped open his wallet and shown me a snapshot. It was going to be gruesome, but I didn't care. I concentrated on the image—and his fear of it. I don't remember ever hearing that Nightmares got off on fear, but part of me kinda did. At least, Phil's did it for me.

Mother.

It washed over me. My skin tingled like my entire body had been asleep and now all the blood was rushing back to my extremities. I was changing, morphing into what Phil feared most.

And what Phil feared most was his mother being able to control him from beyond the grave—getting her revenge for him killing her many years earlier.

My skin felt stretched, and somehow shrunken. I was dry and brittle, light and almost skeletal, but the pain in my jaw and eye were gone. In fact, my eyeballs felt like raisins, rolling in sockets that were too big for them.

Phil squirmed beneath me, white as a ghost, his eyes huge and round. I think he might have pissed himself too—it smelled like it. Thankfully, in this state I couldn't feel it against my flesh. I didn't have much flesh left, and nerve endings were a thing of the past in this form.

"You good for nothing little bastard," I said. I didn't have much left for lips, so it came out stiff, with a lisp that sounded like sheets flapping on a clothes line.

Phil pushed at me, as ineffectually as a moth beating its wings against a boulder. I felt only the slightest tug against my flesh. I think something gave way in the vicinity. I tried not to think about it. I wasn't going to be very effective if I let it get to me.

"Mama?" he squeaked.

I leaned down, joints popping, knees scraping the

rug through muslin-thin flesh. "Come on," I taunted. "Don't you have a kiss for your mother?"

Phil shrank away and I continued. "You used to like it when I kissed you."

"No," he whispered. "I never did. I never did."

"Liar! The first doll you made had my hair, from my head as well as my pussy." This was too twisted, but I kept it going. "You'd be nothing right now without me. You are nothing without me."

He shook his head. There were tears in his eyes. He was truly terrified. I almost felt guilty. Almost.

"Such a disappointment," I said sadly, teeth clacking.

Phil went berserk then and lurched at me with a howl of rage. I screamed back, laughing manically as I did so. Little fucker thought he could turn on *me* like that?

I undulated against him, making all kinds of rude gestures and remarks as I simulated riding him. He began to sob sometime during all of this. Then the sobs turned to a kind of wet babbling. That was when I realized his mind had snapped. When I realized what I had done. He was gone, even though his body kept fighting. Darkness swarmed the edges of my brain—I literally felt unconsciousness coming for me. I didn't want to pass out and be left alone with this . . . mess.

Dear God. Someone help me.

And then, as though in answer to my silent prayer, I heard a familiar voice above me. "What the hell?"

Chapter Sixteen

Noah. It was Noah. I must have called out to him, and beautiful creature that he was he answered, allowing me to draw him into my dream. It was knowing that he was there that enabled me to regain control.

I changed back—just thought about it and let it happen. It hurt a little, but not much. I looked up, slid onto the floor, and met the unreadable gaze of the man I adored. "Noah, meet Phil. The Warden let him into my dream so he could rape me."

To say that Noah's expression was murderous would have been an understatement. It went beyond murderous. Before Phil could move, Noah kicked him in the ribs.

"Fucking son of a bitch!" Noah yelled. Several more kicks made sure the rapist couldn't get up—not that he was capable of it before this. I think I fried his brain pretty good, judging from the glazed look in his eyes. Noah must have noticed too—or maybe it was the drool—but he stopped his kicking and turned back to me.

"What the hell was that?" Noah asked as he helped me to my feet. "You looked like a goddamn zombie."

"I kinda was." My jaw throbbed so I had to speak slowly and carefully. "I was his mother. He's terrified of her, even though he murdered her."

I felt him go still, but only for a second. "Jesus, Doc. Sometimes you scare me."

My heart pinched a little. "Sometimes I scare myself."

He hugged me then, taking away the sting of his words. "I don't care what kind of freaky things you can do, I'm just glad you can do them." He kissed me firmly on the forehead, carefully avoiding my eye and jaw.

"Thanks for coming," I said, my jaw damn near immobile now. I had to heal myself—if only I could concentrate enough to do it. It wouldn't take much, but I was so drained it felt like trying to lift a house. "How did you know?"

He smoothed hair back from my forehead. "I don't know. I just knew you were in trouble and that I had to get to you." Proof positive that he was indeed more than just a lucid dreamer. He was one of the anomalies. No wonder I had been drawn to him.

And he'd come running to my rescue. The thought

made me chuckle—which hurt, but not like it had, so obviously my body was beginning to heal.

"What's so funny?" he demanded, but there wasn't any harshness to it.

I looked up into his beautiful black eyes. "I tried to break up with you because I thought you were the one who was more vulnerable in this world, and I'm the one who needed saving."

He grinned and I knew it meant something to him to hear me say it. "You held your own."

My laughter faded as I thought of what I had done. "I was scared." Scared of Phil. Scared of the Warden. Scared of myself.

Noah hugged me again. "You're safe now."

For a moment I believed him, but I knew it wouldn't last. Breathing slowly, I willed my jaw to mend and my body to heal faster so I'd be in better shape to face what happened next. Both happened with surprising ease—the after effects of the surge of power I'd felt earlier.

Reaching up, I placed a palm on either side of Noah's face, loving the feel of his stubble against my skin. I pulled his head down to mine and kissed him. His lips were firm and smooth, parting easily for my tongue. I tasted him and sighed. It was like coming home again. That was when he took control, wrapping me tight in the warm, hard circle of his arms, claiming my mouth with hot, wet determination. I moaned—from pleasure not from pain—and let him have his way.

When we broke apart, both of us were breathing a little harder. Noah rested his forehead against mine. "Come back to me," he whispered.

Tears burned the backs of my eyes at the catch in his voice. How had we become this entwined in the brief time we'd been together? I cupped my hand around the back of his neck, kneading the tense muscles there. "I didn't really leave," I whispered back.

Behind me someone cleared their throat. I sighed and gave Noah another squeeze before turning in his arms. His hands fell to my hips as he stood behind me, facing this new arrival with me.

It was Verek, of course.

I forced a tight smile. "What took you so long?"

"He can't come with us." Verek's jaw was tight as he glanced at Noah. At this point, I really didn't care if he was jealous or found Noah a threat. I was just glad to have my guy beside me.

"He's coming," I insisted, taking Noah by the hand. "If you're dragging me to face the firing squad, I want him with me."

The Nightmare rolled his eyes. "The Council is assembled, they're waiting for you in the great hall."

"The Council?" I stared at him. "You really are taking me before a firing squad, aren't you?"

He gave me a sympathetic look. "It's been reported that you used your powers to harm a dreamer." He glanced at Phil, still lying upon the floor. "The Council wishes to uncover why."

"I don't have a choice, do I?"

He shook his head. "I'm afraid not." He offered me his hand. "I'm to escort you."

Of course he was. I took his hand, still holding Noah's in the other. "Hold on," I said, closing my eyes. Noah's fingers tightened on mine.

When I opened my eyes we were in the same temple-like building as before. This had to be the Council's chambers. We entered the main room through the open doors, and as we walked, heads turned. The looks I got weren't all that friendly.

"The people in this world really seem to have it in for me," I remarked tightly as we walked up the aisle toward the front of the room.

"You scare them," Verek murmured, his head high. Beside me, Noah kept his gaze lifted as well. Was he scared? Or was he full of defiance? I figured it was probably the latter.

I glanced at Verek out of the corner of my eye. "Do I scare you?"

He looked away. "A little."

Great. Not only did I scare Noah, but Verek as well. My father was probably scared as well. This was just freaking dandy. The whole damn Council was probably terrified that I was going to rain ruination down upon them all. I directed my attention to the front of the great hall, where the Council sat like a sour-faced jury. My father sat to the left of them, flanked by Hadria and the Warden—my sister, who looked all too pleased to see me. She looked pleased to see Noah as well. No doubt she saw his presence as just one more nail in my coffin.

Morpheus looked pained, and I think maybe there were tears in his eyes as his gaze fell on my battered face. Even Hadria, who rarely looked anything but serene, seemed disconcerted by my appearance. At least they were on my side. So I had them along with Verek and Noah to support me. Against the entire Council and an audience of at least two hundred Dreamkin. Fabulous.

Why the hell couldn't I have been born human?

"What's this all about?" I asked, refusing to take one step closer to Padera and her nest of vipers.

My father's shoulders sagged. "A few minutes ago the Warden called the Council together, claiming you used your powers against a dreamer. She's renewed her petition for the Council to order you unmade."

Of course she did. The bitch planned this whole

thing. And I'd played right into her hands, probably even better than she expected.

"And that's it? I'm not given any warning, just brought here and put on trial?"

Were those tears in his eyes? Christ, this was as much to hurt him as it was to get to me. "Yes."

"That really sucks." And it really pissed me off, but there didn't seem to be anything I could do about it other than allow Verek to escort me to the front of the cavernous room where my father and the others waited.

"And she has brought a dreamer with her!" Padera shrilled triumphantly. She turned to the Council. "See! She willfully brings a human into our realm."

"Actually," Noah said before I could. "I came here on my own."

The Warden stiffened, slowly turning her head to fix Noah with a cold stare. "I beg your pardon?"

My hold on Noah's fingers tightened as he stepped forward. He squeezed back. "I was in my own dream when I sensed that Dawn was in trouble. I don't know if she pulled me into her dream or if I walked into hers, but I found her fighting with a convicted rapist." He gestured to my face. "You can plainly see what he did to her."

Red-faced, Padera pointed behind us. "And we all can plainly see what she did to him."

I don't know why I bothered to look when I already

had a good idea of what was going on. Two large Nightmares practically carried Phil into the chambers between them. The rapist was pale and vacant and there was a dark, wet stain on the front of his pants. If you have a dream that you piss yourself, do you wake up wet?

It was a testament to how surreal this all was that I even asked such a question—even if it was only to myself.

Of course murmurs rose up from the crowd as Phil was brought through. I could feel the daggerlike gazes whipped in my direction. At this rate, they weren't going to bother hearing my side of it, they were just going to lynch me.

"It was self-defense," I blurted. It was very difficult to look at my father, but I did. He looked so sorry, so ashamed and pained. "My life was in danger."

"You expect the Council to believe that?" the Warden asked snidely. "You cannot die in this realm."

I turned to her, trying to keep my anger at bay. "But I can be raped, can't I?" I held her gaze, letting her know that I knew she had been behind the attack. She shifted a little, but did not look away.

"It's impossible," she insisted. "No human could come into *your* dream and harm you. Humans can't dreamwalk."

More murmurs. A few council members nodded in

agreement. I wanted to smash their stupid Q-Tip heads together.

"Therefore," my sister continued smugly, "you must have walked into his dream and attacked him."

I ground my teeth. "He came to me."

She just kept smiling.

"Dawn"—it was my father who spoke—"do you have any proof to support your theory?"

My *theory*? Even my own father didn't believe me? Fuck around.

Reaching into the pocket of my jeans I pulled out the broken medallion I had taken from Phil. I offered it to Morpheus. "He was wearing this."

The heavy wooden splinters fell into his open palm. I watched as his expression went from bewilderment to recognition to flushed anger. "Truly?" He raised his head to stare at me with eyes that were more pale and spidery than they had been a moment before. "You took this from him?"

I nodded, resisting the urge to back away from him. Hadria set her hand upon his arm, offering what I hoped was some kind of calm. "I thought you would know what it is."

"I do." His nostrils quivered as he took a deep breath. "I give these amulets to the people I care about. They're imbued with a part of my essence, a talisman against harm."

"This is ridiculous!" Padera broke in. She turned to the Council. "The amulet is probably her own."

"It's not," I replied. "But since you brought it up, where's yours, sis? You do have one, don't you?"

She flushed, but her fingers went to the neckline of her sleeveless blouse and pulled a thin chain free. Dangling from it was a wooden circle exactly like the one I'd destroyed.

Damn. I was really hoping she wouldn't have hers. I was sure she had been the one to supply Phil. She probably was, but she'd obviously gotten the amulet elsewhere.

I turned to Morpheus when I couldn't stand looking at Padera's arrogant face any longer. "How many are there?"

My father shrugged. "A dozen maybe."

"Have you ever given one to a human?"

He frowned, distracted. "Your mother has one. As do you."

"That's probably hers in your hand," Padera drawled.

I glared at her. Our father barely glanced at her, but his tone left no doubt as to how he felt. "Padera, if you cannot control yourself, you will leave these proceedings."

The Warden flushed bright crimson, but she didn't cower. "You cannot brush me aside as you could when

I was a child, my lord. As a Nightmare, your precious daughter is under my jurisdiction."

Morpheus stiffened. Long fingers closed around the broken medallion, going white at the knuckles as he squeezed. "And as my child and subject, you are under my jurisdiction. I may not be able to force you to leave, but I can fix it so you no longer have a mouth to speak with."

It was all I could do not to grin at Padera. Hell, it was all I could do not to scream "Neener-neener-neener" and point my finger at her. And oddly enough, I felt a little sorry for her. Her words had given away a huge glimpse into her emotional state, and now I saw her not only as someone who hated me, but someone who hated me because I'd had the love of a father whom she believed didn't love her.

Padera paled but she wisely held her tongue. I had no doubt that Morpheus would make good on his threat.

My father rose to his feet and turned to the Council. "We will take a break," he told them. "I need to find out how the human came to be in possession of my mark."

I glanced at Phil who was still out of it. "Can you fix him?" I asked. Much as I thought he deserved to rot, I felt a little bad about making him as fully functional as broccoli.

Morpheus shrugged. "It depends on the damage done."

Well, there you go.

The Warden wasn't happy about the recess, obviously, but she didn't say anything except, "What about the Princess?" And even those few words dripped with disdain.

My eyes narrowed. "Technically, aren't you a princess too?"

Bright red lips parted, no doubt to tear me a new one, but Morpheus spoke first: "Dawn will remain at the palace until we reconvene."

I will?

"What is to stop her from leaving?" A council member asked. "She is very powerful in this world, and no one can follow her into the human realm."

My father's expression set into harsh lines. I'd never seen him look like this. "If she leaves, she will be unmade as soon as she sets foot in this realm again."

My mouth fell open. Had he just said that he would willingly unmake me? Son of a bitch! I could go home, but the next time I fell asleep that was it. Fabulous.

"With an invitation like that, how can I refuse?" Snide? You bet I was snide. I was also freaked out. It had to be bad for Morpheus to put my life on the line like that.

"Mr. Clarke can stay with you."

With all that was going on I had almost forgotten that Noah was with me. I had definitely forgotten about

Verek, who made a grunt of disaproval. Noah moved closer. If he objected to my father's decision, he didn't let on. Were the situation reversed I would rather stay with him than return to the "real" world and worry.

Morpheus cast a quick glance over his shoulder at Verek. "Escort her to her room."

I started forward as he walked away, real fear gripping me for the first time. "Morpheus?" He didn't stop. My heart jumped into my throat. "Dad?"

That stopped him. He turned briefly, his face stricken by so many emotions I couldn't even begin to name them all. I ran to him and wrapped my arms around his waist, hugging him for all I was worth.

He hesitated, probably not wanting to show any weakness, but then he folded me into his embrace and rested his cheek on top of my head.

"If you gave Madrene an amulet," I whispered for his ears alone, "you might want to find out if she still has it."

I gave him another squeeze and then let go, stepping away and finally walking back to Verek and Noah.

"Let's go," I said, taking Noah's hand once more. "We're done here."

Verek only escorted Noah and me to the outside of the building, leaving me to take us back to the palace. My mother was waiting there for us. I don't know how she knew what happened, but I guessed that Morpheus had somehow managed to fill her in.

All I know is that her hug did more to make me feel better than any pill or cocktail could have. She offered us tea, or something a little stronger, but all I wanted was to be alone. With Noah.

I guess one positive thing to come out of this was that Mom seemed really taken with Noah.

My room at the palace had changed since the last time I was there. Instead of the furniture and décor of my youth, now the room was done in a more mature manner, with cream-colored walls, walnut furniture, and pale gold curtains and bedding. The bed itself was huge with a towering headboard that looked like something out of Elizabethan England.

I loved it.

"Room for two," Noah commented, sinking down onto the mattress. "You okay, Doc?"

"I don't know," I replied honestly as I walked over to the dresser where my old jewelry box sat—the only thing in the room that was as I remembered it. "I can't quite decide if I'm optimistic or losing it."

I heard him move, sensed him walking up behind me. I sighed when his arms came around my waist, pulling me against him. He felt so good. So solid and warm and strong.

My gaze fell on the jewelry box. It was small and

pink—exactly the kind of thing most little girls want. I touched the lid, pressed the latch and flipped it open. A little ballerina popped up and began to twirl around to a warbly tune.

Against the lining of pink satin lay several little gold rings, a single tiny ruby earring, a handful of delicate chains, and a round, wooden medallion of two crescent moons back to back.

"I found my amulet," I murmured, lifting it out of the box. It hung from a simple leather cord and looked about as special as an eight-year-old would string together.

"Your father seemed really freaked out by the one you gave him."

"He should be. It means someone he trusts is trying to hurt him."

"And you," he added softly.

"Mm. And me." It was that simple agreement that flicked the switch inside my head. I turned in Noah's arms and slipped the leather cord over his head. "There."

His forehead wrinkled. "What are you doing?"

"I'm giving you my medallion."

"I noticed. Why?"

"Because I need to know there's someone I can trust in the Dreaming. Someone who will come when I need them. Someone who can protect me when I need protecting."

His gaze warmed before dropping to the little circle against his T-shirt. "But I'll be able to do things a human shouldn't be able to do. Isn't that against the rules?"

I patted his cheek, beyond caring. "I think we've all learned that no one here plays by the rules. Not anymore. It'll be our secret. Besides, you can already do things most humans can't."

My smile faded when he looked at me again. "I missed you," I confessed. "I'm so sorry for everything."

He nodded. "Me too. I wasn't going to let you get away that easy."

"But you never returned my call."

Now he smiled—crookedly and self-mocking. "Wounded pride makes a man play hard to get."

I smoothed my hands over the solid wall of his chest. "What does a woman swallowing her pride make a man do?"

Apparently that got a woman kissed. Well and good. I sighed again, this time against his mouth, as all the tension rushed from my body. He was better than a glass of wine in a hot bath.

We moved to the bed still wrapped around each other, hands roaming over each other's bodies like we hadn't been together in months rather than just a few days. In my eagerness, I wished our clothes could simply be gone, and as we hit the mattress, they were.

Sometimes being non-human is so cool.

Noah's hands and mouth were everywhere. He turned my nipples into stiff, aching buds—just like in books. I had goose bumps all over as he slid lower, twirling his hot tongue around my belly button, and then between my thighs as his strong fingers held me open.

He made me writhe and twitch and arch in mindless pleasure. If it sounds like I'm bragging, it's because I am. No one had ever made me feel as sexy and sensual as Noah did. No one ever made me come as easily as he did. And when he was done with me and the spasms of orgasm had eased, I came up on my knees over him and returned the favor by taking the satiny length of him into my mouth. I went down on him like he was a fudge stick and it was a hot day in July.

His fingers tangled in my hair, holding my head as he flexed his hips. He groaned, whispering encouragement that consisted mostly of dirty words and suggestions that under most circumstances would have made me blush.

I released him before he could come, but he didn't complain. I kissed my way up the delicious length of his torso, rubbed my face over his chest before burying it in the crook of his neck to breath in the vanilla spice scent that was uniquely him. I couldn't get enough of the smell of him, the feel of him, the taste of him. With him, I believed that everything would work out. I believed in myself. That was almost scarier than anything the Warden could throw at me.

Straddling him, I took him inside and slid down until his hipbones pressed into the backs of my thighs. I felt stretched and full and oh-so good. Noah's fingers gripped my hips and I slid my hands down to clutch his biceps.

"Christ you feel good," he muttered.

I leaned down and kissed him. My hair fell around us, blocking out the lamplight so that everything was muted and shadowed.

"Thank you for being here with me," I whispered against his lips.

One of his hands slid up my back and tugged at a lock of my hair. "No place I'd rather be."

I believed him. He wouldn't rather be hovering over Amanda than be with me. Right now he wouldn't even rather be painting than be here with me—his crazy-assed, half-human girlfriend who always seemed to be landing in otherworldly shit.

At that moment I wanted to tell him I loved him, but I was too chicken. I was afraid that if I said it he wouldn't say it back. Not only would that ruin the mood, but probably also my life. I'd already been rejected by my father's people. I couldn't handle being rejected by my boyfriend as well.

So I pushed all that stuff aside and concentrated on

me and Noah and how our bodies fit together, how they moved together to create such intense feeling. It wasn't a difficult thing to do.

I churned my hips, pushing up and down, the motion pulling through the front of my thighs. I moved slowly, not wanting this moment to end, not wanting to let go of how he felt inside me. Maybe it was just my heightened emotions, but it felt as though we were one. We were connected in more ways than just physically.

Eventually our movements quickened. I braced my hands on the pillow beneath Noah's head, sweat dampening my hairline. Our breath was humid as it mingled in shallow pants. I don't know if half the things we said to each other made sense, but they sure sounded good.

Pressure built between my thighs, deep inside me. I ground myself against Noah, desperate for release. When it finally came—when I came—it was huge. My mind went numb, my body stiff. I cried out, and then Noah did too, his fingers digging into me hard enough to leave bruises as his hips arched against mine. I could feel the heat of him erupt inside me and then we collapsed together, still joined, me on top of his chest.

After a bit, I rolled to face him on my side. I kept my arms wrapped around him, knowing that eventually I'd have no choice but to let go.

"You know you'll wake up in your own bed," I murmured, twirling circles on his chest with my index finger.

The arm he'd slipped around my shoulders tightened. "I'll be back as soon as I can. I promise."

Having him there with me meant a lot. Oddly enough I didn't feel the least bit weak in admitting that I needed his support. I wanted his support. But that didn't stop a little insecurity—a little pettiness from slipping through. "What about Amanda? Don't you have to look after her?"

A strong finger under my chin forced my head up, making it impossible for me to avoid his shrewd, dark gaze. "I'll check in on Mandy, but you're my priority right now, Doc. You're my priority period."

God, that sounded good! I hugged him so he couldn't see the tears in my eyes and settled my head against his shoulder. "Thank you," I said, voice hoarse.

His reply was a gentle kiss on the forehead. And then we drifted off to sleep.

When I woke up he was gone and someone was knocking at my door. Still half asleep, I clutched the sheets to my naked chest and sat up. "What?"

The door opened. It was Verek. He took one look at me and the rumpled bed and his lips tightened. "Lord Morpheus wants to see you," he said flatly. "The Nightmare Council is resuming your trial. *Now.*"

Chapter Seventeen

Before leaving the palace, Morpheus allowed me a brief "escape" to wake up in the human realm and return to the Dreaming corporeally. I was stronger in a physical state, plus it cut back on the chances of Lola coming in and finding me asleep and being unable to wake me. I called Bonnie and had her reschedule today's appointments. Told her I was sick. It was close enough.

Morpheus, Verek, and Hadria were waiting for me just outside the palace when I returned. The men looked severe, the priestess serene. I don't even want to know how I appeared.

We took Hadria's carriage to the council building. I

guess no one trusted me to transport myself and Verek. Maybe they thought I'd kidnap the big Nightmare and use him to barter my freedom.

Because that was so my style.

Morpheus had to show some impartiality and I understood that. It was Hadria who sat beside me and held my hand, who gave me kind smiles and assured me that everything was going to be all right.

"Your mother isn't allowed to join us," my father said from his seat beside Verek. "But she wanted me to give you her love."

I smiled. "I know." I also knew that Morpheus was a little jealous of Hadria on my mother's behalf. He should be thankful the priestess seemed to like me as much as she did.

There weren't any spectators when we arrived at the council chambers. Other than Padera and the Council, the only other person in the room was Madrene. Morpheus obviously took my advice. Padera stood next to her mother, and for the first time I saw the resemblance, despite the difference in coloring. I also saw a slight similarity between the Warden and myself, and it made me a little sad knowing I had a sister who hated me so much.

I took a few moments to study the Council as well. There weren't many young-looking people on it. Padera was perhaps the most youthful, but I knew she was much, much older than me. But this was the body that governed the Nightmares, not the entire Nightmare population, although Verek had told me that their numbers had shrunk over the decades. It seemed Nightmares were often the target of assassination as they tried to protect this realm and the humans that came through it. I would think they would embrace me based on that alone rather than putting all this effort into deciding if I was a threat.

Hadria moved to the front of the room. "Now that we are all here, why don't we settle and begin? Dawn, you will sit here beside me?"

Sure. Following behind her I felt amazingly small and protected—like a kid. We all sat around a large octagon table with a battle scene carved into the stone top. Men and women with spears and swords fought a huge multiheaded monster that towered above them, blotting out the moon.

Once everyone was seated, Hadria turned to an elderly-looking man dressed in flowing blue robes. He was one of the Q-tips I'd noticed last night. His hair was a brilliant mass of white curls and his eyes were almost as pale—except for dark rims. "Gladios, would you begin the proceedings?"

He inclined his head toward her, slowly, like a turtle

drifting off to sleep. "Earlier, Princess Dawn offered evidence that the human she is accused of harming was encouraged to attack her by one of our own. She claimed that he was in possession of an amulet, which our lord Morpheus recognized as one of his creation. My lord, have you determined the original owner of the amulet?"

I turned my attention to my father, who sat almost opposite me across the table. "I have. The human's mind is still too confused to give any valuable information, but after studying the amulet, I discovered it is the same one I gave to Madrene before the birth of our daughter, Padera."

Well, it was probably just as well that my mother wasn't here. I had a feeling there were a lot of kids out there she didn't know about. After all, Morpheus had been around since the beginning of time. In fact, old Gladios there had something of a family resemblance . . .

Attention turned to Madrene. "Did you give the human the amulet, Madrene?"

Madrene looked worried. Hell, she looked scared, but she didn't look all that guilty. "No. I would never do such a thing."

Morpheus turned on her, gaze sharp. "Then how did he get it?"

The succubus shrunk from his anger. "I do not know.

The amulet went missing many years ago. I assumed it lost."

"Lost!" my father thundered. "I trusted you with a piece of myself and you disregarded it like garbage?"

Padera leaned over her mother, shielding the succubus. Her face was hard and angry, and I saw something of myself in her gaze. "She gave that stupid amulet more consideration than you ever gave us."

Ohh. Score a point for my crazy sister.

"That is not what we are discussing here," Gladios intoned brusquely, bringing everyone's attention back to the matter at hand—me. "Madrene, you should have reported the amulet missing."

The beautiful succubus hung her head in shame. I wanted to defend her, even though there was a good chance she was in league with the Warden. The very same Warden who turned her icy jade gaze on me.

"Where is your amulet, Princess?" she demanded haughtily. I noticed she was wearing hers again. Maybe she always did. That was a little sad.

I didn't blame her for drawing attention away from her mother. I would have done the same. I wasn't even angry that she turned her anger on me. Obviously I didn't have my amulet either. In fact, I'd never worn it. "I gave it to Noah."

Morpheus's head whirled around. "What?"

Padera grinned. "You are incredible. You accuse my

mother of giving her amulet to a human to harm you, which breaks a fundamental rule about interacting with humans and yet you do the same thing." She laughed. "I find your audacity amusing, sister."

I held her gaze without remorse. "Actually, there isn't really a rule about such a thing." And I could be confident here because both Verek and Hadria had been drilling rules into me during our sessions. There really weren't that many. "We're not to intentionally harm humans and we are not to reveal the secrets of this world to them, but I gave the amulet to a human who already knew about our world."

"Because you told him."

I shook my head. "Because a Night Terror attacked him several weeks ago and revealed this world to him. A Terror, I might add, who claimed to be part of a larger group intent on disposing Morpheus." I smiled tightly at her. "You wouldn't know anything about that group, would you, Padera?"

At that moment I was really glad looks couldn't kill. She didn't say anything, so I took that opportunity to address the Council: "Someone from this realm gave a similar amulet to a human in order to hurt me, so yes, I gave mine to Noah because I need all the friends I can get. With the exception of Hadria, Verek, and Madrene no one from this world has shown me the slightest amount of kindness or even courtesy." I shot a glance at Padera. "Not even my own sister. I've been treated like a monster for no other reason than the fact that I'm different. Where I come from, that makes the lot of you bullies. And I don't know if you're up on the concept, but no one likes a bully."

"Especially not you, Dawn." It was Padera who spoke. "We know what you did to the last person who bullied you."

I stared at her. I knew who she meant. "That was an accident."

She snorted and turned to address the Council. "Thirteen years ago a girl named Jackey Jenkins teased the Princess at school. That night Dawn went into the girl's dreams and tortured her for hours. Miss Jenkins has never recovered."

"It was a mistake," I insisted. "I didn't know what I was capable of doing. I never meant to hurt her that badly."

"What about Phil Durdan?" she asked sweetly. "Did you mean to hurt him?"

I glared at her, but I kept a firm grip on my control. "Not as much as you meant for him to hurt me."

Her gaze raked over me and obviously found me lacking. "Since you're not drooling and are able to form coherent sentences I'd say you weren't in half the danger as Mr. Durdan."

"Enough," Hadria's voice echoed through the chambers. I admit I jumped at the sheer volume and strength of it. Gone was the serene expression I was accustomed to, replaced by a fierce resolve that made me realize that she was *not* someone to mess with.

"This trial is about whether or not Dawn is a threat to this world now, not if she made mistakes as a child. Now, the evidence supports her claim that Phil Durdan was given that amulet by one of our own. Madrene says she has no idea how the amulet came to leave her possession. If that's true, then Dawn is not the only so-called threat this world may face."

Padera snorted. "Maybe Dawn gave the human the amulet herself. So she'd have an excuse to give one to her lover."

I rolled my eyes. "I suppose I asked him to beat the snot out of me and try to rape me as well?"

The Warden shrugged. "How do I know what lengths you'll go to in order to achieve your own goals?"

"That's more your style, not mine. Tell them about your visit to Noah."

Hadria turned her swirling gaze on my sister. "What is this?"

Padera refused to speak as she glared at me, so I replied for her: "The Warden threatened Noah as a message to me. How many rules does that break?"

Madrene turned to her daughter. "Padera, is that true?"

The Warden remained stubbornly silent.

Gladios shook his head. "I find this all very distressing, and this constant bickering gives my head an ache. Allow me to detail what is at stake here, so we all understand. Padera, your position as Warden is at stake if this accusation proves to be true. Dawn, if it is indeed a habit of yours to endanger humans and disregard the sanctity of this realm, you will be unmade and stripped of your remarkable abilities."

Hadria spoke before I could, "I do not think that would be wise."

Everyone stared at the priestess as she continued, "There is no way to know if Dawn can be unmade, let alone if the process will strip her of her abilities. An attempt to do so might have catastrophic effects on this world."

Padera scowled. "I don't believe it."

"Explain," Gladios encouraged. "Has this to do with the prophecy?"

Oh, not this again.

Hadria nodded. "I believe Dawn will be the savior of this realm. I do not believe that she has any intention of harming it. I've seen what she can do—amazing things. And I've seen her resist the allure of temptation and corruption. Even the Eve fruit couldn't sway her. In fact, I believe she will be all that stands between us and destruction."

Oh, good lord. No one but me and Padera seemed to think this a load of bull.

Gladios nodded sagely. "We will take that into consideration, Hadria. Madrene, your amulet allowed a human to do harm and be harmed in this world. It was your responsibility, which you obviously did not take seriously. Therefore, if it is decided that the human did come to this world with the intent to harm Dawn, then the punishment will be yours as well."

Padera squeezed her mother's hand.

"And now," continued the old Nightmare, "we will convene." He rose from his chair and the rest of the Council followed, their robes swirling as they left the room.

I looked at Padera. "How come you're not going with them?"

She flushed. "Because of my personal . . . relationship to you, it's been decided that I cannot be impartial and therefore do not get to vote on your fate."

"Well," I said caustically. "That sucks, doesn't it?"

She actually made a face at me, but I only smiled. At least one thing was in my favor.

We sat there for what felt like hours. In reality I think it was maybe half of one. I played with my fingernails and tried to respond to Hadria's optimistic small talk as we waited.

Finally the Nightmare Council returned.

"You've heard the arguments," Morpheus told the Council as he moved to stand beside me once more. I was flanked by him and Hadria—who held my cold hand in hers. My father placed his hands on the back of my chair. "Make your judgment. No, Padera, you don't get to speak again."

The Warden glared at me, as though Morpheus coming to my side meant he had completely turned on her, but she kept her mouth shut. I didn't even smirk at her. To be honest, I was too nervous to do anything but chew the inside of my lip and wait as Gladios came to stand at his place at the table. "We've made a decision."

And? It was all I could do not to kick it out of him.

"We have decided that Dawn Riley acted out of self-defense and without intent to do harm to this world. We will take no disciplinary action against her."

"What?" The Warden's shrill cry sliced my ears like shards of glass. "Are you all stupid?"

The council head held up a hand, his expression unchanging from its blankness. "However, we do find that Madrene must take responsibility for the loss of the King's amulet. Allowing such power to fall into the wrong hands is inexcusable. I'm going to recommend to the Matron that she be sentenced to imprisonment for one hundred years, in the Dark Lands."

Who the hell was the Matron? And what were the Dark Lands? It didn't seem anyone was going to explain, but it was obviously bad judging from the expression on Madrene's face—and Morpheus's as well.

"No!" Padera shouted, jumping to her feet. "You can't! You have no right—no jurisdiction over her as a succubus."

Gladios showed no emotion in the face of hers. "Which is why I intend to take my findings to the Matron. She will see that the sentence is handed out. As for you, Padera . . ."

"No." The Warden cut him off, shaking her head. "I will not allow you to punish my mother for something she didn't do! She did not give that amulet to the human."

"She did not respect it. She allowed it to be stolen and did not report it. That is crime enough." Gladios looked at Verek. "Please escort Madrene to the brothel."

Padera stepped between her mother and the big Nightmare. I knew from the look on her face that she'd kill Verek to protect her mother. And what about Antwoine? What was I going to tell him now that I'd gotten his lover arrested? He'd die without ever seeing her again, her imprisonment would last out the remainder of this lifetime and part of his next.

"You can't take her," Padera insisted. "I won't let you. I'm the one who stole the amulet. I gave it to the human." She looked right at me when she spoke. "I only wish he had done his job before you destroyed his mind."

Chapter Eighteen

Padera's confession put a halt to everything. The Council wanted to have a private conversation with Morpheus and Hadria about matters, and that meant that I was sent back to the palace. I have no idea where Madrene and Padera were taken, but I bet they had a lot to talk about. Madrene looked both enraged and devastated, and somehow managed to still look beautiful. She and my father would have made an incredible-looking couple.

That thought was still swimming around my head as Verek took me home. What had Madrene seen in Antwoine that made her give up a god? I suppose the same things I saw in Noah that made him so much more appealing to me than the beautiful hunk of man sitting beside me. Verek was lovely, but he wasn't Noah. And my father wasn't Antwoine. And for my mother, the man whom she married couldn't compare with the man of her dreams. We don't get to pick and choose who we love. That was something both humans and Dreamkin had in common.

Look at me being all philosophical. Easy to do when the Council's decided you don't have to be ripped apart and rebuilt into something new.

"I'm glad they sided in your favor," Verek said, not looking at me.

"Thanks. Hopefully they won't change their minds."

"I doubt it. You should increase your training—learn all you can about this world. It will keep them off your back."

"Hey," I said with a lift of my hands. "I'm trying."

He smiled. "I'll help you."

I snorted. I'd be better off with Antwoine for knowledge of the world, but Verek knew how to fight. "You just want an excuse to kick my ass."

"You know me so well."

We grinned at each other and I could sense the truce forming, the bridges rebuilding. Verek, for some reason known only to himself, wanted me. But he wasn't about to let that get in the way of us being friends. Or, maybe the big brute was so arrogant he assumed that if he was patient enough I'd eventually give in. I hope he didn't hold his breath.

Funny, but two months ago—not even that long—I would have never believed that a guy who looked like him would be into someone like me. Now, the fact that he was occurred to me as just another part of my life. Huh.

"I'll come for you when the Council reconvenes," Verek promised as he left me just inside the palace doors. The obsidian-skinned guards stood outside, their thick velvety wings tucked around them like living cloaks.

I felt safe with them out there protecting me, but I had no illusions that they were under orders to stop me should I try to leave. Of course, my father was probably the only person who could stop me from doing whatever I wanted. I wasn't going to test that theory, especially since it had already been decided that I could go ahead and escape—if I was willing to face being unmade once I entered the Dreaming again. There was no way to avoid that. Even when I made my own little dreamworld when I turned my back on what I was after Jackey Jenkins, I still came into the Dreaming, just like everyone else. It was one of those things—like death and taxes.

I gave Verek a hug and thanked him for everything. Once he was gone, I didn't feel like going to my room and obsessing over everything that might or might not happen. Instead I went to the library, where I was sure to find something to occupy my mind.

What I found was my mother, stretched out on one of the large sofas, a fuzzy purple blanket pulled up around her shoulders. Her eyes fluttered open when the door closed behind me.

"You okay?" I asked as I approached.

"Mm-hm." Groggily, she sat up, smoothing her mussed hair with her hand. Her pale peach pants and cream blouse were wrinkled—something I found oddly disturbing.

"I didn't know you slept in this world," I remarked. Obviously I did, but I was part of it. Mom was just another dreamer.

"Cat naps," she replied with a yawn. "I guess I'm getting old. I seem to need them more than I used to."

She was trying to make light, but I knew without asking that these "naps" had become more frequent once the doctor started work on her case back home. If Morpheus's hold on her broke . . . Man, I did not want to think about that. My father would lose it.

"How did things go with the Council. Did your father fix everything?"

God, what line of BS was he feeding her? This was so beyond his control. "They're taking a break," I replied honestly. "Padera jumped up and admitted that she gave Durdan the amulet that gave him power in this realm."

Mom's face hardened. She looked tired. Worse, she looked old. "Bitch. I'm surprised she confessed."

I don't think I'd ever heard my mother use such a harsh tone before. It surprised me. I guess I truly meant something to her after all. "Only because they were going to punish Madrene for it—it was her amulet."

The lines around her mouth deepened. "Ah." She ran her hands over her blouse, brushing away some of the wrinkles. "I think I'd like some tea. What about you? Shall I ring for some?"

She wasn't going to avoid the topic that easily. I concentrated on the coffee table before her, imagining her favorite tea set on top, loaded with a plate of sandwiches and another of scones, jam, and cream. The air shivered a little, then actually blurred before pulling back into focus once more. When it did, the tea service sat upon the table, the pot steaming. There was a cup, saucer, and small plate for each of us. Silverware as well.

Mom's jaw dropped as her eyes widened. She looked up at me from her seat on the sofa with a look of awe and maternal pride. "Dawnie! Look what you did!"

I almost expected her to start clapping for her little girl. It wasn't a big deal, but I puffed up with pride and beamed under her approval anyway.

I sat next to her on the sofa, fixed her a cup of tea the

way she liked it, and filled a plate for her before doing the same for myself. As I plunked a second scone on my plate beside the three sandwiches I'd already placed on the fine china, I leaned back and looked at Mom. "You didn't know, huh?"

She didn't bother to pretend ignorance. We were blood—she knew what I was talking about.

"I didn't want to know," she amended with just a touch of bitterness as she plopped a large dollop of clotted cream onto a jam-dripping scone. So this is where I got my emotional eating. "I knew he had been with Madrene, just like I know there have been others. I know there are other children as well."

Regardless, I wasn't about to mention my suspicions about Gladios. That was too weird. "So what's the issue?"

She scowled, suddenly a lot fiercer than I ever remember her being. "The difference is that his kid is bullying my little girl and he never saw fit to tell me that one little detail."

I smiled in sympathy. "He wasn't exactly open with either of us, but in his defense, it probably never occurred to him."

Mom snorted. "You give him more credit than I do. I love that man, Dawnie, but I know his flaws to the last, insignificant one. He was hoping we'd never find out."

You know, maybe I underestimated my mother. I'm

not saying I was ready to forgive her for everything—
like abandoning her family—but I was starting to like
her a whole lot more. "Did he apologize?"

Her face transformed with a sly smile. "He did. He
still is."

And then we both laughed, because, let's face it, he
deserved it. That's what being all high and godly will
get you.

We talked about the trial and about Noah. At least
Mom thought I was right in giving him the amulet. "I'll
feel so much better knowing he's around to help you in
this place."

I frowned. "You make it sound like you're going somewhere." I thought of our conversation when she asked
me to look after Morpheus if anything should happen to
her. "Is there something you need to tell me?"

She merely smiled—a little sadly I thought. "I worry
about you."

A little lump formed in my throat. Not enough to start
me bawling, but just enough to bring that damn, all-too-
familiar burn to my eyes. "I worry about you too."

I didn't stop her when she put her arm around my
shoulders. Our plates and cups were on the table, so
there was nothing to stop me from sliding closer to her.
She was so little compared to me, so delicate and fragile, and yet I'd never felt more protected in all my life as
I did that moment, in my mommy's embrace.

"I hate this, Mom," I whispered, knowing no one else would ever know of my confession. "How come no one ever seems to like me?"

I felt her smile as she stroked my hair. "They don't know you, babe." My throat tightened again. She hadn't called me that in years.

"They don't want to know me," I complained bitterly. "They just want to hate me."

"People here are no different than people anywhere. They hate what they don't understand. You just have to make them understand."

"Great," I replied caustically. "That shouldn't be difficult."

"No," she agreed with a soft chuckle. "Once you find your way, I don't think it will be difficult at all."

I fell silent, lost in my thoughts and anxieties—and trying to figure out when "finding my way" just might happen. I was tired, so frigging tired of all this drama.

"You know what you need?" Mom asked in that distinctly maternal tone that said *she* knew what I needed even if I didn't. "You need a nap. Everything will be better after you get a little sleep."

"I don't think I could sleep right now." Tired as I was, I was just too jittery.

"Nonsense," she replied, and much to the dismay of my fragile emotional state, she began to hum what we always used to call a "dee-dee-dee" song. A soothing melody, uttered low and sweet, made entirely of dees, das, and dos.

I was asleep before the second refrain.

Mom was right. A nap made everything better. When I woke up sometime later, I was on the sofa, but this time I was the one laid out with the soft, fluffy blanket pulled up to my chin. My mother sat in a large wing-back chair on the other side of the coffee table. Noah sat in its twin. They talked in hushed tones.

They didn't notice I was awake, so I took advantage of the time to watch Noah without him being aware. He chatted easily with my mother, the exotic lines and contours of his face open and without judgment. How did he see her? I resented that she left us, but did he see her as a woman who'd had the guts to leave a bad situation—who was anything but a victim? Even now, she fought to hold on to what she had.

When I looked at her that way, I didn't feel half so angry anymore.

And when I looked at Noah, I saw someone worth fighting for. I had given him that amulet not only because I trusted him to watch my back, but because it put us on a more equal footing in this world, and that's what I wanted for us to be—equals. I didn't know if it would work, but I was willing to try. I could only hope that he would find that more appealing than being a knight in shining armor, because I didn't want to be rescued all the time and I didn't want a guy who based his self-worth on whether or not he could save someone.

And I knew that Noah didn't want someone who kept things from him because she was afraid of how he would react. Because she was afraid he would finally see her for a freak and leave. And I'd be lying if I didn't say that I was still worried about that one. My issue, not his.

"You guys are talking about me, aren't you?" I yawned as I sat up.

"You know it," Noah replied with a lopsided grin that made my panties melt. "How you doing, Doc?"

I mussed my hair, scratched my head. "Okay. I'd like to go home."

His smile faded. "I'd like that too."

Our gazes locked, charging the air with all that was unsaid, but still communicated.

My mother cleared her throat and rose to her feet. "Well, if the two of you will excuse me, I have some things to do."

I'm pretty sure that wasn't true, but I appreciated her saying it all the same. "Thanks, Mom."

She ran a hand over my hair and said good-bye to Noah before leaving. The second the door clicked shut behind her I was on Noah's lap, my arms wrapped around his neck, showing him just how happy I was to see him with a kiss that shook me right down to my toes.

"How are you doing really?" he asked when we broke apart. His hands rubbed slow circles on my back.

I rested my head against his. "I want it over, but I'm scared of how it's going to end. Padera confessed to giving Durdan the amulet, but the Council isn't impressed that I gave mine to you."

"You told them?"

I shrugged. "They asked. It didn't occur to me to lie."

From the look on his face I knew that was exactly what Noah would have had me do. Not to protect him, but to protect myself.

"If I'd lied and they found out I'd be in even more trouble, Noah."

"I know. I just don't like being a part of it."

Sighing, I slid off his lap and stood. I didn't want to go through this again. "Well, since the Council knows that my sister threatened you, you are part of it all."

Noah's brows shot up. "Your *sister*?"

Oh hell. I winced. "Didn't I tell you?"

He made a sound that might have been laughter—or maybe a curse. "Any thing else you forgot to mention?"

I managed a half-assed grin. "I'll let you know if I remember anything else."

He shook his head, running a hand through his hair. "Jesus, Doc. Warren and I aren't even related and we'd never do anything like this to each other."

I shrugged my eyebrows. "Yeah, well Warren doesn't think you're the Anti-Christ."

He rubbed his jaw. "What's your father saying about all of this?"

"Not a helluva lot. To be honest, I haven't talked to him about it."

Frowning, Noah tilted his head. "He's on your side, isn't he?"

"Oh yeah. It can't be easy for him, though. Think about how conflicted and responsible he must be feeling."

This time the sound he made was unmistakably laughter. "Analyzing the God of Dreams. Yeah, you're okay."

I smiled sheepishly. I would have gone to him and hugged him again if Verek hadn't walked in at that exact moment.

"Excuse me," the big guy said, giving Noah a narrow look. "The Council has reconvened."

I exhaled a shaky breath. "Time to get this over with." I held out my hand. "C'mon, Noah."

Verek raised his brows but said nothing about me taking Noah with us. I suppose he knew there was no point in arguing. Noah was coming with me and that was that. Against the rules? I'm pretty sure there wasn't one about taking a human before the Council, since it technically "couldn't" be done. Also, Padera had threatened him, so he had a stake in this as well.

I "zapped" us to the council chambers, as Noah like to call it. It was quicker than taking the carriage, and quite frankly, I really just wanted this over with. Sometimes the wait to be punished is worse than the punishment itself.

Everyone was already around the table when we walked in. None of them looked particularly surprised that I had Noah with me again. Padera didn't even give me a haughty smirk. In fact, she looked fairly subdued sitting next to her mother, whose beautiful face was strained and drawn.

I looked at Hadria, who gave me that familiar but strangely comforting serene smile. Then to my father, who looked like I felt. I couldn't tell from his expression if he was hopeful or not.

Gladios rose from his seat. He wasn't very tall—maybe five foot ten or so, but he had wide shoulders and a presence that made him seem much larger.

"Mr. Clarke. You will hand over the amulet Princess Dawn gave you."

Noah shook his head. "No."

Okay, so this wasn't entirely unexpected, nor was I all that surprised by Noah's refusal, but it all made me anxious anyway.

"This is not up for discussion, young man."

Noah gave Gladios a wry grin. "You're right. I'm not giving you what was a gift to me. I've already been attacked and almost killed by one of your kind. And threatened by your Warden. Next time I'm going to be better able to defend myself."

"You expect there will be a 'next time'?" Gladios demanded haughtily.

Noah's grin widened as he nodded his head toward me. "I'm dating public enemy number one. Yeah, I expect there to be a next time."

Despite the pessimism behind the remark, I grinned too. Because Noah was sticking with me, no matter what. And damn it, I was going to stick with him.

"Leave him, Gladios," Morpheus said in a voice that was as dark as the shadows on the wall behind him. He rubbed his eyes with his thumb and index finger. "My enemies don't care about the rules; Noah should be able to defend himself, and my daughter."

"With all due respect, Lord Morpheus," the elder Nightmare remarked. "I do not believe there is much the Princess needs defending from."

My father's pale gaze went from me to Padera. "Except perhaps her own kin."

Padera didn't flinch. "But will you give this domain leave to protect itself against her?"

With a bored expression Morpheus turned back to the Council. "If you have made your judgment let us have it. I'm weary of this drama."

Gladios nodded in acquiescence. "Although the Council does not approve of her methods or behavior, we cannot find Princess Dawn guilty of any willful wrongdoing. Given Padera's confession, we find that Dawn acted in self-defense, and all prior offenses were committed out of ignorance or genuine concern for humans."

Oh, thank God. I sagged against Noah. He supported me with a strong arm around my waist.

"As for the Warden, Padera's actions were a blatant abuse of power with intent to harm, not only to influence dreamers but to harm a member of the royal family as well. We find her guilty of Treason. She will be stripped her of her position as Warden. We leave any other punishment for her crimes in the hands of Lord Morpheus."

My eyes widened. Damn. That was throwing her to the lions, wasn't it? I looked at my father. I half expected him to look pleased, but he was anything but.

"What do you think should happen to her, Dawn?" he asked.

Oh sure, leave it to me rather than take responsibility

for your own rotten kid, I thought. There were all kinds of horrible things I could do to her, all kinds of punishment I thought she deserved, but in the end I wasn't that vengeful. Not really.

"I think stripping her of her power is sufficient." Knowing how arrogant she was of her power, that seemed fitting. "Maybe she should have some solitary confinement so she can think about what she's risked and lost."

Morpheus smiled proudly at me. Obviously he thought I'd made a strong but generous judgment. His daughter would be punished, but not permanently harmed. "A fair judgment."

I turned my gaze to my sister. "But if she ever threatens me or anyone I care about again, I want her unmade." I turned that gaze to Morpheus. "Agreed?"

He looked a little surprised—maybe that I would think of such a thing, but I wasn't dicking around, not when it came to the people I cared about. "Agreed."

Padera practically snarled at me—and at Morpheus. "It doesn't matter what you do. Another will take my place. You will fall, my lord." She glared at me. "And you, you abomination, you will be destroyed."

Her words put a chill in my chest. This wasn't over, then? I turned to my father with an expression that no doubt bordered on psychotic panic. "What the hell is she talking about?"

Morpheus was grim. "Unless the current Warden is challenged for the title, a new Warden will be appointed from the appropriate candidates."

I glanced at him. "And there's a fifty-fifty chance that whoever is appointed will be an enemy of yours?"

He turned his face to mine. "Judging from her expression, and recent events, I'd say the odds are better than that. She wouldn't have risked her position if there wasn't another already set to take her place."

I swallowed. Great. Then, with a sense of finality that really, really ticked me off, I stepped forward, glaring at the woman who'd tried to end my life. "I challenge you for the position of Warden."

That's when she lost it.

Chapter Nineteen

Padera came at me like a lioness pouncing on a dumb-struck lamb. I truly wasn't prepared, though I should have been given our history and my not-so-subtle challenge.

What else could I do? It was the only way I could think of to protect my father, Noah, myself, and everyone else I care about. Verek hadn't offered to do it, so I had to.

Speaking of Verek, he and Noah were the ones who caught Padera and stopped her from taking my face off. I was surprised Noah was able to hold her—he must be more powerful in this world than we originally thought. Surprise, surprise. And I must have been in a thin state of shock to continue standing there like nothing had even happened.

"Do you accept my challenge?" I asked the redhead struggling against the strong arms that held her from either side.

Pale eyes glittered like shards of glass. "I accept."

"She cannot challenge for the position of Warden!" A council member I didn't know shouted as he leaped to his feet. "She's not one of us!"

Wrong thing to say. My father's face was impassive, but I knew he'd be watching this man from now on, and Ama would help him if Morpheus found him lacking. "She is of my blood. That makes her Dreamkin. And there is nothing written that states who can and cannot challenge for the position."

Sour-faced, the man reluctantly resumed his seat.

I turned to Morpheus. "How do we do this?"

"It's a physical and mental contest," my father explained. "Whoever proves themselves superior in strength, speed, stamina and, above all, sheer power, will be the victor." To be honest, he looked a little dubious. I guess his other daughter was pretty kick-ass. Great.

OK, so I could fight physically. I knew I had some degree of power. What this contest meant was letting what I referred to as "Dark Dawn" out to do her worst. That was what was going to be hard—giving over my control to sheer instinct. I didn't have a choice. Either I won, or the next person who took the position picked up where Padera left off.

Noah walked up to me. He looked worried. He looked a little angry too. "I don't suppose you have any idea what you're doing?"

I shook my head with a faint smile. "None whatsoever."

He watched me for what felt like forever, dark gaze searching my face. I'm not sure what he saw there, but I think it might have been fear with a healthy dose of determination. And I think he realized that I was going to do this—no matter what.

"She's a dirty fighter," he said in a low tone, taking one of my hands in his and massaging it. "Watch her legs. She'll be fast, but unsteady. Use her anger against her to throw her off balance. Get her feet out from under her and you'll dominate her physically."

I smiled just a little. "You like talking dirty like that?"

He chuckled briefly, more like a breath of laughter, but it was there all the same. Then his humor vanished. "Don't hesitate, Doc. Take every advantage. She's going to fuck you up if she can."

I saw how serious he was—how worried. Throat tight, I nodded. "I will."

Verek approached us. Apparently someone else had guardianship of the Warden now. "It's time," he said. His light gaze met mine, piercing and intense. "Good luck, Princess."

Noah watched the big Nightmare as he walked away. "So that's my competition, huh? Am I going to have to fight him when this is over?"

I think he was joking, but it was hard to tell. "No. There's no contest."

He smiled at me, his obvious relief like a punch to the chest. Then he hugged me and kissed me on the forehead. "Protect yourself."

"I will." God, I hoped I could.

No one seemed to care that Noah was going to stay for the event. I guess having a human in their midst was the least of the Council's concerns right now.

While I'd been talking to Noah, my father had turned part of the room into stadiumlike structure. There was a large mat in the center where Padera and I would square off—and seats off to the side for those watching.

There were more people than I remembered as well. The Nightmare guild was in attendance. There weren't many of them as Verek had said. But more than Nightmares were there—it looked like a good two hundred Dreamkin were in attendance as well. Who the hell were they?

And there was my mother, sitting next to Morpheus on the sidelines. Fabulous. Like I didn't have enough pressure on me.

"The opponents will come to the center of the circle," Gladios intoned, in a voice that filled the room.

Noah gave me another hug and kiss before taking a seat on the stands beside my parents.

Padera had changed her clothes. She wore loose pants and a tunic suited for fighting. I willed my own clothing to change as well—into a pair of calf-length sweatpants, flats and a T-shirt. My hair was up in a clip—no ponytail for the bitch to grab.

We faced off, both braced and tensed for action. When the council head boomed, "Begin" I almost jumped right out of my skin.

Noah was right. The Warden was fast, but her rage messed with her control. She also used her legs a lot. I figured that one out the second her foot connected with my skull and knocked me onto my back on the mat.

Stars danced before my eyes. And then a sharp pain tore through my side. She'd kicked me. Kicked me while I was down!

"*Get up,*" a voice in my head insisted. "*Get up and kick her ass.*"

It was easier said than done, but I managed to roll to my feet and avoid another kick at the same time. The next time I saw her foot flying at me, I grabbed it and the leg it was attached to. I twisted it hard and kicked her other one out from underneath her, throwing her away from me as she fell.

Noah shouted out in encouragement. His voice filled me, mixing with the adrenaline coursing through my veins. I bounced on the balls of my feet, stretching my neck like I'd seen boxers do in the ring. I felt confident. Hell, I felt cocky.

Big mistake.

Padera was back on her feet and snarling like a pissed-off tiger. She ran at me and I leaped to meet her halfway. We grappled, clutching at each other's arms. She pivoted her upper body and I had a second of disbelief as my feet left the mat. The next thing I knew I was sailing through the air, the wall on the far side of the room coming fast to meet me.

I hit the wall hard. I think I heard it splinter under the impact, but that might have been my teeth knocking together. I fell to the ground in a great breathless, agonized heap.

That shouldn't have happened. You should have reacted better.

The voice was right. The Nightmare part of me that I had buried for so long knew what to do—it was in my blood the same as knowing how to breathe. I just had to let it take over. It shouldn't be too hard—I'd let that part of me out during the fight with Karatos. I could do it now.

I rose to my feet, refusing to stagger. When I raised my head I saw the Warden coming at me with lightning speed. She was smiling. It was the smile that ignited that familiar burning in my eyes, the fire in my soul.

She stopped smiling when I picked her up and tossed her like I had tossed Verek before. Watching her hit the wall above the spectators gave me something to grin about. I cast a glance at Noah and saw him watching me in astonishment. Did I scare him? My confidence wavered, and then he grinned, and sweet relief washed over me.

"Dawn!" It was my mother who cried out. I turned my head in time to see Padera launching a new attack. This time she had a sword. I recognized it as a Morae blade, the weapon of all Nightmares.

I managed to duck, dodging the razor-sharp blade as it swung at my head. I couldn't die here, but I didn't want to test the theory of whether or not I could be decapitated. Pain was pain, no matter the outcome. Plus, if she took my head, I was pretty sure that would count as a win for her.

I rolled to my feet—me, the kid who could never do a summersault in gym class, tucked and rolled in one perfect, graceful movement. When I jumped to my feet,

I had my own blade in my hand, having summoned it without being aware. Usually it took the form of a dagger, but since my opponent had a sword, I made mine a sword as well.

When the blades met it was like that scene out of the first Highlander movie when Chris Lambert and Clancy Brown are fighting on top of the sign. Sparks flew. Metal screeched against metal and I felt the reverberation all the way up my arms. It must have made the Warden's arms feel like noodles.

Or maybe not. She whipped that sword around and sliced my cheek with a swiftness that dropped my jaw.

"First blood goes to the defender," the council head boomed.

First blood? That insinuated that there was more blood to come, didn't it? OK, so this didn't count as a win for her. I could still do this. I could still win, but I had to get a grip on myself.

When she came at me again, grinning like a maniac, my first reaction was to keep my blade up in deflection, but my arms wanted to do something. I listened to my arms, bringing the sword down in a wide arc and twisted my body in a swirling turn so that the tip of my blade severed her Achilles tendon. Padera stumbled, but didn't fall. Her cry of pain echoed throughout the room. I shouldn't have felt so self-satisfied, but I did.

"Second blood goes to the challenger," I taunted as she limped around for another go. Her blood pooled onto the floor just as mine ran down my cheek and neck, soaking my shirt. This might not be a battle to the actual death, but it sure as hell felt like it.

She stopped and faced me, sweaty and flushed. "Let's try this another way, shall we?"

What now? Like a dolt, I stood there and watched as she held her hands out to her sides and begin to chant in a low voice. Behind me I heard Verek shout, but I couldn't make out what he said above the noise of the crowd and my heart pounding in my ears. Shit, what now?

By the time I figured it out, it was too late. As my heart leaped into my throat I knew that Padera was going to kick my ass well and good.

She had summoned the mist. I should have known. She'd used it against me before, and being the kind to always exploit a weakness, she'd brought it back for a second go at me.

My sister actually smiled at me as the undulating wisps of fog wove around her like little puppies wanting attention. To me, they were piranhas circling, waiting for blood.

What the hell was I going to do? As the mist slowly moved toward me, my mind went blank. I didn't know what to do. It was going to bite and claw and rip me apart and no one would stop it. Oh, I'd heal at the end, but the damage would be done.

I stood still as the first tendrils brushed against me, closing my eyes against the fear that rose up in my chest, flushing my cheeks and making my head swim. Just kill me and get it over with.

Padera was still talking. What was she saying? Urging it on, commanding it to do its worse. I should have told Morpheus to fry her ass. I don't care if she's blood—she's a fucking psycho.

A sharp sting on my wrist made me flinch. Third blood goes to the mist. Fourth and fifth as well—on my ankle and the side of my neck. Blood trickled from the wounds, and I imagined the mist's aggression mounting, like sharks moving in for the kill.

In my head Verek's voice rang out. *"You have to command it to respect you."*

Okay, there are ways to conquer fear, and the first is to face that which you are afraid of. I opened my eyes and forced myself to look into the mist.

And gasped as wispy claws raked my back. At this rate the venom would get me before anything else did.

I concentrated on my breathing, trying to ignore the sweat pouring down my face and neck. The wounds stung and burned, and fever was already heating my blood. I had to act fast, and that was so not my strong suit. I was impulsive, yes, but for the most part I thought too much, and that was my problem now.

Clearing your mind is a lot harder than it sounds, especially on demand, but I really didn't have much of a choice. Right now I had to let go of everything that I thought and let instinct take over—and not the instinct that told me to slice at it. That was my human instinct. I had to reach deep down inside and let that part of me that I thought of as dark take over. In this world, she knew what she was doing. I just hoped I could control her once I let her out.

I didn't have to dig far. I think she was waiting. I was so going to have to get into some Dissociative Identity Disorder therapy when this was over.

Another bite to the back of the knee, scratches to the face. I stumbled as the mist wrapped itself around me and squeezed. All the while, the multitude of voices within hissed and cursed at me.

I was on my hands and knees, panting for breath when I felt heat explode behind my eyes. At first I thought my retinas had exploded from the poison. Then I realized that I could see better, sharper. I could make out shapes in the mist—faces both monstrous and sweet, hands and mouths, eyes and ears. Creepy. Some of these shapes were humanoid and some weren't. There was a little bit of everything in the mist.

Wait. Hadn't Hadria said that there was a little bit of everything in me? That's when it hit me.

I didn't have to fight the mist. I didn't have to defend against it. All I had to do was become it. The mist thought I didn't belong. I had to make it see that I did. God, it was so simple! Why hadn't I thought of it before? That time at Hadria's I had reached out to it—and absorbed part of it. That's why it had left—why it stopped hurting me.

Suddenly it wasn't so hard to concentrate. The part of me rooted in this world had no problem with such things. She grabbed on to the idea and held on for dear life, pushing and pulling the fabric of the Dreaming—of me—until I was no longer whole. I was no longer me. I was mist—light and insubstantial, yet sharp as razor wire and strong as steel. Stronger.

The rest of the mist sparkled with confusion. I could hear the voices inside me, and I added my own to it. "I don't want to harm you," I whispered. "I'm not a threat to you or this world."

I entwined myself with other tendrils as I spoke, rubbing against them as I had witnessed them behave with Verek and Padera. I felt like part of something—something so special and strange I couldn't help but laugh with glee. How could I have hated this incredible, powerful being—these *beings*?

Thin strands like smoke began to curl around me as

well, dancing and weaving through me as well. And the voices that had once been so cutting and harsh were now soft and welcoming. The mist understood what I was. And for the first time, I think I did too.

I was the Dreaming.

When I came back into my own form, my wounds were healed as though they'd never existed. How long had I been gone? I stood in the center of that arena floor with the mist banked around my feet, climbing around me like the scent of sunshine or baking bread.

Now I smiled at Padera. "That all you got?" I asked, oh-so arrogantly. I urged the mist away. Now that I understood, I didn't want it getting between us. I didn't want it to get hurt. It only wanted to love and save this world. And now, it only wanted to love and save me.

The Warden's face was pale, but severe, as she raised her sword. Obviously, that wasn't all she had.

"Watch your boyfriend," she muttered. "He knows he has power, and he's not above using you to reach his full potential."

She was trying to throw me off, I knew that. She almost succeeded. "Shut up."

She shrugged. Her blade never wavered—so much for thinking her skinny little arms were weak. "Believe what you will. You probably believe our father would never turn his back on you either."

I gritted my teeth. "I know he wouldn't."

She smiled, but it wasn't taunting, it was pitying. "I *knew* that once too." Her gaze locked with mine. "You have no idea what he is. No idea what a monster you truly are."

Right there things got a little fuzzy. I remember her going into an immediate and quick offense, striking while I was still stunned by her verbal blows. The burning in my eyes and stomach spread to each arm and leg, every finger and toe. I felt as though my hair was made of flames. A searing pain tore through my shoulder and I roared in response. All that fire that had rushed out, came pouring back into my center. My arms came up. My blade, weightless yet impossibly heavy, moved like it was an extension of my body. I pivoted and whirled, turned and feinted, all the while slashing wildly with my sword. I shoved it downward, holding it parallel to my body so that the tip pointed at my toes. It sliced like a hot knife through butter.

I heard a gasp—and Noah yelled my name.

I blinked, bringing the room back into focus as my chest heaved and my lungs greedily sucked air. Everyone was staring at me. Some—like my father—looked triumphant. Others, like Noah and my mother, looked slightly shocked. There were others who glared at me with blatant hatred.

A gurgling sound at my feet drew my gaze down. On the mat, Padera lie pinned like a butterfly, my sword sticking out of the middle of her chest, leaking bubbles of blood as she tried to breathe.

"Oh shit!" I pulled the sword out of her and tossed it aside as I fell to my knees beside my sister. I pressed my hands over the flooding wound in her chest. I wasn't a killer. I wasn't. I knew she couldn't die, but I had hurt her, badly. Seeing her suffer made the base of my skull prickle with pins and needles, filled me with a hot chill that made me think I really was a monster after all.

I tried to fix her, but I couldn't think straight. I hovered on the brink of hysteria.

Suddenly, Morpheus was there beside me, pushing aside my bloody hands. He placed his palm over Padera's wound and I watched as the blood flow stopped, as her expression eased from pain and terror to discomfort and awareness. She looked at me and blinked. She didn't look so mean anymore. She didn't look cold or pinched or scary.

She looked young and bewildered. She looked like my sister.

I managed to lurch a few feet away from her before I threw up. Amazingly, a large bowl had appeared in front of me at the exact moment my stomach emptied itself. How convenient.

"Doc!" I heard Noah's voice, lifted my head to search for him. I saw him jumping off the stands and running toward me. One of the Nightmares tried to stop him only to be stopped by a wall that appeared between them.

Noah had power. Real power. Was it because of the amulet or was it his own? And what kind of trouble was that going to get me into?

Noah rushed to kneel beside me. "Doc, are you all right? Say something."

I nodded, my hands stiff and clumsy as they closed around his arms. He'd have bloody prints on his sleeves. "I'm okay. Noah, I'm okay." As long as you didn't count the shaking in my limbs, the pain in my shoulder where I'd been cut, and the strange burning feeling on the back of my neck that I couldn't explain.

He crushed me to his chest, his hands running over my back. I was sore from the fight, but I wasn't about to tell him to stop. Slowly, the heat from his body filled mine and I began to feel a little like myself again.

I think I'd lost some of myself as well.

Morpheus knelt down. "Noah, I need to tend to Dawn's injuries."

He didn't want to let me go anymore than I wanted him to, but Noah reluctantly drew back so my father could close the shallow cut on my cheek and the much deeper gash in my left shoulder. I made the mistake of looking at it as he worked and almost puked again. Was that bone?

Not only did he heal me, but he took away the pain

as well. Except for the tingling on the back of my neck. Jesus, what was that?

"What did you do to her?" I asked. "She changed. Did you unmake her?"

"More like I reset her," he replied. I'd never noticed the lines around his eyes as much as I did right then. He hadn't been able to bring himself to destroy his daughter, even if he could remake her in another image, because doing so would mean taking away everything she was, or ever had been, and obviously he still had a lot of love for those parts of her.

"I hope you don't expect me to invite her for a slumber party or anything," I remarked drily as he helped me to my feet. "It's going to be a long frigging time before I can look at her and not think of all she did to me." I tried not to lean on him. I didn't want to need him. Didn't want to put myself in his hands at that moment, but I didn't have a choice.

He nodded. "Me too."

But he had saved her regardless. Hmm. Maybe he was father material after all.

My mother rushed up to me, engulfing me in her slender arms despite her pristine clothing and my bloody, sweaty state. "I knew you'd protect him," she whispered tearfully before kissing my cheek. "I feel so much better knowing you can protect yourself as well."

I frowned, but before I could say anything, she pulled

away, gifted me with a tearful smile, and then walked away to keep Noah company while my father and I talked.

I glanced over at Padera. "Are you still going to confine her?"

"For a while, yes."

I looked at him closely. "You're going to help her, aren't you?"

He nodded. "I am. I'm sorry if that hurts you."

Oddly enough it didn't. "She's your responsibility. You should help her."

Morpheus smiled. "You always were too bossy for your own good."

That made me smile. "Morpheus . . . Dad . . ." I didn't get a chance to say anything else because he cut me off with a fierce hug that robbed me of breath let alone speech. I guess we really didn't need to say anything else anyway.

When he finally released me and I could breathe, I said, "Can I talk to her for a moment?"

His brow puckered, but he nodded. "For a moment."

Noah shot me a quizzical glance when I didn't come to him, but I held up a finger for him to wait for me. I'd explain later.

My sister sat alone. Not even those who had served under her as Nightmares moved to assist her. Only a few of my father's guards stood near her, ready to take her away when Morpheus gave the command. Her injuries had been healed as well, but I suspected her chest still felt like a horse had kicked it, and probably would for a while.

I knelt in front of her. "Do you know our other siblings?"

Her eyes were wary as she raised her gaze to mine, but there was no longer the hate that had been there before. It really was like our father had hit her reset button. "Yes."

"How many are there?"

She laughed—a genuine laugh. "Fifty. That I know of."

Fifty? Shit. I guess that wasn't so bad for a guy who'd been around forever.

I wanted to know my siblings in this world as well as I knew them in the human realm. Family was good to have close—whether you let them guard your back or to remind you not to turn it on them.

"Someday, when I ask you to," I began, "will you take me to them?"

I couldn't read her expression as she regarded me carefully. She didn't trust me, I imagine—no more than I trusted her. But we were sisters, and blood counted for something.

"I will," she said just as the guards helped her to her feet. I guess Morpheus had decided we'd talked long enough.

I rose as well and watched them take her away. Our gazes never looked away from each other until she was gone from the room. That's when I went to Noah and gratefully melted into his arms.

"It has been settled." Once again Gladios's huge voice filled the room. "Dawn Riley is the new Warden of the Nightmares."

There were some cheers, a few polite applauses, and some glares. I faced them all with a neutral expression with Noah by my side. I was Warden and I had no idea what that was. I had power though I didn't know its full extent. I had people who would look to me to lead them.

And I had enemies. How long would it be before someone challenged me for the title? I had to learn and learn fast if I was going to hang on to the position, if I was going to use it to help my father keep his throne.

"Praise Ama," came a voice from behind me.

I turned just as Hadria swept down upon me, took me by the shoulders—easily dislodging me from Noah's hold—and turned me around. That's when she gasped.

"What?" I demanded, thinking some kind of parasite had burrowed into my flesh and that was why the spot burned like it did.

Turning me around again, the huge priestess cupped my face in her long hands and kissed both my cheeks. "Congratulations, Dawn. You have received your mark."

Chapter Twenty

So now I'm the Warden.

What does that mean exactly? Well, I'm not quite sure. I know that it means a lot of responsibility and power—yee-haw. And I know that there are people not exactly thrilled with the regime change. I've met with the Council and the Nightmare guild itself, and Verek's been assigned to help me ease into the position. Noah's not too crazy about that, as you can imagine. I kinda like him being jealous. It's nice it not being me for a change.

I'm having a meeting with the Council tomorrow night to discuss the particulars now that things have calmed down, and by the end of the month I'll make my official debut. I hope I know what I'm doing by then.

You'd think the change in status would have made my life even more crazy, but in truth, things calmed down a lot after the fight with Padera—who Morpheus says is doing well. I wouldn't know. I haven't seen her, and I didn't intend to, not for a while. She and my fifty other siblings could wait for the time being.

Right now I was enjoying the downtime. Soon enough I expected to encounter some of those who publicly hated my father, and in turn me, and then things would get ugly again. That was just how things were going to be for me, the strange little half-breed.

That was why I resolved to take advantage of the quiet. The exception to this was the visit Noah and I made to Antwoine and Madrene in Antwoine's garden. I had promised Noah I'd help him figure out what he was capable of, and I meant it—we just had to do it in his dreams. Under the radar. Madrene and Antwoine were the picture of bliss, though it was weird seeing him as she saw him—as he was in his own mind, young and vital once more. Still, I was glad to see him so happy.

As for my mother and father, things seemed pretty status quo. Morpheus was proud as hell that I was the new Warden, but if he thought I was going to do everything he wanted, he was going to be very disappointed. Mom was pleased as well, and hadn't made any other remarks about me being able to look after myself or Morpheus.

Oh, and that mark I'd suddenly developed? Hadria thinks it happened after I melded with the mist—not when I pinned my sister to the floor like a tail on a paper donkey. That's good. I'd like not to think that I'd come into my power or destiny or whatever after doing something so violent. Anyway, from what I could tell, the mark looked similar to the OM symbol, without the squiggling bits coming out—sort of like a stylized 3. Hadria says it represents the waking state, the dreaming state and the connection between the two.

She's very excited because basically she thinks it means that I am the key to dealing with the thinning of the veil between the human world and the Dreaming. She thinks I'll be able to protect both worlds from each other and eventually lead to rebuilding the separation between the dimensions, or lead to the assimilation of the two.

I'm thinking either way it sounds like a lot of work. And I'm hoping that it's just a symbol of my birth, or maybe my lucky number.

Thanksgiving rolled around a couple of weeks after my ascension to Warden. Noah and I were invited to Amanda's apartment for dinner, along with the rest of Noah's family and Amanda's as well.

Warren answered the door. Dressed in khaki trousers and a white shirt, he looked like he just stepped off the pages of *GQ*. Of course, he couldn't hold a candle to Noah, but I'm biased. He grinned when he saw it was us.

"Hey, guys. You're early."

"Dawn hates to be late," Noah drawled as we stepped inside. He wore black pants, a white shirt and black leather jacket. Very sexy. Things had been good with us since the big showdown, but I hadn't forgotten what Padera said. I trusted her as much as I'd trust a rat. God knew. I trusted Noah infinitely more, but that didn't mean he didn't have his own agenda. It didn't make that wrong either. I didn't spend much time brooding over it. I'd find out in time.

Noah handed his stepbrother the two bottles of wine we'd brought. "Smells good in here."

It did too—like savory and stuffing and moist turkey. My mouth watered in anticipation.

"I did an amazing job with the turkey," Warren replied without a hint of modesty. "Wait till you taste my gravy."

Noah's smile tipped to one side. "That just sounds wrong."

I took the wine from Warren and left the two of them to trade barbs while I went into the kitchen to see if I could help Amanda. She was standing over a huge pot, mashing the contents as she poured cream over them.

A stick of real butter sat on a paper wrapper on the counter beside her. My stomach growled in delight. I didn't care if I gained forty pounds, I was eating whatever I wanted today.

"Can I help?" I asked.

She jumped at the sound of my voice. "Good lord, Dawn! You walk like a cat."

Amanda looked great. She'd started to gain a little weight and her face was softer. Most of the bruises and swelling were completely gone now, and except for the odd time she shied away from a touch, or the times she seemed to drift off with a haunted look on her face, you'd never know she'd survived the horror she had. Her hair was growing back and she'd discovered all kinds of styles and accessories to hide the stubble.

First time anyone's ever told me that. "Sorry," I said sheepishly. "I thought you heard me. Is there anything you need a hand with?"

She gestured to another pot on the stove. "You can drain the veggies and spoon some butter in there with them if you don't mind."

"I can do that." I took the pot to the sink, leaning back from the steam as I emptied the water from it around the cover I held at an angle. "How are you doing?"

The masher rested against the side of the pot as she turned her gaze to mine. "Good," she replied with equal amounts certainty and wonder. "Really good. Is that weird?"

I smiled. "Not at all." In fact, it was lovely to hear. Amanda and I had begun therapy again almost immediately after Durdan (still confused but no longer drooling) was locked up; and I'd been doing things the old-fashioned way this time, rather than messing around in her head. I let her talk things out and work them out on her own. I needed to find a balance between what I did in dreams and in the waking world, especially now with everyone in the Dreaming watching my every move.

"How are *you*?" she asked. This time, her gaze was fixed on the potatoes she was mashing the crap out of.

I had to think about that. Did I wake up on occasion sweating? Did the image of Phil's face sometimes pop unbidden into my head? Yes. Did it affect my life? Not really. He would fade, just like Karatos was fading—just like everything that didn't kill me eventually would.

Right now I was having a harder time dealing with how I felt about Padera. She had tried to kill me, but she was my sister. Talk about conflict.

"I'm OK," I replied as I sliced off a generous pat of butter and dropped it into the vegetables. "I'm just glad it's over."

Amanda nodded with a slight smile. "Why don't you pour us each a glass of wine?"

The wineglasses were on the counter, so I took two of the delicate peach designs and poured a generous amount of the German white Noah and I had brought into each.

"So," I began as we leaned with our backs against the counter, "how are things with Warren?"

I think she might have blushed a little—either that or she was flushed from the cooking. "Slow. Right now he's being a very good friend. He seems to know all the right things to say."

"Occupational perk," I quipped. Then seriously, "I know I'm being nosy, but do you see a future with him?"

She shrugged, a sad look in her eyes. "All I know is that someday I want to be able to have a man touch me again and not think about how the last one hurt me."

I reached out and squeezed the hand near mine. "You'll get there. I promise." And I meant it. I was in a position now where I could help her—and others like her.

And as Warden, there were very few who could stop me. How was that for a power trip? Part of me couldn't wait to get into the politics of the job and start weeding out those who were trying to usurp Morpheus. Another part was scared I'd discover that my father deserved usurping.

I also worried—on occasion—about Noah. He had

demonstrated real power in the Dreaming when he bent the world to his will, even if it was slightly. What if some zealot decided anomalies like him should be terminated? I don't think my heart could take another threat to his safety.

But, that wasn't something I needed to fret over today. Today, everything was good. Very good. Like one of those dreams you just want to go on forever, it filled you with such a sense of peace. That's what I felt today; peaceful.

Amanda polished off her wine. "Want to help me load up some bowls and take them to the table?"

"You bet." I finished my wine as well. The doorbell had rung twice while we were in the kitchen. The rest of the families had arrived, and Warren played host to them, slipping easily into the role of man of the house. I wondered how Amanda felt about that.

I wondered how Noah felt about it too.

Speak of the devil. Noah and Warren chose that exact moment to come into the kitchen. "We're here to offer our services," Warren said. "Apparently Mia is about to start gnawing on the coffee table, she's so hungry."

"We can't have that," I said, handing Noah the huge bowl Amanda had just filled with potatoes, and a slice of turkey to appease his ravenous teenage sister. "You wanna get your gravy made?"

A few minutes later the lot of us were sitting around

the extended table, passing around the bowls and platters of delicious food. Warren was right, his gravy was amazing.

"A toast," Amanda's father began, raising his glass. He waited until we all joined him before continuing, "To friends and family. I'm very thankful for both."

We chorused in agreement and drank.

Noah favored me with a loving smile. "Speaking of thankful . . ." The look in his eyes made my heart jump into full gallop as he raised his glass to me.

"And to life sentences," Warren added, interrupting what could have been a much too intimate moment to share in front of family. "I'm thankful for those as well."

And of course, we all drank to that as well. Phil Durdan was going to be locked away for a very, very long time. In fact, it was very likely he'd never see the outside world again, given he'd been denied parole. Of course, his lawyer would appeal that, but I had a strong suspicion he'd fail.

After all, Durdan was pretty messed up, thanks to me. He wouldn't be going anywhere until he recovered—if he ever recovered.

Did I feel guilty? Not one little bit.

"I owe you an apology," I said it as Noah and I were lying in bed later that night, the lights of the city illuminating his bedroom with a soft, murky glow.

He turned and propped himself up on his elbow, resting his head on his hand. He was all highlights and shadows, smooth and silky. He really was quite possibly the most beautiful thing I'd ever seen—even more beautiful than Verek's perfection. "What have you done now?"

I smiled a little at the teasing in his voice. It helped ease the shit feeling I had for having been such an idiot to him at times. "I've been so hard on you for wanting to protect the people you care about, and I'm exactly the same way. We both have a savior complex." And to think it had only taken nearly being raped, killed, and unmade to figure that out.

"It's good to have something in common." His eyes twinkled with humor. "You don't have to apologize, Doc. I've been pretty hard on you too at times."

My brows drew together. "Yeah, but I think I deserved it."

Noah laughed—a sound I loved, and reached out to pull me closer. "I think I love you, Doc."

It was like bands of steel had wrapped around my chest, as David Cassidy began to sing in my head. "I think I love you too." Who was I trying to kid? I knew I loved him. I *thought* I'd been in love before, but it hadn't felt like this. It hadn't felt this right. "I just don't understand why you put up with me."

"You make me lose control and you drive me nuts,

but I like it." He chuckled. "It's crazy, but I like it. I like *you*."

I guess it didn't get much easier or more straightforward than that, did it? Okay, so note to self—no more worrying about Amanda. "Fair enough," I said. "I won't question it again."

He grinned. "Smart girl." And then he kissed me.

I kissed him back—eagerly. It seemed like it had been too long since we'd been together in this dimension—without anything hanging over our heads.

He pulled my boxers down over my hips and legs, tossing them halfway across the room when they finally came off. Then he kissed his way up my stomach and chest as he inched my tank top higher and higher. I sat up so he could pull it over my head, and lay back with a sigh as his mouth found the hollow just below my ear.

His lips were soft and warm, so sweet and gentle against my feverish skin. He kissed and nibbled along the length of my neck, applying just enough pressure with his teeth to make me shiver and clutch at his shoulders. Down, down he moved until one of my nipples was engulfed in the wet heat of his mouth. I arched upward as he sucked, little spikes of pleasure jolting me from chest to groin. I was already damp and achy, wanting him inside me. But Noah wasn't done with me. He kissed my ribs, my waist, and my stomach. He trailed his tongue along the crevice between my thigh and body, the curls between my legs. He kissed the tops of my thighs and calves, and the tops of my feet.

And then, just when I thought I couldn't melt anymore, he rolled me over and began kissing his way back up. His tongue tickled the sensitive skin behind my knee, up to the curve of my backside. He kissed each cheek and then the small of my back, rubbed his stubble against the dip in my spine before moving up to my shoulders and the back of my neck, where the swirling backward 3 tattoo had appeared the day after I claimed the position of Warden. The hot length of his cock pressed against the apex of my thighs. Instinctively, I spread my legs and lifted my hips, angling one knee a little higher on the bed.

He slipped a hand between my legs, his fingers sliding easily into my wetness. I gasped in delight as he expertly found my g-spot. Damn, that was intense.

He fingered me for a few minutes, until I was pushing against his hand, beyond caring and ready to pop. Then he withdrew his hand and replaced it with his erection. The thick length eased inside me, stretching me in a way that sent a shiver down my spine. When he was fully inside, he wrapped his fingers around my cocked thigh, holding our bodies tight together as he began to move.

The position made me so tight I could feel the ridge

of the head of his cock as it pushed deep into me. I was panting and gasping, lifting myself on my hands to better bear down on him, to force him to my rhythm rather than submit to his.

The hand that held my thigh slid around to my front, reaching beneath my hips to find my sweet spot, the aching little button that thrilled the second he touched it. He stroked firmly but gently, knowing exactly how to build the fire within me with slow deliberation. Noah was all about my pleasure, but he liked to make me wait for it, the jerk.

I moaned. I think I might have drooled on the pillow too. Did I care? Hell no. He leaned over me, the hair on his chest tickling my side. "Do you like that?" he whispered. When I nodded he said, "How much?"

"A lot," I managed to rasp.

"Tell me what you want."

Talking dirty was still fairly new to me, so I wasn't totally confident in it, but I sure liked hearing him do it. "You," I told him, meeting his hot gaze over my shoulder. "I want you."

I think it must have been the eye contact that did it, because he rammed himself deep inside me and moved his fingers with increased ferocity. My body was humming, arching in response to every touch and thrust. My skin dampened with sweat as I moved closer and closer to climax.

And then I exploded. I cried out as orgasm ripped through me, so intense I couldn't think. I was vaguely aware of Noah stiffening above me, his groans mixing with my own noises.

God, I think I could have died right then and would have been all right with it, I felt so damn good.

Afterward, we lay together; breathing heavy, sated.

"Bet Verek couldn't do that," Noah remarked drily after a few seconds, his voice breathy.

I laughed even as I gave him a soft nudge to the ribs with my elbow. "I don't plan on ever finding out." He liked to make jokes at the handsome Nightmare's expense on occasion. I didn't mind his jealousy, or his insecurity. It was kind of sweet knowing he wanted to keep me—that he was worried someone else might actually steal me away. That someone might *want* to steal me.

It was really nice having someone who thought I was that great of a catch. Of course, I thought the same about him. I would never have reacted to Amanda as I did at first if I didn't.

Hadn't I said no more worrying about Amanda?

"I'm glad you're mine," I told him, threading my fingers through the thick, silky black of his hair.

"Me too," he replied, kissing the top of my head. It was too soon to be making declarations of forever. Hell, sometimes I think it's too soon to be in love, but I guess that's just one more thing that's out of our control as humans.

I was going to cling to my inability to control everything. Sometimes, late at night, I'm scared that that's the only thing that can keep me human—or at least half of me.

But you see, oddly enough, I don't mind so much anymore. I mean, sure, when I think about it I get freaked out, so I try not to think about it. I am half Dreamkin, half human, and that's okay. It's me. I vow to no longer worry about not belonging to either world and focus on the fact that I actually do belong in both. When you think of it, that's pretty damn cool.

My cell phone rang, surprising me so much that I jumped as the ringtone blared, ruining the silence and relaxation of the moment. "Damn it!" I cried. I thought I had turned the bloody thing off.

"Better grab it," Noah said, casting a glance at the alarm. It was after one. "It might be important."

It had better be important, I thought as I snatched up the offending technology. I flipped it open. "Hello?"

"Dawnie." It was my brother, Mark. Instantly all the fight and annoyance drained out of me. I knew from the sound of his voice that it was important after all.

"What's wrong?" I asked.

He explained quickly and efficiently—that was his job as eldest. I listened without interruption, which was hard for me as the youngest, but I did. I couldn't believe what he told me. In fact, it filled me with such a deep sense of dread and foreboding that I didn't understand it.

But I knew I had to do something about it.

"I'll be there as soon as I can," I promised. "I'll call you when I've booked a flight. Love you too."

When I closed the phone, Noah's hand came down on the back of my neck, his fingers tracing the tattoo-like figure there. "Who was it?"

"Mark," I replied, somewhere on the verge of feeling nothing and feeling too much. "My brother."

"Is something wrong?"

I looked at him, but didn't really see him. "My mother's awake."

At Avon Books, we know your passion for romance—once you finish one of our novels, you find yourself wanting more.

May we tempt you with . . .

- **Excerpts** from our upcoming releases.

- Entertaining **extras**, including authors' personal photo albums and book lists.

- Behind-the-scenes **scoop** on your favorite characters and series.

- **Sweepstakes** for the chance to win free books, romantic getaways, and other fun prizes.

- Writing **tips** from our authors and editors.

- **Blog** with our authors and find out why they love to write romance.

- **Exclusive content** that's not contained within the pages of our novels.

Join us at
www.avonbooks.com